La Charca

La Charca

by Manuel Zeno-Gandía

Translated by Kal Wagenheim

Waterfront Press

Published by
WATERFRONT PRESS
52 Maple Avenue
Maplewood, New Jersey 07040

English-language translation
Copyright 1982 by Kal Wagenheim

ISBN: 0-943862-03-5 (Clothbound)
         0-943862-04-3 (Paperbound)

Printed in the United States of America.
Second printing 1985

Major Characters in *La Charca*

Silvina, a beautiful teen-age country girl.

Leandra, Silvina's mother.

Pequeñín, Leandra's young son.

Galante, Leandra's common-law husband.

Gaspar, Silvina's common-law husband.

Juan del Salto, wealthy, cultured owner of a coffee plantation.

Marcelo, a young sickly peon on Juan's farm.

Jacobo, Juan's only son, who is studying in Europe.

Montesa, the stern foreman on Juan's farm.

Old Marta, a miser woman, who lives with a starving grandson.

Deblás, a fugitive from the law.

Padre Esteban, a Catholic priest, and friend of Juan.

Ciro, Marcelo's younger brother, who loves Silvina.

Andújar, the greedy owner of the country store.

Inés Marcante, a peon on Juan's farm.

Doctor Pintado, a doctor from town.

Preface

Before the turn of the century, while the rich in Madrid, Paris and Rome capped their sumptuous dinners with sips of Puerto Rico's exquisite black *café*—"the best in America," according to a popular Spanish *zarzuela* of the period—the anemic men, women and children who harvested the precious crop lived in squalid huts, and rarely saw a scrap of meat.

Brutalized by grinding poverty, theirs was a harsh world: the world of Manuel Zeno-Gandía's *La Charca*, published in 1894, and widely acknowledged as the first major novel to emerge from Puerto Rico.

First, what does *La Charca* mean? In the colloquial Spanish of Puerto Rico's hill country, *una charca* is a stagnant pond, a small body of brackish water that emits a miasmic stench.

Puerto Rico's Spanish colonial society, says Zeno-Gandía, was an immense *charca* of human beings, oppressed by poverty, ignorance and disease.

His bitter melodrama offers stark contrasts: the beautiful Puerto Rican countryside, blessed by nature, a veritable Garden of Eden, "a jewel that adorns the bosom of the Earth," with lush foliage, sparkling rivers, blue skies and dazzling sunsets; yet within that "regal panorama," starved, diseased human beings clung desperately to life. *La Charca* is a disturbing document of life in a particular time and place, but its outraged cry against oppression and injustice is still relevant today.

* * *

The new French writers of the 19th century, particularly Emile Zola, with their "new wave" of realism and social protest, profoundly influenced the Spanish-American literary world, until then dominated by the romantic style of expression. As Argentine novelist Vicente Fidel Lopez (1815-1903) wrote, French literature

7

"inoculated in us young men ... the very ardour for social revolution and the realm of new ideas."[1]

Anselmo Suárez Romero in Cuba, Alberto Blest Gana in Chile, Javier de Viana in Uruguay, and dozens of other writers, from the Río Grande to Tierra del Fuego, were soon "inoculated" with the stirring idea that literature should document the ills of the world, and point towards reform. Zeno-Gandía's *La Charca* stands firmly in the mainstream of this 19th century protest movement.

Manuel Antonio Zeno-Gandía was born January 10, 1855 in the port town of Arecibo, on Puerto Rico's northwest coast. The son of *don* Manuel Zeno Correa and of *doña* Concepción Gandía Balseiro, his family roots traced back to the Duke Renairo Zeno, of Venice.

During his youth, Zeno's family moved to Spain, and he completed his undergraduate studies in Barcelona; he earned his doctorate in medicine and surgery in Madrid, and served part of his internship in Paris. By 1876, he returned to his Caribbean *patria* and was soon helping to combat widespread epidemics of smallpox and yellow fever. After a brief return to Europe, he settled in Ponce, on Puerto Rico's south coast, where he raised a large family, and spent two decades in the practice of medicine.

But Zeno-Gandía was a restless man of many talents. He read widely in Italian, French, English and Hebrew. And from his prolific pen there flowed scientific papers on medicine, anthropology, geology, and philology; philosophical essays, literary reviews, poems and short plays. He authored a Spanish grammar text, and later a book on infant hygiene that won him membership in Moscow's Imperial Society of Pediatrics. He founded a scientific-literary journal, was a correspondent for magazines and newspapers, and later became owner and director of Ponce's daily newspaper, *La Correspondencia*.

After 1898, when the United States invaded Puerto Rico and took the island as its prize in the Spanish-American War, Zeno-

---

[1]Cited in Jean Franco, *An Introduction to Spanish-American Literature,* New York: Cambridge University, 1969, p. 46.

Gandía formed part of a commission—with Eugenio María De Hostos and Dr. Julio J. Henna—that journeyed to Washington, D.C. to seek reforms of the colonial regime. In 1902 he retired from medicine, served as Arecibo's representative in the insular legislature, and was a founding member of the Unionist Party, which for years protested against U.S. domination of the island's political system.

On January 30, 1930, when Zeno-Gandía died at the age of 75, and scores of friends filed past his candlelit funeral bier in San Juan's Atheneum, they paid tribute to a man who had led a full, fruitful life, combining scholarship with action in the public arena. The most important legacy that he left them, and to all of the Puerto Rican people, was a quartet of novels upon which he had labored for much of his lifetime.

They were part of a grand design which he called his "chronicles of a sick world."

The first chronicle of this tetralogy, published in 1894, was *La Charca*; earlier he had written *Garduña,* a scathing novel about the intrigues of a wicked small-town lawyer, which was published in 1896. Then came *El Negocio* (The Business), in 1916, which draws upon some of the characters of *La Charca,* but this time in an urban setting. Next, in 1925, came *Los Redentores* (The Redeemers), whose ironic title refers to the North Americans, who had come to "redeem" the island from the evils of Spanish tyranny, only to submit it to their own more subtle brand of rule. A fifth novel, *Hubo un escándalo en Nueva York,* about Puerto Ricans in New York City (conceived far before the mass migration took place following World War II) remained incomplete at his death.

In all of these works, "the great concerns of our people were echoed in their pages," wrote literary critic Francisco Manrique Cabrera.[2]

La Charca, most critics agree, was the best of all his books. It was by no means a perfect work of art. Despite its pungent realism,

[2]Francisco Manrique Cabrera, *Historia de la Literatura Puertorriquena,* Río Piedras: Editorial Cultural, 1965, p. 180.

there are long florid passages that tend to be overdone (remnants, no doubt, of Zeno-Gandía's earlier formation in the romantic literary style). Most of the characters, though memorable, are like "marionettes . . . lacking in depth," says the contemporary critic-novelist Enrique A. Laguerre.[3] But Laguerre, who laments the thinness of the characterizations, and the constant moralizing of the author, concludes with: "whoever wishes to reconstruct Puerto Rico's social situation in the 19th century will find in Zeno-Gandía's work . . . a documentary of enormous value."[4]

Nilita Vientós Gastón, the distinguished critic and editor, has commented that Zeno-Gandía's novels "helped us to see more clearly what we are and how we are . . . because the novel is one of the literary genres that best reflects the spirit of a people or an era. . . . One of the best portraits of our society in one of the most decisive and interesting periods of its history is contained in the work of Zeno Gandía."[5]

Despite its flaws, one cannot read *La Charca* without being moved, without "seeing" what Puerto Rico was like a century ago, in all its fierce beauty and tragedy. The key characters are, indeed, allegorical types, but how memorable they are! Silvina, the young maiden, symbolizing all that is innocent and beautiful, who is raped and humiliated, who yearns for just a moment's peace and kindness before her death. Leandra, her long-suffering mother, inured to cruelty. Andújar, the scheming owner of the country store. Brutish Gaspar and Galante. Marta, the wrinkled old miser woman, who hides gold in the forest, while her emaciated grandson starves to death. And, perhaps most complex of all, Juan del Salto, the wealthy, aristocratic plantation owner; a liberal man, whose conscience is seared by the misery around him,

[3]*Revista Asomante*, San Juan: Asociación de Graduadas de la Universidad de Puerto Rico, Vol. 4, 1955, p. 49.
[4]op. cit. p. 53.
[5]op. cit. p. 7.

but who remains silent, paralyzed by the immensity of the problem, and by his own self-interest. Padre Esteban, the jovial country priest, and Pintado, the dour doctor from town, who—in one of the novel's most ironic moments—gather around Juan del Salto's dinner table, and with rhetoric solve the problems of the starved peons huddled in the shacks outside, whereupon they enjoy a huge feast of meat and wine. There are scenes of theft, rape, murder, heroism, all chorused by the sounds of the river, of the "winged insects of the night," and the eternal sing-song of Puerto Rico's ubiquitous tree toad: *co-quí! co-quí!*

Today about two million persons of Puerto Rican birth or origin live in the United States. Many are unable to read their Spanish mother tongue. It is hoped that this English translation of *La Charca* will make accessible to them, and others, a treasured part of Puerto Rico's literary heritage.

Because some of the archaic prose employed by Zeno-Gandía might, in my opinion, rebuff the very readers (young students) who would profit most from reading *La Charca*, I have lightly edited the original text, substituting modern idioms here and there, abridging an occasional long passage. But I have taken care not to alter any vital dialogue or episode, and I have tried to maintain much of the 19th century "patina" of the original.

Special thanks to: Amilcar Tirado, who one sunny afternoon in 1961, at El Patio de Sam in Old San Juan, first suggested this project; to Professor Manrique Cabrera, gentleman, scholar and patriot; to Pedro Juan Soto, who gave so generously of his time to review my first draft and caught numerous errors (all those remaining are, of course, my full responsibility); and to my wife, Olga Jiménez de Wagenheim, whose patience, encouragement, and knowledge of the colloquial Spanish of Puerto Rico's hills were indispensable. Perhaps someday, *si Dios quiere,* we shall see English-language translations of Zeno-Gandia's entire "chronicles of a sick world."

—*Kal Wagenheim*
Maplewood, N.J.

Introduction

Juan del Salto and Silvina never meet, yet *La charca* is essentially the story of their interlocking worlds. The two ends of the social spectrum—the rich hacendado and the poor peasant girl—are set in narrative counterpoint, the protagonists at no point actually coming into direct contact but always implying each other as the associations and analogies mount. Intermediate characters like Marcelo and Ciro, Galante and Gaspar, Dr. Pintado and Old Marta, and the suggestive coincidence of events, bring their disparate lives gradually to converge through the distance. Toward the end we even hear Juan del Salto speak sympathetically of Silvina—whose sad story he knows, at least "in part"—and it is significant that the last chapter begins by locating them at close range: "Two years later, Silvina was living in a hut situated in the heights of Juan del Salto's farm."

But, as the epileptic Silvina finally collapses and crashes to her death, Juan del Salto is off in Europe to attend the university graduation of his idolized son. *La charca,* in fact, seems to build toward their rapprochement, only to accentuate the unbridgeable gulf between them, the mutual irrelevance and exclusion of their lives and concerns. Silvina, the defenseless victim, may get a warm, comforting feeling when she gazes off in the direction of his hacienda and vast coffee plantation; and Juan del Salto, the powerful caballero, is typically wracked with pity and liberal outrage when he is made to think of the likes of suffering Silvina. But the story shows that their relation is ultimately one of contrast and conflict, not harmony, since they inhabit opposing extremes in an antagonistic class system.

This dynamic polarity between the two main characters forms the basic compositional principle of *La charca,* and is a feature of

the book to which scant attention has been paid in previous critical
writings. Even recent interpretations and relevant historical
studies, while contributing valuable new insights on social and
stylistic aspects, still largely overlook the specific elements of plot
structure and characterization. (A selective bibliography of writings
about, and relevant to, *La charca* is included.) The present comments will take the structured action and character relations of the
novel as a springboard for reassessing some of its sociohistorical
and ideological dimensions, and then turn to the issue of its literary
placement. Only occasional reference will be possible to the rich
symbolical and stylistic qualities of *La charca,* a fascinating topic
entered into by some earlier critics, but still awaiting more coherent
analysis.

In addition to the central contrast between landowners and
peasants, and mediating between them, there is a third social force
at work in the novel. It is the world of *"el negocio,"* a single term
referring to all the various deals and schemes—from business
transactions, usury and hoarding to outright larceny and
murder—which serve to propel the action. The characters here—
Andújar, Galante, Gaspar and Deblás—are treated with an unqual-
ified disdain, often cast in pejorative racial tones. As befits their
lack of spiritual and human depth, they tend to be flat and
allegorical, varied incarnations of evil driven by a singular emotion,
greed. It is only in the sequel to *La charca,* in the novel entitled *El
negocio,* that these characters take on any psychological complexity
and come to occupy the center of fictional interest.

In *La charca,* this business sector appears in its earliest, em-
bryonic stage. Their names suggest that they are immigrants,
signalling the preponderance of entrepeneurs from Spain in the
unfolding of Puerto Rican commerce during the late 19th century. Indeed, they typically appear on the scene as foreigners
intruding ominously and violently upon the native setting. But they
are not outsiders to the plot. Rather, they are the collective catalyst
of events, their abiding influence impinging on both Silvina and
Juan del Salto and binding their disparate worlds into one indissol-
uble dramatic web.

These three class constellations—landowning elite, rural laborers and petty entrepeneurs—comprise the social ensemble of the
novel; together, they are the human components of "*la charca.*"
Along with Juan del Salto, the *hacendados* are represented by his
companions, Dr. Pintado and Father Esteban and, as extensions of
his "ideal" and "practical" selves, his son Jacobo and his foreman
Montesa, respectively. Silvina's world of the peasants and day
laborers includes her mother Leandra, her beloved Ciro and his
brother Marcelo, as well as Inés Marcante and a mass of other,
nameless characters. The stagnation and pollution of the title
indicates that the whole society is seen as a "sick world," though its
moral affliction is overtly attributable to the contaminating role of
"*el negocio.*" The pollutant is the force of commercial greed, and the
schemers and usurers who introduce and represent that motive.
But the landed aristocracy and the helpless peasantry are equally
caught up in the general social miasma. Their social interaction, in
fact, makes for the very stagnation needed to allow the sickness to
fester. And it is this relation that is of utmost interest in the novel.
The stature and dimension accorded Juan del Salto and Silvina and
the narrative structure by which their fates are systematically
interwoven, make it clear that the story is really about them.

It is especially important to call attention to Silvina because she is
so overshadowed by the commanding presence of the *hacendado*.
She lurks, frail and almost indiscernible, at the edge of the forest
(her name associates her with *la selva*), while he confidently
oversees his vast plantation and ponders deep philosophical truths.
Juan del Salto bears so much of the intellectual weight of *La charca,*
and so strongly suggests its author, that most interpretations have
focused primarily on him. His words and thoughts are often
quoted as those of Zeno Gandía himself, and in ideological and
political discussions of the book it is assumed that he is the one who
defines and embodies its deeper problematic. If he is not the
raisonneur, the assumption goes, he is by far the most conscious
and articulate figure in the novel, and his ideas, however contradictory, correspond to its broader perspective and meaning.

In terms of the plot and narrative structure, however, it is Silvina who occupies the central role, and Juan del Salto is most conspicuous for his absence. The story begins and ends with her, in precisely the same setting, the young girl's despairing stance on the cliff above the river forming an emblematic frame around the intervening events. More significant, though perhaps less obvious, is Silvina's centrality to the climax of the book. It is Chapter 7, that traumatic "night of crime and love," when the young peasant girl experiences, in blinding succession, a bloody murder and an act of sexual passion. That is the point in the action—evoked in the motto as "the serene summer night"—toward which all the emotional tension gathers, and after which the pace noticeably slackens and the moral and personal knots are unravelled. And through all those middle chapters of the book—during the flood scene, on that crucial summer's night, and at the trial of conscience that ensues— Juan del Salto is hardly even mentioned by name, and he plays no part in the events. He surfaces again only later, after the dust has settled, his aloofness from what transpires all the more blatant.

At times, as in the memorable flood scene immediately preceding the climax, his remoteness from the action seems to be the very point at issue. Torrential rains have caused the river to overflow its banks, and a young boy is about to be carried away in the deluge. Hearing the desperate cry for help, Juan del Salto comes forth to witness the scene. Rather than leaping to the rescue, though, he remains on the sideline, enraptured by the noble humanity of his courageous peasants. Even the language here, with its ironic play on his name, goes to accentuate his physical inactivity, and to underscore the hypocrisy inherent in his fervent idealism:

> "Juan del Salto felt wonder, not surprise. He had witnessed similar things many times before. Inés Marcante, the one who had been whipped by Montesa earlier in the day, jumped into the water from the left shore. Almost simultaneously, six more *campesinos* jumped in. The liquid monster parted, allowing a few shreds of humanity, ennobled by heroism, to penetrate its depths."

Only intellectually, in his chronic mental leaps from lofty ideals to practical self-interest, is Juan del Salto true to his name. When it comes to real life-and-death plunges, like Silvinia's *salto mortal* at the end, he is far away, or as in the flood scene, he can only feel and think, immobilized by his own internal rhetoric.

For there, too, in the face of physical danger and heroic humanity, he is encountering Silvina's world, even though she herself is not directly present. The terrified little 14-year-old (a boy of her age) is seen clinging for life, as she does, from the limbs of a tree. Silvina is further associated with the episode through its hero, Inés Marcante, with whom she later comes to spend the last years of her brief life. The whole scene, in fact, which stands out as the only instance of strong moral affirmation in the book, seems to prefigure symbolically the entire course of events. Silvina, of course, ends succumbing to the catastrophe while the young boy is saved; but the same disconnection between the threatened state of the peasant and the aloof world of the *hacendado* is strongly evident again as the story concludes.

The distinctive quality of *La charca* rests on this basic contradiction, represented by the contrasting protagonists, but also engrained throughout in the narrative structure and texture. That is, it is a disconnection not only between Juan del Salto and Silvina, but between the intellectual and dramatic dimensions of the fictional world itself. When ideas are expressed and philosophies expounded, the figure of the educated *hacendado* dominates, and there is relatively little action; while the main events, centering around the experience of Silvina, transpire unaccompanied by the rhetoric of reflection and explanation.

This contrast is also the source of the central irony in *La charca,* for the mute bearers and sufferers of the action actually do more to articulate the moral thrust of the novel than does its apparent spokesman. To refer again to the flood scene, where the two worlds come closest to colliding, the aftermath of that feat of heroism is different for the two main characters. Juan del Salto's ray of optimism and paean to humanity is but a momentary flash, after which he quickly returns to his real interests: he is off with his *mayordomo* Montesa, who had just whipped the heroic laborer Inés Marcante into obedience, to take stock of the damages the flood has brought to his plantation. Typically, the burst of idealism and human sympathy gives way to his more pressing concern for property and, of course, for the security of his son.

For Silvina, on the other hand, the image of the imperiled boy is but another foreboding of her own eventual downfall. The flooding river is to him what the engulfing social reality is to Silvina, for even Inés Marcante turns out to be anything but a hero in his treatment of her. The one-time embodiment of Juan del Salto's ideal is arrogant and abusive, to the point where Silvina, just before her end, chooses to leave him rather than share him, and their bed, with another woman. This final refusal, the act of a young woman—she is about 18 by the end—rejecting the burden of entrenched sexual oppression, represents an act of real heroism and humanity. Though characteristically mute and unreflected, it raises her moral stature in the book above that of the patriarchal Juan del Salto.

* * *

Like its intellectual protagonist, though, the narrator of *La charca* also maintains a distance from the immediate tragedy. For it would be misleading to presume the class perspective of the novel to be that of the downtrodden peasantry. It has rightly been viewed, especially in recent studies, as a rather elitist work, saturated with the prejudices and apologetics of a frustrated colonial ruling class. Though total disdain is reserved for the criminal, inhuman world of "*el negocio*," the portrayal of the peasantry and of women is also by and large a demeaning one: they are an inert, ignorant mass, open game for the corruption and disease that surround them. This class and sexual bias, buttressed as it is by overtones of racial determinism, is explicit and unconcealed. Yet the ironic treatment of Juan del Salto, the very embodiment of these hierarchies, points to greater complexity than would be suggested by such outwardly reactionary associations.

The historical dating of the novel is of interest in approaching its ideological perspective and ambiguities. It is known that Zeno Gandía wrote *La charca* in the early 1890s, the years preceding its publication in 1894. What has not been adequately noted is that the only historical reference in the book places the action much earlier, in the late 1860s and early 1870s. Later on in the story, Juan del Salto is engaged in a lively dinner conversation with his respected friends Dr. Pintado and Father Esteban. The discussion is spirited and wide-ranging, finally turning to the politics of the day. "The three friends," it is said, "were inspired by the progressive nature of the September revolution." The dramatic events of the "Glorious Revolution" in Spain, which occurred in September of 1868, must have been recent, as the three liberals are still reeling with enthusiasm for the spirit and rhetoric of reforms ushered in at the time. "No'more guardianship," they proclaim in unison, thinking of both the Spanish motherland and the colony. "They spoke of rights and duties, of equality, of the need to equalize before the law all sons of the nation, all groups, all people."

Such was the language and tone of the liberal colonial elite at that stage of Puerto Rican history, and it would not be so for long. By 1873 the theme would more likely have been the new constitution and the abolition of slavery, and in the 1880s, closer to when *La charca* was written, it would surely have been the serious economic crisis and political repression that ensued, culminating in the "Terrible Year" of 1887. From his vantage-point in the early 1890s, Zeno Gandía was evidently harkening back a full generation, setting up the span of elapsed time between authorial and narrative present that was typical of much 19th century realist fiction.

Perhaps too much might be made of the coincidences that emerge from this more precise dating of the novel's action, beginning with the fact that as a child of Silvina's age Zeno Gandía himself witnessed the September Revolution first-hand in the streets of Barcelona (an experience which he was to recall vividly much later in life). In the years around 1868 when the novel is set, his other protagonist, Juan del Salto, is somewhere around the author's age when he is writing it. And, in a more political vein, is it not at least possible that "el Grito de Lares" passed through the author's mind, that first major political assertion of Puerto Rican nationality which occurred only two weeks after the September events in Spain? And if we bear in mind the words of the motto, "such was the cry that he called out on the serene summer night" and their subtle bearing on Silvina's despairing outcries, *La charca* reads almost like a testament to the Puerto Rico of that early, national affirmation.

The very absence of any mention of Lares in a novel so explicitly set in just those years is actually rather remarkable, though it is in line with the silence that long surrounded that event in the island's official culture. Could it be, as the eminent Venezuelan critic César Zumeta (a contemporary of Zeno Gandía) suggested when *La charca* first appeared, that the author "was well aware that the *guardia civil* was reading over his shoulder"? One recent critic, in fact, has gone so far as to see in *La charca* "a tacit desire to create a national consciousness and to foment anti-colonial revolution."

But such deductions are still largely conjectural, and better left to future study to either substantiate or discard. The point of specifying dates and time-spans is not to arrive at some telling chronological details, however charged they may seem with symbolical implication. The goal, rather, is a more satisfactory notion of the sociohistorical field of the novel, which encompasses the period between its portrayed action and its eventual composition. *La charca* represents Puerto Rican society—or rather, a certain aspect of that society—in the years between the late 1860s and the early 1890s. On one end of that frame is the four-year period—say 1867 to 1871—during which the fictional action occurs and when major legal and political strides were made toward the formation of Puerto Rican nationhood; the other pole comprises the years just prior to 1894 when Zeno Gandía was writing, on the eve of the transfer of the colonial nation from Spanish to North American hands. A critical interpretation of the novel must obviously have both periods in view, and certainly not assume them to be interchangeable. But what is most essential is the relation between them: how is the Puerto Rico of 1867-71 altered by being portrayed from a hindsight of some 25 years? And what form does the ideological and literary viewpoint of a Zeno Gandía in the 1890s assume when it sets out to represent Puerto Rico in those earlier times? Changes and developments occurring in the intervening years, and the extent to which they bear on the fictional rendering, are of central interest.

Another important qualification has to do with the scope of Puerto Rican society represented in *La charca*. Perhaps because of its uncontested stature as the "flower" of the Puerto Rican novel, the work is customarily read as a metaphor for the whole Island society. Zeno Gandía was the first to caution against that assumption, having conceived *La charca* as but one installment in an ambitious novelistic project that originally was to comprise eleven volumes, each intended to focus on a different aspect of social reality. The author of course could not have foreseen that he would never complete his project, nor that his portrait of coffee-growing Puerto Rico would continue to draw greater acclaim than the other *"crónicas"*—*Garduña, El negocio* and *Los redentores*—as the supreme literary achievement.

La charca refers to a specific portion, or aspect, of Puerto Rican society. As has been pointed out—by Francisco Manrique Cabrera and other critics—*"la charca"* and *"el café"* are intricately associated at a metaphorical and sensual level, and the sense of morbid inertia implies first of all life in the coffee regions. The title refers to the whole society only by extension: *"la charca"* is Puerto Rico itself insofar as the country's most stagnant, self-enclosed sector, coffee cultivation, epitomizes the condition of the entire national economy. This generalization must of course take account of the relation of the part to the whole, that is, the extent to which the delimited world of Juan del Salto and Silvina is set against the larger social panorama of Puerto Rico and its colonial status. The novel itself gives us little basis for this contextualization, since the universe surrounding the coffee plantations is presented as such a self-contained unit. For the inhabitants of that world, the author is saying, it appeared self-contained and disconnected, which of course contributes to the isolation and inertia to which he is drawing attention. But the novel contains no mention of other economic and social sectors and their active bearing on the world of coffee.

Yet, far more than coffee, it was sugar production and international commerce, that were the central, moving forces in Puerto
Rican economic life for all those years, from the 1860s through the
1890s. While it is true that coffee claimed the highest monetary
value on the world market, especially in the late 1880s when it
reached its peak, at no point did it surpass those other areas of
economic activity in terms of its defining role in overall social
development. As regards both the productive forces and the
relations of production, the coffee-producing sector had long been
representative not of change and the advent of modern classes, but
of the old world of small scale production, servility, and patriarchal
authority.

The question of the ideological orientation of *La charca*—the
subject of widely divergent interpretations—may perhaps be more
fruitfully approached with such a guiding framework of the
historical field and specified social horizon. Omissions, from this
vantage point, turn out to be as revealing as what is actually
presented. For one thing, the very isolation of the world of coffee,
its virtual disconnection from other forces comprising the totality,
indicates an ideological distortion of some magnitude. There are
no slaves, no sprawling canefields or sugar mills, no burgeoning
commerical establishments, no artisan trades, no movement of
rural workers to the coastal towns with its gradual formation of an
agricultural proletariat. Even within the system of coffee production, in fact, there is no hint of the widespread and particularly
exploitative employment of women and children for all stages of
labor on the plantation.

All of these factors, seemingly extraneous in *La charca,* would
bear directly on the fictional experience portrayed, perhaps lend-
ing some dynamic to the immobile reality thus viewed largely from
within. Furthermore, those neglected dimensions were also active
tendencies within the historical field. Between 1868 and 1894, the
institution of slavery and its aftermath (following abolition in
1873), the continual expansion of sugar holdings, the restricted
growth of colonial commerce and the faltering proletarization of
the masses, all assumed increasing importance in the definition of

national life, as did the many political changes to which those processes gave rise. Yet none of these tendencies, of which the author was assuredly aware when writing, comes to figure in the unfolding and outcome of the book.

Zeno Gandía was once characterized as an "aristocrat with liberal tendencies," and the ambivalence suggested in that epithet still seems remarkably apt. His merciless anatomy of *"el Puerto Rico del café"* leads to what sounds like an all-round condemnation, and a view of a social world doomed by its own internal corruption and passivity. On the other hand there is a protectiveness, and more than a hint of nostalgia, in the treatment of that threatened world, especially as it is invaded and superseded by the steady awakening of commerce (represented at the end of the novel with the establishment of Andújar & Galante, Inc. off in the coastal city of Ponce). For no matter how sickly and stagnant the "swamp" of rural life may be, it remains morally and spiritually preferable to the scheming, parasitic world of *"el negocio."*

There are thus many ways to approach a critical understanding of *La charca* and its ideology, and the present round of debate is indeed opening up suggestive new ones. Of particular relevance is the important recent work in 19th-century Puerto Rican history by such writers as Fernando Picó, Astrid Cubano and Laird W. Bergad, some of which focuses specifically on the coffee-producing areas during the same period. With all due qualification, the novel seems to be another example, so prevalent in the tradition of 19th-century realism, of a critique of emerging capitalism from the standpoint of earlier, pre-capitalist relations. It may tend to idealize and sentimentalize that antecedent world, but the weight of its narrative force is directed against the impending inhumanity and reification being ushered in by the incipient bourgeoisie. The rural world is condemned, to be sure, but mainly because it is so easily overrun by the corruptive influence of private property and money. Reference to pre-capitalist conditions—including the empathetic treatment of the peasantry—thus conveys a sense of criticism and rejection of bourgeois society. It implies an alternative, though residual and mystified, to the decadence and inhu-

manity of the social order that is taking its place. For this reason the
ideological position of *La charca* cannot be dismissed as an unam-
biguously reactionary one.

It was an historically futile position, though, as was that of the
class it represented, which accounts for the defeatism and pessimism of the book's guiding tone and metaphor. The colony's
coffee-growing elite, in fact, appears to be the very embodiment of
the stagnant social order that surrounds it; though voicing the
ideals of autonomy and reform and claiming Zeno Gandía's lifelong allegiance, the *hacendados* prove ultimately ineffectual because
of their structural dependence on both the destitution of the
peasantry and the vagaries of international commerce. And this
sense of hopelessness could only have been reinforced by the
nagging colonial bondage under which Puerto Rico continued to
languish: direct subjection to metropolitan power constituted the
main obstacle to any kind of autonomous national development
and independent initiative on the part of the emerging classes.

Through a familiar ideological transfer, of course, it is the servile
masses who bear the brunt of this historical frustration. In terms
that resonate through much elitist thinking in Puerto Rico, the
poor and working people are characterized as pathologically docile
and held directly responsible for their own lowly condition. This
derogatory attribution defines the main tenor of the novel, being
voiced not only by Juan del Salto, Montesa and Dr. Pintado, but by
the narrator as well. However, closer reading and attention to the
book's thematic composition suggest that the fatalistic title and
determinist rhetoric are not all there is to *La charca*. For there can
be no denying the undercurrent of sympathy and even admiration
for the humble masses, especially as manifest in the implicit moral
elevation, however subdued and paternalistic, of the tragic Silvina.

* * *

This political and philosophical ambivalence is further reflected
in the complex literary placement of *La charca*. During the same
historical span, 1870–1890, a major shift occurred in Puerto Rican
literature. The years in which the novel is set saw the height of

romanticism, with its Edenic exhaltation of the Puerto Rican landscape expressed in elegiac tones and styles. In the ensuing decades came the gradual ascendancy of literary realism aimed at providing an objective representation of colonial society. Zeno Gandía and Alejandro Tapia y Rivera, the two major figures in late 19th-century Puerto Rican literature, both exemplify in their own careers this transition from a romantic to a realist mode of writing.

Some writers, like Zeno Gandía, carried the realistic project even further, seeking not only a description of social forces but their clinical anatomy: the society was regarded as "sick" (*"un mundo enfermo"*) and the task of literature was to get to the root of this pathological state in order to "cure" it; as the motto begins, "to tell everything so as to know everything, so as to cure everything." This is the program of naturalism, and *La charca* is readily identified as an example of the "roman experimental" as prescribed by Zola, the founder of that movement. Much has been made of the influence of Zola in Latin America, an influence which was particularly strong and direct in the case of Zeno Gandía because of his career as a medical scientist and his extensive familiarity with French literature. Those words from the motto of *La charca* are a quote from Zola's *Dr. Pascal* (1893), the last and summary novel of the Rougon-Macquart series after which Zeno Gandía obviously fashioned his "chronicles of a sick world." (The motto, I would argue, forms an integral part of *La charca,* both in terms of its literary identification with Zola and because of its subtle, poetic anticipation of the story to follow. It should continue to be included even though the author evidently authorized its omission from the last edition published during his lifetime, in 1930.)

Still greater critical attention has gone to the many deviations from the naturalist model, evidence of countervailing movements coming to the author from Spain and the other Latin American countries. The general consensus is that *La charca* is actually a hybrid, eclectic naturalism whose theoretical program is modified in practice by prominent shades of Spanish realism, lingering romanticism, and anticipations of prose *modernismo*. This tracing of influences and movements is of value in its own right in the case of a country like Puerto Rico, whose whole literary life has been so diminished and distorted by uninterrupted colonial rule. It is important to ascertain that *La charca* is not just the "great Puerto Rican novel," springing sui generis from native traditions and not inspired by promising new developments in other countries. It is also necessary to recognize that Zeno Gandía's work is not merely an imitation or offshoot of a European source but has its own distinctive qualities, deriving from its precise historical and cultural context.

But literary classification should also serve to shed light on political processes and to deepen our understanding of the work itself. Zeno Gandía and many other Latin American writers of his day saw in naturalism a way of rigorously exposing social conditions in their totality, and particularly the "lower depths" of those societies, the peasantry. They were no longer satisfied with the superficial, folkloric populism of the "cuadros de costumbres," nor with the rhapsodic idealism of the romantic mode. They wanted to go deeper, and their clinical sight was usually riveted on those most victimized by the social pathology, the rural laborers.

In this sense, *La charca* must be read in relation to other works of naturalist fiction in Latin America. *La charca*, in fact, was not the first example of that genre to appear in Puerto Rico, nor did its publication in 1894 usher in a new movement. Naturalist ideas were introduced in 1882 in *El Buscapié,* a prominent literary journal edited by Manuel Fernández Juncos. As in most Latin American countries the movement caught on in Puerto Rico, and in the ensuing years there appeared a spate of second-rate naturalist novels by Zeno Gandía's precursors and immediate contemporaries, largely forgotten authors like Francisco del Valle Atiles, Matias Gonzalez Garcia, Carmela Eulate Sanjurjo and Federico Degetau. Naturalist writing continued on into the early 20th century in occasionally interesting works by Ramón Juliá Marín, José Pérez Lozada and José Elias Levis. All of this literature had in common a focus on the social world of the Puerto Rican peasantry, and that emphasis would remain central to Puerto Rican fiction through the 1940s, long after the naturalist fever subsided.

More pertinent still is the work of Salvador Brau, a figure more of Zeno Gandía's intellectual stature; Brau's short naturalist novel *¿Pecadora?* (1890) and especially his important sociological essays, *Las clases jornaleras en Puerto Rico* (1882) and *La campesina* (1886), were instrumental in drawing the attention of the Island's liberal intelligentsia to the pitiable conditions of the peasant masses. The very vocabulary and political tone contained in those observations on the situation of peasant women seem to resonate in many passages of *La charca*.

The turn from romanticism to realism and naturalism was thus more than a matter of changing literary fashions. Rather, it was representative of a larger reorientation of the educated elite, away from the aloofness and subjective idealism of the earlier stage and toward a more concrete, objective definition of the national problematic. Not that there was a total abandonment of the romantic temper, nor that the authors suddenly took up the interest of the impoverished classes and saw the historical project from their perspective. But there was a new dynamic at work, the critical focus of realism and awakened concern for the peasantry going to deflate the rhetorical excesses and evasions of the romantic vision. It is important to mention that this tendency toward realism and naturalism in the national literature was also prevalent in the emerging artisan and working-class fiction in the 1890s and especially in the first two decades of the 20th century.

The dynamic interplay between contending literary and social orientations is directly present in *La charca,* and in fact corresponds to that distinctive narrative tension between the book's protagonists. For Juan del Salto and Silvina view the world, and particularly the natural setting, in different ways—one typically romantic, the other realist and social. The *hacendado's* experience of nature, in his own words and as attributed to him by the narrator, is elegiac: the aesthetic exterior of the landscape sends him into a state of mystical enthusiasm, and the language is charged with poetic cadences and metaphysical correspondences. Such passages are directly reminiscent of the rhapsodic writings of José Gautier Benítez, the young Hostos, and the earlier verse and prose of Zeno Gandía himself.

But the opening scene of the novel, where we encounter nature

from the viewpoint of Silvina, explicitly contraverts this familiar
romantic optic. The young peasant girl is left cold and unmoved by
that beautiful spring sunset, which the narrator has just presented
to us in all its enchanting splendor: "The trees, ever alive, wore
pink vestments and red trappings; the landscape was like a dreamworld, fashioned by the hand of Spring." But Silvina, we are
immediately told, "looked, but did not see. That poetic scene, so
familiar to her, offered no distraction. The peaceful sunset was of
no interest to the fourteen-year-old girl."

What Silvina "discovers" in observing the natural setting, behind
and beneath its outer surface, is the world of people who inhabit it.
The very lay of the landscape, which she surveys as though through
the lens of a movie camera, reveals to her and to the reader the full
range of hierarchies and contradictions in the surrounding society.
The long paragraphs which follow, presenting nature through
Silvina's eyes and on the basis of her social experience, serve as a
convenient introduction to the cast of characters. More than merely
a literary device, though, they also provide a detailed map of the
prevailing structure of class and sexual power. Silvina's own
subordinate, precarious place in that social panorama, even more
than her epileptic condition, already implies her final end. For she
sees all of this, after all, while leaning against the branches of a tree
"so as not to fall," the passive verbs *"asida"* and later *"sujeta"*
somehow epithetic of her dependent, defenseless position.

This collision of class perceptions could hardly be more dramatic, and the importance attached to it is stressed by its occur-
rence at the outset of the story. It serves as an initial cue that we are
to witness sharply contrasting human experiences of the same
social and natural reality. And this difference, embodied in the
main characters and representative of their divergent class
perspectives, is also expressive of differing literary styles and
philosophical imaginations. Romanticism and realism, the main
tendencies prevailing in Puerto Rican letters, are thus set into
dynamic counterpoint in *La charca*. Rather than merely external
influences or contending alternatives, they are woven into the
poetic and thematic fabric of the book.

True to its naturalist credo, the outcome and overriding tenor of *La charca* seem fatalistic—the guiding metaphor of the title indicates that it is a world pathologically doomed to stagnation and moral pollution. But, significantly, it is not naturalism in any doctrinaire, deterministic sense that goes to expose and satirize the romantic tone and posture. *La charca* may be most appropriately considered a work of critical realism, since the forces impinging on the course of events are overwhelmingly social and not biological or ecological. The role of race, heredity and climate—which prevail in strict naturalist terms—is marginal when compared with the decisive weight of lived social experience. The fate of Silvina, to take the most obvious instance, is not haunted by any "ghosts" inherited from her mother Leandra. On the contrary, her character is one of refusal and rebellion which, though ending in futility, is diametrically opposed to that of her grotesquely submissive parent.

This placement of *La charca* in the realist tradition—which has also been suggested by some of the most astute readers of Zeno Gandía—should help to overcome its facile identification with the naturalist school and the prescriptions of Zola. At the same time, it also serves to counteract the common tendency of highlighting examples of romantic and modernist writing as poetic exceptions to the mechanical laws of naturalism. Rather, *La charca* may be seen to range freely yet cautiously between those stylistic poles, activating both but yielding to the excesses of neither. It is this balance, this interplay of contrasting human possibilities, that lends the novel its enduring fascination, making it still today the most penetrating literary portrayal we have of 19th-century Puerto Rican society.

But the interest of *La charca* to contemporary readers goes beyond the insights it provides as a social document, or even its place at the threshold of modern Puerto Rican fiction. For in that book, and in the other installments of the "crónicas de un mundo enfermo," Zeno Gandía lent profound literary representation to a key stage in a protracted historical process which we are still living through in the present day. The final third of the 19th century saw the decisive formation of Puerto Rico as a colonial nation. It was the time when the emerging social classes first arrived at a collective—

and then a differentiated—political and cultural expression. And it was the time when the whole society entered into its definitive position in the international economic system.

Since then, of course, the whole colonial orbit has changed from Spain to the United States, and all of Puerto Rican life has been altered by sweeping industrialization and mass emigration. But the world of *La charca* is still with us today in the pervasive and unrelenting affliction of imperialist rule. Zeno Gandía diagnosed it as "sick," and sought in vain for a "cure." Or rather, as the author would have it, the cure is the novel itself—the endlessly flowing river—which goes on "telling it all" even after the sad story has been told. Bearing witness to colonial misery in its deeper psychological dimensions, the novelist also uncovers rays of hope and change. Despite his pessimism Zeno Gandía always detected this glimmer of affirmation. This was true in *La charca* and it was also evident toward the end of his life, when he again took stock of his country's pitiable condition. Writing in 1929, Zeno Gandía concluded his gloomy account by reminding us that for all of the oppression endured by Puerto Rico "there is some reaction. At times a latent fire flares up, efforts in the right direction are made—utterings that could perhaps lead our mother island to a better future."

We would thus do well to keep returning *La charca*. For what it says, and leaves unsaid, still illuminates our present struggle.

—*Juan Flores*
  Center for Puerto Rican Studies (Hunter College–CUNY)
  and Queens College

Selected Bibliography Relevant to La Charca

Alvarez, Ernesto. *Manuel Zeno Gandía: Estética y sociedad.* Ph.D. dissertation, New York University, 1978.

Algarín, Pedro. *El naturalismo en Manuel Zeno Gandía.* Ph.D. dissertation, University of Illinois, 1972.

Aponte, Marta. "Hacia una interpretación ideológica de 'La charca'," *Sin Nombre*

Ara, Guillermo. *La novela naturalista hispanoamericana.* Buenos Aires: Editorial Universitaria, 1965.

Barradas, Efraín. "La naturaleza en *'La charca'*," *Sin Nombre* V, 1 (1974), pp. 30–42.

Barrera, Héctor. *"La charca* (Osario de vivos o generación de fantasmas)," *Asomante,* XI, 4 (1955), pp. 59–72.

Beauchamp, José Juan. *Imagen del puertorriqueño en la novela (En Alejandro Tapia y Rivera, Manuel Zeno Gandía y Enrique Laguerre).* (Río Piedras, Editorial Universitario), 1976, pp. 29–69.

Bergad, Laird W. "Hacia el Grito de Lares: Café, estratificación social y conflictos de clase 1828–1868" in Scarano, *Inmigración y clases sociales,* pp. 143–185.

Colón, José M. "La naturaleza en La charca," *Asomante,* V, 2 (1949), pp. 50–60.

Cubano Iquina, Astrid J. "Economía y sociedad en Arecibo en el siglo XIX: los grandes productores y la inmigración de comerciantes" in Scarano, *Inmigración y clases sociales,* pp. 67–124.

Gardón Francheschi, Margarita. *Manuel Zeno Gandía, vida y poesía.* San Juan: Coquí, 1969.

Gómez Tejera, Carmen. *La novela en Puerto Rico: Apuntes para su historia.* San Juan: Imprenta Venezuela, 1947.

González, José Luis, "Manuel Zeno Gandía" in *Literatura y sociedad en Puerto Rico* (Mexico, D.F.: Fondo de cultura económica, 1976), pp. 193–202.

Guzmán, Julia M. "Realismo y naturalismo en Puerto Rico," *Literatura puertorriqueña: 21 conferencias* (San Juan: Instituto de cultura puertorriqueña, 1969), pp. 151–177.

Laguerre, Enrique. "El arte de novelar en Zeno Gandía," *Asomante* XI, 4 (1955), pp. 48—53.

————. "Pròlogo" to Manuel Zeno Gandía, *La charca* (Carácas: Ayacucho, 1978), pp. ix—xlix.

López, Mariano. "El perfil humano de 'La charca'," *Sin Nombre* IX, 4 (1979), pp. 46—61.

Manrique Cabrera, Francisco. "Manuel Zeno Gandía: poeta del novelar isleño," *Asomante*, XI, 4 (1955) pp. 19—47.

Méndez, José Luis. "La estructura social y la literatura puertorriquena," *Casa de las Américas*, no. 115 (1979) pp. 38—45.

Picó, Fernando. *Libertad y servidumbre en el Puerto Rico del siglo XIX*. Río Piedras: Huracán, 1979.

————. *Amargo café*. Río Piedras: Huracán, 1981.

Quiñones, Samuel R. "Manuel Zeno Gandía y la novela en Puerto Rico," *Temas y letras* (San Juan: Biblioteca de autores puertorriqueños, 1955), pp. 11—38.

Rivera Valdés, Sonia. "Relecturas: 'La charca' de Manuel Zeno Gandía," *Areito*, VIII, 31 (1982), pp. 50—52.

Scarano, Francisco A., ed. *Inmigración y clases sociales en el Puerto Rico del siglo XIX*. Río Piedras: Huracán, 1981.

Torres Santiago, José Manuel. "Nueva visión de Manuel Zeno Gandía," *Claridad* (Oct. 14, 1973), p. 19.

Vázquez Vázquez, Luis Fernando. *Discrímenes y prejuicios en las 'Crónicas de un mundo enfermo' de Manuel Zeno Gandía*. M.A. thesis, Centro de Estudios Avanzados de Puerto Rico y el Caribe, 1982.

Zeno de Matos, Elena. *Manuel Zeno Gandía: Documentos biográficos y críticos*. San Juan, 1955.

To tell everything so as to know everything, so as to cure everything: such was the cry that he called out on the serene summer night.

. . . and human was his effort, filled with the immense anguish of beings and things.

—*From* Doctor Pascal, *by Emile Zola*

Rural Puerto Rico,
in the late 1860's . . .

Chapter One

Clinging to two trees so as not to fall, Silvina leaned over the cliff's edge and gazed anxiously below to the river bed. She shouted with all her strength:

"Leandra! Leandra!"

She stood on a mountain in the deep woods, a labyrinthine wilderness which resembled a staircase leading to the altar of heaven.

"Leandra! Leandra! Come up, Pequeñín is hungry. Come up, come up . . ."

Her voice echoed in the hills and fell to the river bed, where it was muted by murmuring cascades and whirlpools. By the shore, Leandra crouched over a smooth flat stone and laboriously did the wash. Her dress was gathered and pinned behind her knees; the soapy water splashed her bare legs. Finally, she heard the cries, and sighted Silvina.

"What do you want?" she asked, gesturing with her hands.

Silvina told Leandra that her youngest son, Pequeñín, lay face down on the floor of the hut, crying from hunger.

"Look!" Leandra trumpeted, cupping her hands to her mouth, "try to quiet him . . ."

"But he doesn't *want* to."

"Entertain him, woman; I still have work to do . . ."

"You've got to come up. I've stuck my finger in his mouth, and instead of sucking he's *biting* it. Come quickly!"

In an ugly mood, Leandra rose, letting the dress fall on her wet legs. She quickly bundled together the damp clothes and began to climb a steep narrow trail that weaved through the coffee grove on the hillside.

Trying to ignore Pequeñín's wailing, Silvina gazed languidly at the landscape. The surroundings, cooled by the breeze of approaching eventide, glowed with the last ardors of the setting sun.

Behind her, a vast expanse of virgin forest ended in an abrupt peak; ahead, on the far side of the river, a grayish mountain sloped gently left and right towards the sea, forming small valleys and fierce ravines. The colors danced about like sparks, jumbling into subdued tints, leaping apart in gay contrasts. The spray of colors in the fields resembled an immense palette where the Supreme Artist might dip his brush. An inimitable blue drifted down from the sky like a nuptial gift; a gentle green blinked in the fields like a slave offering. The blend of those two hues formed the soft gray of the distance and the tepid gold of the foreground. The trees, ever alive, wore pink vestments and red trappings; the landscape was like a dreamworld fashioned by the hand of Spring.

Silvina looked, but did not see. That poetic scene, so familiar to her, offered no distraction. The peaceful sunset was of no interest to the fourteen-year-old girl; she was lost in her own private thoughts. The regal panorama of the mountains quivered in front of her like a flock of swallows before a statue. Looking straight ahead, near the mountain's peak, she saw the dark smudge of Galante's opulent coffee grove. She felt repulsion and hatred as she recalled the painful history of her thwarted love, brusquely cut short by Gaspar, that terrible man to whom she, still so young, owed the duties of a wife. Gaspar: his presence made her tremble, his image filled her with dread. She studied the valley down below, far away, where Andújar's settlement nestled. She could see the store, with its grimy entrance and filthy counter; the shed for the threshing machine, the four small shacks for storing provisions and lodging the workers. She saw Andújar, with his bare arms and grease-stained undershirt, behind the counter arguing over the price of a single bean, begrudging a grain of rice, weighing out light pounds of provisions and measuring short yards of cloth. Her gaze fell to another knoll spattered with shanties: the tiny dwellings of the peasants who roved the mountains barefoot and toiled on the large farms. They were ever in debt to Andújar, the swindler of the *barrio*, since they bought from his store. For them, time passed without their having recourse, nor spirit, to work their own lands where—thanks to nature's fecundity—coffee and banana grew with abandon, and fields of forage or thicket rippled in the wind. Her gaze continued down the mountainside, which stretched smoothly to the plain; like a giant kneeling to kiss the base which sustains him, the huge earthen mass humbled itself to the level of the flatlands, which stretched to the sea.

Still grasping the trees, Silvina took in the panorama. In the depths of the ravine, the river sent up a commotion with its galloping force and watery leaps. To the left, on the side where Silvina stood, was a small woodland that belonged to Old Marta, a wrinkled, aged *campesina* who lived in a beggarly hut shaded by a coffee orchard, and whose reputation as a miser was matched by her deeds. Her sole companion was an emaciated, almost skeletal grandchild. Over to the right was another large farm, belonging to Juan del Salto. Staring at those fields, she thought of Ciro, the man she loved. Ciro was a young *campesino,* scarcely twenty years old, who worked on that farm, felling the tall trees, carrying timber, handling the bark stripping machine. Memories filed by in her thoughts. Galante. Gaspar. Andújar, Juan del Salto, Leandra, Old Marta; her submission to a man she despised and feared; her unyielding passion for Ciro, who was beyond reach; the monotonous slavery of her life with Leandra; the burdens of her daily existence, full of hard work and stress, which overwhelmed her weak spirit; the well-being of Galante, of Juan del Salto, of Andújar, which made her envious; everything flitted through her mind, like a ribbon of light brimming with vibrant images.

At last, Leandra emerged from the green depths of the slope. She was tired from the climb. Barefoot, she leaned to the left, supporting the bundle of clothes that she bore on her right side. Her blouse was pitched far forward, nearly baring her bosom.

Leandra entered the hut, Silvina behind her, and hurled the bundle in a corner. Pequeñín sent up a deafening, tearless cry.

"I'm at my limit," she said, thrusting a breast into the little boy's mouth. "I'm tired of your laziness!"

"That's all I need, for you to pick on me now," Silvina answered. "Is it my fault that you have no milk, that the boy is always hungry?"

"Useless!"

"Before going down to the river you gave him to suck, and look . . ."

"You're worthless. You don't help me, you don't care about all the work I have to do. All day long, you sit with your arms folded, thinking of the . . ."

"Come now, mother, are you going to insult me?"

"It's easy to see that you don't know what it is to work, to have children . . ."

"You can be sure of that. God help me! Why should I want children? It's enough to put up with that brute . . ."

"That *brute* is your husband, the man who supports you."

"Ah yes! One *peseta* a week. All he supports are Andújar's card games and bottles. He gives me what he can spare from the game . . . after he loses. And, oh yes, a whipping. What's more, he makes me want to throw up."

"Don't be a fool, Silvina. Your husband is a man of respect, who looks after us. Women who live alone only suffer abuse."

"What more abuses could I suffer that I haven't already?"

"That's because you're not the woman of your house; all you do is idle about. Since you married Gaspar, you lie around, needing nothing, your mouth always stuffed full. Why, in the last harvest, you didn't even take to the fields and help pick the coffee. Gaspar didn't want you to, because he cares for you. But you're ungrateful. Ah, if only you were as serious and moral as your mother!"

"Moral?" Silvina burst into laughter. "Look, Leandra, I'm losing my patience. I may be worthless, but I only take after you. Between Gaspar, you and your lover . . ."

"My *husband*, you mean . . ."

"But he's not."

"All right, he's not, but it's the same as if he were."

"Well, between the three of you, you're driving me crazy."

In a bad mood, Silvina shut herself up in the shed which was used as a kitchen.

It was the same old scene. Leandra and her daughter lived in continual discord, hurling curses and complaints at each other. They could not live harmoniously in the small shack where habit and misery held them. Leandra, still buxom for her forty years, had fought her campaign. Nine children conceived under the harsh labor of the fields. Seven of them were already gone. Some had died, others had run away, their whereabouts unknown, and others had been "stolen": carried off from their mother at an early age in order to form a new concubinage. Children of different fathers, each following his or her destiny. Silvina and Pequeñín remained. Pequeñín's father was Galante, the rich landowner who kept a mistress in every nook and cranny of the mountain and was, for the time being, Leandra's "man." Silvina never knew her father, a chance scoundrel who, in the free polygamy of the woods, took advantage of a propitious moment.

But the great secret of the family, which caused Silvina untold grief, was a somber tale. When the first enchantments of womanhood adorned Silvina, Galante was already the man of the house. By threatening to abandon Leandra, Galante forced her into a wicked act. Silvina and Ciro were engaged at the time, and Silvina, reposing in her reveries, dreamed of the future. The future arrived one night of torrential rain, when the shack was flooded. The family was forced to huddle together in one of the house's two rooms. Silvina, seized by surprise while half asleep, tried to resist, but she heard Leandra whisper in her ear:

"Daughter, don't be a fool . . . don't you be the cause of us dying of hunger."

In the darkness, punctuated by bursts of lighting, Galante subdued the virgin.

Afterwards, Silvina bit her fists with rage. What would Ciro think? Galante, on the other hand, promised to help marry off Silvina, and then Gaspar appeared on the scene. The young girl resisted for a few days, but Leandra finally convinced her and took her to the church. With the aloofness of ignorance, Silvina succumbed to her husband, as she had before to Galante. The will, the stirring of desire, the self-judgment; those awoke in her later, when it was too late. Gaspar, fifty years old, awkward and repulsive looking, with tangled hair and drunken breath, was not a gentle mate. The young girl had fallen into the hands of a perverse, churlish beast, with fist ever poised to strike, lips ever parted to hurl an insult. When Silvina reflected upon her misfortune, she swore to guide the course of her new life. But Gaspar enslaved her even more, dominating her completely with his despotic temperament. She hated him, she damned him, she yearned to tear him to shreds as though he were a tattered, filthy rag; but when she faced him and heard the biting acrimony of his words, she timidly lowered her eyes, trembling like a young ewe before a bird of prey. Gaspar had entered into matrimony as though he were blustering into a tavern. He worked on Galante's farm whenever his alcoholic daze lifted. One day Galante asked him:

"What do you think of Silvina, Leandra's girl?"

"*Baray*! Some girl . . . a sugarplum!"

"Do you want her?"

"*Cómo*! Do you think she could ever love me?"

"Do you want her?"

"If only I could have her!"

"Listen, Leandra and I are *good friends*. That girl of hers will fly off any day. Take her now, marry her. I'll arrange it."

"Fine, but I'm clean of 'chips' and women eat like the plague."

"Don't worry; you'll live in their house, and you'll also care for the mother. I'll settle your trouble with the court. I'll pay the fine they have over your head, so you won't go to jail. And I'll throw in one hundred *pesos* to boot."

"Fine, fine," answered Gaspar, who was dazzled. "There's nothing more to say."

Then, as though it had suddenly occurred to him, Gaspar asked, in a wicked tone:

"Tell me, has Leandra taken good care of her little girl?"

"That's none of your affair. Forget it."

"All right; it is agreed."

The pact was sealed, and the knot was soon tied in the church of the town, which was the district capital. Gaspar consumed Silvina as though he were guzzling a drink, soiling her with his vile breath.

She lived unhappily. At times she was irascible; other times she mourned and sighed, and shed furtive tears. Her sole comfort was the forest, walks along lonely trails, the rapture of contemplating—without understanding—the fierce panorama of the region, and concocting impossible schemes to run off with Ciro.

When Pequeñín tired of vainly sucking on Leandra's breast, he fell asleep. She laid him down in a miserable crib filled with dirty rags and descended the steps of the shack to where Silvina, with a wooden spoon, taciturnly stirred an unsavory *salcocho,* a banana stew in which thorny scraps of food sporadically bubbled to the surface.

The storm clouds between mother and daughter passed quickly. A few moments after their argument, they were chatting amicably. Leandra mentioned that she had heard shouts and insults coming from down near Andújar's store, but did not know the cause. Some drunken brawl, no doubt. Since it was Saturday and the men had collected their wages, they thought only of drink. They went to Andújar's to pay their debts of the week and, glass after glass, spent their time and money

Leandra cursed them. Disgusting loafers! The women heating and re-heating the miserable broth, the children lifeless and waxen, and *them* wasting the fruits of their labor, running the risk of going to jail for some act of tomfoolery. That was why Leandra claimed to be content with her lot; her "friend" was rich, he gave her money each day and avoided brawls. True, she had to tolerate his promiscuity, the insatiable hunger of a robust *macho,* and resignedly allow him to keep other *campesinas* in the same predicament of intimate friendship. But what could she do? Better to be tolerant than expose herself to the outrages of some barbarian, such as many she knew. Silvina, meanwhile, grieved over her unlucky stars: wife of an old man, so gross, so ugly! Had there been trouble at Andújar's store? Undoubtedly Gaspar was there. Her husband was old and ugly, and shameless, too. For if he had one jot of pride he would not have married her. And conceding that he sold himself for money, to pick at someone else's castoff scraps, the greatest disgrace of all was his tolerance of Galante's demands. On this point, Leandra argued that Silvina was wrong. If Galante had occasional "whims" for her, it was unimportant. This kept him happy, and he protected them.

"A woman must know how to hold on to a man," Leandra said.

"I know all too well that Galante prefers you to me, but I keep quiet; if I complain he would abandon me and we would lose everything."

This was an atrocity, Silvina argued. In the same house, while pretending to love the mother, to pursue the daughter; a girl who loathed him, who was married to an even more despicable man, who would consent to such filth, against the girl's will. The talk ended as always. There was no other choice: it was better than dying of hunger.

They heard a man approach the small esplanade in front of the house. It was Gaspar; as he came closer he hacked his long machete into a tree and left it there quivering.

"Nothing to eat around here?" he said, slumping down on the stone that served as a doorstep.

The women served him a heaping plateful of stew. Gaspar gobbled it down, talking while he ate:

"That pig Montesa is lucky I didn't kill him this afternoon. Meddler! We were by the river, just a few friends, enjoying a small game of cards. I was winning, and if I'd played my jack I would have broken the bank. Deblás shuffled and was about to deal when Montesa happens to pass by. He stops, looks at us and says:

" 'What are you bandits doing over there?'

" 'Whatever we have a mind to.'

" 'You're breaking the law. What if the deputy comes?'

" 'Figure it out yourself! Andujar is the deputy, and whenever we play he charges us one *chavo* for each . . .'

" 'And who asked you to mix into what is none of your business?'

" 'Quiet, you scoundrel!' he says to Deblás. 'Waggle your tongue and I'll twist it off; I can't stomach a runaway like you.' "

"His haughtiness made me angry. Of course, Montesa was talking like that because he knows that Deblás is hiding from the law, that he can't afford trouble, and that if they lay their hands on him they'll throw him back into jail. The coward! I wanted to see if Montesa would dare get smart with *me*. I jumped up and reached for my machete, but he was ready. When I was about to split him in half, he gave me a mean kick in the belly and knocked me down. What a fuss! The game was ruined. Everyone ran off, and Montesa was cowardly enough to call me a shameless good-for-nothing . . . *me,* lying on the ground, unable to defend myself. Ah! I'll get him yet. When I got up, Andújar held me back and asked me to please not get mixed up with that idiot Montesa. Then, since it was best to keep quiet about the card game, and since I'm already up to my neck in problems that have cost me dearly, I held myself back. But there is time; someday I'll cut him to *pieces* . . ."

Gaspar seized the machete and gave the tree another slash. A dark resinous fluid oozed from the wound in the bark.

Silvina, who was squatting in the corner, followed Gaspar's violent gestures with anxious eyes, as though she feared that the threats would be directed against her.

"Here," Gaspar said, handing a few coins to Silvina. "I made nothing this week, and then in the fight I lost my winnings. Maybe Montesa himself robbed me. But anyway, here are thirty-two *chavos.* If you need more during the week, ask *mamá* Leandra to give you. And if she doesn't have, let me know so I can 'touch' Galante. Better yet, *you* do it, he'll be more willing with you."

Leandra advised Gaspar to be more prudent. It was better to go straight home after a day's work. As Gaspar stubbornly argued back, Silvina again drifted off to her dreamworld, and saw how the light slowly dimmed in the sky, and how the shadows were slowly closing in.

Gaspar made Leandra laugh when he told her how Old Marta had been at the card game, with a handful of *chavos* bound in the corner of a kerchief. When the fists began to fly, Marta suffered a slap in the neck that tore the kerchief from her head, leaving her tangled hair waving in the breeze.

"But," Gaspar said, "that devil of an old woman has such luck that despite everything she'll surely stash away half a *peso* on the mountain tonight. Ah, if I could only find her hiding place!"

The night was advancing. Gaspar stretched, yawned. He told the women to be ready for a dance in Vegaplana. Everyone would go; it was time they went on a lark, he said. It was good now and then to shake off one's boredom and have some fun, drinking a bit and stepping off a *contradanza*.

The neighboring *barrio* of Vegaplana always had good dances. Upon leaving home, they would remove their shoes, so as not to dirty them, and put them back on in order to make a proper entrance into the dance hall.

Leandra went down to the shed. As though he had been waiting for his chance, Gaspar motioned to Silvina with his hand. She came close.

"As I've told you," Gaspar whispered. "Deblás is eager, and I won't back out; so be ready."

"But Gaspar," said Silvina, turning pale, "it's horrible . . ."

"Horrible no! This is a business affair, like any other."

"My God! My God!"

"You've got to help us, it's the only way."

"Why don't you two arrange it between yourselves, now that you've decided to go ahead? Why force me, if you know that I'm scared to death?"

"Because no one will suspect a woman. No objections, now. You'll come, and that's all there is to it."

Since Leandra was returning, Gaspar raised a finger to his lips. He was sure of her silence. Then he went inside and lay down upon the floor, on a bed made of clothes spread across a mat, with folded sacks for pillows.

Moments later, he was snoring. Leandra lay down in the other room, in a shaky, but real bed, which was the luxury of the household. Silvina remained where she was, facing the starry night, contemplating it from her rustic dwelling. Inside, deep slumber drugged Gaspar and Leandra; outside, the strident clamor of the night insects—the choir of the crickets, the dirge of the toads, the rubbing of winged violins—chorused a night psalm in the forest's wild expanse.

Chapter Two

Riding a mule, Juan del Salto arrived at his plantation where the brigade of *campesinos* weeded and cleaned the fields. A prudent master, he came to oversee the work so that no one whiled away his time picking at the edges of the thicket and ignored the weeds in the center. He left his mount on the trail and stepped into the woods. A group of laborers echeloned along the slope swung their machetes, laying waste the weeds and vines.

Juan scanned the scene with a practiced gaze. Some of the men sang monotonous *coplas*[1], others wielded the blade silently, and those nearest him chatted animatedly.

"We're short of men here, don Juan," said one of them, as he rooted out a bellflower in a stroke. "Harvest time is near, and if the cleaning is not hastened much will be lost."

"How clever you are!" replied Juan in a benevolent tone. "Do you think we land owners find help so easily? Tell your companions what you've just said; the ones who don't work on Mondays because they're too tired from Sunday's carousing; the ones who scandalize the *barrio* with outrages like last Saturday's in Andújar's store; the ones who spend the week chewing tobacco, stretched out in their hammocks . . ."

"Ah, but I'm not one of them!"

"Agreed, but I don't speak of you. Your trouble is that you mistake the harshness of my words for an accusation."

"But I . . ."

"Yes, I know what you're going to say; that you are hard working and honorable. Correct? Evidently you are. But it's no less true that there are irresponsible loafers among you. If it were not for them, we would always have more than enough help."

Juan turned his back on the *campesino*. He realized the futility

[1]*copla,* a type of country ballad, or couplet.

45

of trying to improve these mountainfolk, but he never stopped trying. It was his ideal to reform them, to mold men who could defend themselves from the whip, to give citizenship to the common people, to make them strong.

Juan's ideal was like a weighty burden in his head, and constantly in conflict with reality. Wherever he saw evil, he was stirred to protest; wherever he discovered error, his urge to right it was like that of a drowning man, gasping for air.

Ascending the bluff, Juan continued to inspect the day's labor. A few times he told the workers to cut deeper; if not, the ferocious weeds would soon make the cleaning useless. The soil was rich and the forest growth was energetic; where a weed was pulled, it would soon rise again. Other times he restrained a worker's arm who, in the confusion of his labor, had slashed the stalk of a coffee shrub. Where would such a thing lead to? Each of those bushes represented a sacrifice. To mutilate a plant was like mutilating one's hopes. They should be more careful with the machete, or they would make short work of the bushes that thrived on the mountainside. The worker would pause, and continue cutting with more caution.

Juan roamed the slope, climbing with the help of the tree trunks, descending carefully so as not to fall. It was not uncommon to see him drop to his knees when he spied the root of a coffee plant surging up from the earth. Crouched there, he himself would bury it, explaining to the *campesino* the importance of such a detail. Yes, the roots must go deep so that they may drink the juices of the earth. On the surface, they crawl like serpents and the plant quickly wastes away. He had no patience for the stupidities of the seed sowers. He oversaw every detail on the plantation that constituted his wealth, with the pure affection of a father caressing the tiny heads of his offspring. The workers loved and respected him. They knew him as the benefactor who brought money and medicine up to the shack that harbored the sick. They also knew that, in moments of indignation, he arrogantly displayed his inexorable authority. The good sought refuge at his side and lodging in the settlement of his farm, they competed for the honor of helping him with the household chores or with the work on his machines. The bad, the suspicious ones, feared him.

During his jaunt, Juan happened upon a spot where several *campesinos* were talking. Confronting one of them, he asked:

"Where is your son?"

"My son," answered the man in a vacillating tone, "well, he feels a bit sickly . . ."

"Sickly, eh?"

"Yes, *señor*. Since he suffered . . . a *fall* . . ."

"Still the fall! Listen, though your lazy son gets drunk and falls in ditches, crippling himself; though he doesn't come to work afterwards, not knowing whether the wound hurts him; though he delights in the leisure of your hut, eating your plantains without helping you . . . this is not so bad. It is unfortunate that you should suffer the consequences. But what is worse is that you should permit his excesses; that you should consent to his evil ways, and that you should *lie*, trying to excuse his misconduct."

"My God! I . . ."

"Yes, it's true. When will you finally understand that you corrupt the young when you coddle them? If you had trained him when he was young, your son would not be lost today. But you thought that your own work was enough to feed the family, and today you have on your hands an unruly brute, whose behavior sickens you, who wastes his life on the guitar and liquor, on cards and women . . ."

"Don Juan . . . what do you want of me! I have done everything to make a working man of that worthless . . ."

"You have done nothing. You have favored his bad instincts, letting his drunken sprees go unpunished, perhaps even laughing at his jokes. You have consented to his lawlessness. He has even taken into your own home—close to his mother and sisters—a mistress, and you have tolerated that."

"Only to see if it settled him down."

"No, it is because of your condescendence, which is part ignorance, but is more laziness. The world falls upon your head, and it is nothing . . . You are stoics. You don't know what the word *stoic* means; I will tell you in another way: you are indifferent to good or bad; you are apathetic; you are *shame* . . ."

Juan contained himself. The other men were smiling, and the *campesino* suffered the verbal squall cringingly, mouthing excuses in incoherent monosyllables.

"And worst of all," Juan continued, "is that you don't hesitate to lie in order to conceal the boy's faults. Tell the truth: 'my son got drunk in Andújar's bar; my son couldn't get up for work this morning.' In that way, you at least don't make yourself a party to his depravation. Bah! I can see that I'm wasting my time. You are all accomplices! You stay together in a tight little clan, the good and the bad. Has a mule been stolen? You know who the thief is, but you keep quiet. Has someone intentionally damaged the crops? You know the guilty one, but . . . silence. If a crime were committed, even a murder, you could watch it happen and never utter a word . . ."

As Juan spoke these words, a lean, sickly-looking laborer, about twenty-five years old, paled intensely, dropped his machete, and stiffened, terrified. It was a quick, untamable movement, like the shuddering of a surprised nervous system. Juan noticed the gesture, and though the youth tried to smile, to conceal his distress, the landowner realized the impact of his words. A few minutes later, as twilight approached and the men prepared to suspend their labors, Juan came up to the youth and whispered:

"What is it, Marcelo?"

"I . . ."

"Just a moment ago, when I mentioned crime, you turned white. You're cold, your hands are trembling; what's the matter?"

"Nothing, nothing . . ."

"Don't lie," said Juan emphatically. "Tonight, when everyone is asleep, come to my room. I want to see you . . ."

"Yes, I'll come."

The youth disappeared among the cluster of workers who were returning to their humble shanties.

At ten in the evening, when all were asleep, Juan del Salto meditated in his bedroom.

He sat at a table illuminated by a small lamp, his forehead resting in his hands, his elbows on the table. He was absorbed, as though the wings of thought had carried him far away, leaving behind the inert statue of his body. He was slender and strong, with a high forehead and skin tanned by the sun. His hands were strong and his eyes were large and penetrating, although they were often veiled by melancholy. Neither his genial countenance, nor his benevolent character could blot out that sadness. His inner world dispatched reflections of nostalgia to his countenance, and secret sorrows and worries flowed across his face.

With the lights out in all the dwellings, the night spread its mysteries across the landscape. The stars probed the secrets of the earth. The cool gentle breeze crystallized the dampness into tiny droplets.

It was a time of mystery: of repose for some, of turbulence and passion for others. The spirit of loneliness wafted over the fronds, bathing itself in perfumes. Moths fluttered about joyously in the sunless hours. A few came in through the window, flew about and collided rudely with the lamp; others, dazzled, died as their wings were consumed. The murmers of the outdoors floated in the atmosphere with endless monotony and almost melodic dissonance as the crackle of the waters, which threw themselves headlong down the river bed, dominated the jumble of sounds.

As he waited for Marcelo, Juan lost himself in memories, bitter and pleasant. He thought about his hopes for the future, when already his sufferings and labor had aged him. He recalled the days of his youth, the opulent home of his infancy, destroyed by adversity. He hazily recalled the rich sugar cane plantation where he was born; his early years, his parents' efforts to cultivate his mind, the sojourn in Europe devoted to study; his career, interrupted later when misfortune impoverished them and forced his return. He thought of that woeful homecoming, of the cruel junction of mishaps that heaped ruin upon his family; of the poverty that came later, and the death of his parents. Then came another phase of his life: a series of relentless struggles to conquer misfortune; his efforts realized in business ventures; the day love beckoned his heart; the sweet wife he chose as his companion; the

unforgettable happiness over their first son; the joy in their home
over the first sum of money saved; and then—in methodical
order—the purchase of a coffee farm, the fatiguing tasks of cultivation; the unforeseen death of his loving companion; the departure of his grown son to begin professional studies in the capital
of Spain; his fanatical devotion to work, in order to build an in-
heritance to assure his son's future; and now his painful solitude
as he patiently awaited that future, the fruition of so many
dreams, the return of his absent son, at whose side he would enjoy
calm and comfort. His whole life filed by in those pensive hours.
Each night, upon going to bed, his flights of fancy would soar
upward and explore the past. Juan's passions were already cold,
wounded by anguish, smothered by intellect. He lived for work,
for memories, for dreams, for loving his absent son.

His abstractions were a second life for him, and in that life a
formidable struggle often arose. His travels and studies had
taught him to think, and his cultivated mind had lifted him above
the society around him. His eyes and his heart were in constant
protest against the twisted currents that swept up men and things,
feelings and hopes. Were those poor people clustered on the
spurs of the mountains human beings, or merely shreds of life
launched forth by chance? Were they rabble? Were they swine?
Were they sheep? What moved them? Where were they going?

He probed the past, present and future of his native soil; the
generations to come, begotten in the maelstrom of the present;
the struggle of a helpless people, powerless to lift its head and
inhale the fresh air of culture, forced to submerge itself in a
swamp, weighted down by the infinite burden of ignorance and
disease; and added to the bulk of their immense misfortune were
the laws of nature, brutally shoving them, kneading with tears a
sickly future and an even deeper degeneration for their race.

In studying the people of the mountains, Juan was witness to
the evolutionary development of a race: its prehistory, its obscure
origin, its migrations, and then—upon contact with the
Europeans—its mixtures and transformations.

He was well acquainted with the life these people led in the colony. He saw them descend in a straight line of ethnic mixtures whose end product was contaminated with a deadly, invincible weakness, leaving its arteries anemic, the brain sluggish, the arms without strength.

He felt pessimistic. Such beautiful fields, such brilliant flora, such superb fauna! But what did they all mean to an anemic soul, treading barefoot upon such an exquisite landscape, without even the strength to ponder the generous, opulent handiwork of nature? At times he thought: perhaps their spirits are dormant. Culture, more culture was lacking. Schools . . . schools! Then he looked at it as strictly a psychological problem, and he mentally enacted laws and statutes to uplift the unfortunate masses.

Other times, his ideas followed a different course. No, it was not the spirit. The contaminated, the feeble, the deformed, was the body. It was a physical problem.

Never has the rosebush sprouted from a stone, and never could the full splendor of civilization flower forth from such a sick, undernourished people.

Thus, Juan spent long hours reviewing the history of the colony, searching for remedies, ways to prepare for the future, measures to conserve the good and curtail the bad; and in all his labor there was infinite love for his blessed native land, for the provident soil upon which he lived, and whose happiness and misery he felt to be his own.

But other times the struggle took on another aspect. Faced with collective evil, what should men of cultivated spirits do? Two viewpoints engaged in a brutal match. On the one side, the *ideal:* abandon one's self to the search for cures, clamor for the common good, voice one's feelings of outrage, submit to personal sacrifice before the sacred altar of the common good, of the mother earth of one's native land. On the other hand, the *practical:* be indifferent, turn away, work for one's own welfare; abandon one's self to that eagle which soars highest, to one's personal aspirations; since sacrifice for others bears with it self torment, pain, hunger for one's own children, and is like the hurricane that scatters seeds of ingratitude and treachery, let the stern god of selfishness reign supreme; stay silent, abandon one's self to the miasma that fills the immense stagnant pond of social decay with poisonous sediments. Abandon one's soul and conscience.

Juan bounced like a ball from one attitude to the other. Such anxiety, such impatience for good in his hours of idealism; such pessimism, such cowardice when it was time to act! Reason and a good heart pointed out the enormous duties of patriotism; greed and selfishness detoured his instincts and threw them to their knees in retreat or obeisance.

Juan was sometimes seized by a brief burst of energy and he would try to counsel the impoverished workers. But on other days, he would lapse into dismay: he alone could achieve nothing. And so, his mission on the mountain was exclusively *practical*. His son, his beloved son, should occupy his heart and mind. Of what importance were philosophical speculations? Coffee, plenty of coffee, should be converted into gold and then planted in the by-ways where his son—the sole image on the altar of his affection—would travel.

Juan was so indecisive about such matters that he finally came to laugh at himself, as though he had a Voltaire inside him, mocking his doubts. Bah! That entire world outside the balcony house was nothing more than an immense hospital. Hunger reigned, and life was barely sustained by the miserable alms of a banana. It was a tomb for the living. That great pale mass of people was a multitude of vague silhouettes, dregs . . . a bundle of twisted vines with the vices and virtues so tangled that they were inseparable. Ah! How can one define them? The hurricanes lash them in their simple huts; the steaming humidity of the night lurks treacherously; during the day, the white-hot sun chars them with its silent fire. Everything seemed to push them towards destruction. Juan shrugged his shoulders, feigning indifference. Yes, they were condemned to extinction; a lifeless race succumbing to the selective action of the species; a gigantic stomach, perishing of hunger. What did all those sorrows mean to him? He was but an atom, and evil was as huge as the cordillera. No one listened to him, no one understood him, and the extreme misery around him seemed to menace him with its touch, threatening to destroy his strength and obliterate his spirit.

So he, Juan del Salto, who ate well, who surrounded himself with comforts and always proceeded according to the counselings of good hygiene, often came to believe that he, too, was sick; he imagined himself to be suffering from some nervous disease which prevented him from arriving at just solutions in socio-philosophical matters.

Engrossed in such thoughts, he waited for Marcelo. The night slipped by with the precision of its eternal cycle, illuminated by a tenuous, mysterious light that descended from the sky like a timid kiss, a furtive love. A few glowworms traced luminous zigzags in the emptiness, or perched upon the shrubs and were brilliant dots, like sparkling fairy eyes or spangles adorning earth's vestments. Nature dozed, free from the impulse of man's hand. All alone, it stirred under the force of the divine breath. Juan waited.

The door creaked and Marcelo's lean figure appeared.

"Sit down," said Juan, "and be prepared to speak frankly."

The youth's face still betrayed the emotion he displayed that afternoon. His usual listless color, and the broad rings beneath his eyes, were even more intense, as though he were panic-stricken.

"Yes, be frank, don't hide the truth from me," the land owner continued. "This afternoon, when I made a general reference to crime, you paled and trembled. I was saying that all of you—with your silence—are often accomplices to wrongdoings; and when I suggested that you would perhaps be capable of witnessing a crime and then not help the police in their investigation, you trembled. You are still trembling. Why did my words affect you so deeply?"

"It's that . . ."

"Marcelo, you've seen a crime."

"Me?"

"Yes, and you've said nothing about it."

"But . . ."

"I've told you it's useless to pretend. I can read it in your face. You ought not to hide it from me. I only want to know in order to

save you, if there is still time. I would never hand you over to the
police . . ."

"No, I'm not a criminal, don Juan . . ."

"I am neither a judge nor a policeman. I can be your friend, as
I always am to all my good workers. I have always considered you
to be an honorable man, a faultless worker, even more so than
your brother Ciro . . ."

"Oh, thank you, thank you . . ."

"Speak, then. Lighten the burden in your heart."

"It's true, don Juan. I've seen a terrible thing. Yes, I'm a coward
and I know it. It frightens me to be alone, or to walk in deserted
places, and the thought of crime terrifies me."

"Have you ever thought of it?"

"Yes, I've always dreamed many times that someone was killing
me or that I was killing another: and those dreams frighten me so
much that I feel chills when I see a gun, and the sight of a hunting knife or a dagger makes me dizzy."

"Come now, it's only your nerves. You're the gentle type and
not born for evil!"

"But ever since I saw . . . what I saw, I barely sleep, and when I
finally doze off, I have horrible nightmares."

"Tell me what you saw; every detail."

Then, in an emotional tone, Marcelo related a gloomy tale.
Some time ago, his brother Ciro and he were living in a small
hilltop shack on Galante's farm. To get there, it was necessary to
descend a slope, cross the river by hopping from stone to stone,
and then climb a steep hill. The narrow trail was heavily pocked
by the footsteps of travelers on the muddy, mountainous terrains.
Dense woods covered the paths, and one could virtually be sure
that the direct rays of the sun had never bathed the earth there.

In another hut, still higher than Marcelo's, there lived Ginés: a
young man whose modest property adjoined Galante's. Ginés
lived there with Aurelia, his wife, one of the most beautiful *campesinas* in the region. After the day's labors, Marcelo usually ate in
the home of some friend, since in his hut there was no woman to
take charge of domestic affairs. As for Ciro, he did the same. At

nightfall, the brothers would meet at their dwelling on the hill, where they slept.

One night, following a day of heavy rains, Marcelo was returning to his little home. The muddy path caused him to slip every step of the way, and when he brushed against the plants waterdrops from the rain-soaked foliage fell upon him.

While wading across the river, Marcelo heard footsteps. Frightened, he stopped and huddled behind a shrub. It was a very dark night, but a few faint rays filtered down from the brilliant stars. Then, Marcelo saw a man appear on the path. It was Galante, and he carried a very thin rope in his hand. The frightened youth trembled in his hiding place. He had heard that Galante was a terrible man, with a considerable reputation for suspicious deeds. What could Galante be doing there, and at such an unlikely hour? Why would he forsake the comfort of his dwelling to rove the mountains on such a dark night?

Marcelo waited fearfully while Galante crossed the river in a few bounds and began to climb the path on the other side. Hardly had he taken a few strides, when he stopped. He groped about on the ground as though in search of something, and stood up with a large sharp-cornered rock in his hands. Then he did something Marcelo couldn't distinguish, and the youth watched as Galante dropped the rock to the ground once more, and clambered up a low bushy tree overhanging the trail.

Marcelo was puzzled. Galante, the rich land owner, perched in a tree on a dark and dreadful night! What did it mean? Galante mounted one of the tree branches and Marcelo watched how—as if by magic—the stone floated upward from the earth. Undoubtedly Galante had tied it firmly to one end of the rope and was hoisting it up.

Then, much time passed, with Galante in the tree and Marcelo shivering with fear in his hideout. Suddenly there was the sound of footsteps trampling the thicket, and a fresh harmonious voice broke into song. It was Ginés, returning home after a long day's labor at Juan del Salto's machines.

In the little home on the height of the hill Aurelia awaited her husband, as their supper steamed in the pots. Ginés' song unfolded across the mountainside in a hundred resonances: it gushed gaily, festively, sonorously, and the hollows of the mountain echoed it melancholically, sadly, faintly . . .

Marcelo watched Ginés wade the river and begin the uphill ascent. Now he reached the spot where Galante hid, a place he was compelled to pass. From the branch of the tree, Galante let the rock fall. Ginés howled and fell athwart on the trail, horribly wounded.

He was dead. Galante came down from the trees, examined the corpse, dragged it by its feet to the edge of a ravine and cast it into an abyss. Frozen with horror, Marcelo watched as Galante untied the murderous rock, returned along the same path by which he had come, and disappeared in the darkness of the woods.

As he listened to Marcelo's story, Juan del Salto struggled to contain himself. Ginés had been a model worker. He had toiled honorably and intelligently at the machines for a long time. The day he was found dead in a ravine, everyone supposed the death was due to some accident. He could not have been intoxicated, because he didn't drink. But it was not impossible that on dark nights and slippery trails even the most able of men should stumble.

That night, Aurelia had heard her husband's singing, but she suspected nothing. The corpse was taken to the nearby town and the autopsy by Doctor Pintado revealed that a monstrous fracture of the cranium and contusions of the nerve center had caused death. It was taken for granted that during the fall his head had smashed against a rocky mound. Soon, people forgot about Ginés.

Juan was boiling with anger over such an infamous deed. He looked out the window and searched in the shadows for Galante's farm. On the face of the neighboring mountain, it evanesced in the blackness of the night. There it was: expansive, prosperous, the succulent coffee beans already ripening with abundant riches. Every year at harvest time a river of gold bubbled forth from that place.

"Wretch!" exclaimed Juan, shaking his clenched fists in the air. "You wanted riches and you've gotten them. You first came here a beggar, but you put your tiger's paw in the door, and with trickery and plunder you've built a fortune. Miserable wretch! Never has an honorable thought guided your actions. Gold, always gold, was your religion, and in exchange you offered only ingratitude and wickedness. Great man you are, great man! All lives are at the mercy of your whims, all honors prey to your appetite. Such an example, such a horrible example! How can one hope to improve the lot of the people when these poisoners, these mute teachers, corrupt everything around them with their example, sculpting evil into their hearts and killing all hope of goodness!"

Then he fell silent. He had unleashed a tempest of ideas, which collided with reality and were powerless. It was his dream to redeem, to regenerate. But when his ideas tried to take shape and exercise their influence in actual practice, he felt wrath and pain as he considered the immensity of the task, and recognized the defeat of his ideals.

Meanwhile, the night blurred the contours of the mountains. The monstrous cordillera—its rude peaks and fertile valleys, its worm-like linkings—was like a black brush stroke applied to the deep gray canvas of the sky.

But the landscape's black death contained the lovely whiteness of the coming dawn and the quietude of slumber which anesthetized all about it; it gave promise of the smiling life of the nearing daybreak: a life filled with wing-flappings, perfumes and flowery nuptials; a renascence celebrated by the pure joys of nature.

Marcelo was trembling. His hands were cold and his gaze vacant. His simple mind offered no balm to his predicament. He feared with an impulsive dread, sometimes without even knowing why, conjuring up giant ghastly phantoms.

Emotionally, Marcelo had been severely wounded by witnessing the horrible scene. Each time his memory re-sketched the drama, the wound festered once more, his dormant emotions awoke, his heart thumped uncontrollably, and his nerves quivered as though

electrified. Marcelo felt sick; he tottered dizzily; he was a bundle
of nerves, a shapeless mass that was equally prone to good or evil,
a rudderless soul that was prey to the winds.

Dominating his anger, Juan turned to Marcelo.

"All right," he said. "Galante killed Ginés. But why? Did you
ever find out the reason for the crime?"

"Never. Although what happened later . . ."

"What happened?"

"Not long after, Aurelia took up with Galante."

"She left her home?"

"No. Galante would visit her and take care of her. Then I heard
that he bought her land."

"Yes, this I know to be true."

". . . and that he paid for it in supplies and goods that they gave
her, on Galante's account, in a store in Vegaplana."

"And then?"

"They quarreled. Since Galante owned the farm, he threw Aurelia out. She left in search of some relatives, taking with her a
little boy, Galante's son, whom he didn't want. Now Aurelia lives
here and there, almost on charity."

"And the money from the farm she sold?"

"All gone up in smoke; she is in misery . . ."

They remained silent while Juan meditated deeply. Marcelo
watched him, trembling.

"Marcelo," said Juan at last, in a reassuring tone, "what you've
just told me is terrible. You saw a crime, but you're not a criminal.
If you could prove the truth of such a terrible deed I would say,
do your duty and tell the police. But you have no proof. It happened in such a lonely hidden place that your efforts to prove the
truth would be useless. Keep silent, then, and don't fear. Try to
control yourself, and don't let another man's guilt rob you of
sleep. Work, work all the time: nothing distracts and controls a
man better than work. Are you married?"

"No."

"But a woman lives with you, right?"

"One lived at my side for a few months, but I separated from
her. Now I live with Ciro, who is away most of the nights."

"Didn't she behave well with you?"

"In the beginning, yes. Then she gave me trouble because she liked to drink, and I tried to stop her."

"Don't you drink?"

"Never. One day, to please that woman, I drank and learned a lesson."

"I should say so; you were drunk for a week."

"I don't know what came over me. I lost control of myself. They told me that I spent the whole day picking fights with everyone. Rum burns my throat, it makes me want to jump around and bite; I hate everyone when I drink."

"It's good that you don't. Liquor is slow poison, like a drop of fire. A man who lets himself be dominated by drink is lost."

"Ah, God free me! It's a hateful vice."

"You must work, and you must eat in order to be strong. Understand? You're alone; everything you earn is your own. You're thin and pale. Try to feed yourself better; eat meat. On Sunday, at sunrise, go to town and see Doctor Pintado. I'll give you a card so that he sees you and prescribes something. You need medicines to give you strength, to cure your nightmares and your pallor. To sleep now. Until tomorrow."

Marcelo left and Juan remained alone with his thoughts.

Chapter Three

The next day, with the first streaks of light, work resumed on don Juan's farm.

The morning wet the earth with tremulous drops of dew. A rainbow of colors in the sky gave an imperial reception to the sun. The cool, damp dawn enriched the forests and gave them strength for the new day, kindling the hues of the flowers, enhancing the green of the leaves, raising erect the tall slender stems of the plants, enticing the flowers in the fields to show their opulent finery to the sun. The serene new day smiled upon the hillocks and valleys; the eternal force turned the wheel of life with the inexorable patience of the infinite.

The brigades of workers moved with a haste that stimulated the foreman, as though the night's interruption had damaged the crop, as though the hours of sleep had slowed the growth of the coffee plants. Montesa, the foreman, drove them hard: he spoke harshly to the sawyers, demanding that the planks cut from the thick tree trunks be of an exact length, equal in breadth; the men, protesting and promising, disappeared in the hills, in search of the cutters, where the trees condemned to the ax rose skyward; he shouted at the drovers whose animals were laden with banana seedlings and coffee grains, urging them to hurry to the planting sites, but without uselessly whipping the patient mules, or the powerful hinny that could haul the cargo of three animals; he flung curses at the men who cleaned the fields, and rebuked them for their stupidity. When they threw crushed rocks on the ground to make a footpath girdling the orchard, they had destroyed some of the precious stalks, which had to be replanted. Then he scolded the carpenters for their poor work the week before. To Montesa, they were all drones, sloths, with neither eyes nor senses, and often even lacking in good intention.

Montesa was one of them; a compatriot of that mass of pale country folk who so preoccupied Juan del Salto; but he had seen the world. As a boy, he would often descend to the plain, to the capital of the district. From the crests he had gazed southward and seen a silver fringe of water set ablaze by the noonday sun. He contemplated that immense surface which disappeared in the distance, in the land of mysteries on the horizons of the unknown. But the day he went down and beheld the sea from the shore, he stood there mute with astonishment. He arched his head back, straining up on his toes, to see even farther, anxiously inhaling the sea breeze. That day, the sea filled his dreams, and became the theme of his stories, related while squatting together with the other lank youths of the mountain. To him, the sea was grand and beautiful. Lacking in education, he was unable to find points of comparison on the land, so he sought them in the sky. To Montesa, the sea was as huge as the celestial roof, it was hypnotic. One day, he went down to the plain with some *campesinos* who were driving a pack of beasts laden with fruit. He did not return to the mountain. His family learned later that he had decided to pursue another type of work. They soon forgot him.

The boy, in the meantime, ran the gamut: he served as a horse groom, stable boy, shop clerk and in a thousand other jobs.

Finally—older and stronger—he secured work as a stevedore. From that day, loading and unloading ships in the heat of the warehouses and holds, rowing boats and poling launches, he no longer thought of his native woods: the sea, his master, was out there, captivating him with its murmurs, enrapturing him with its frothy leaps.

One day, the captain of a ship anchored in the port was carried ashore gravely ill. Montesa was chosen to watch over the man, and nurse him back to health.

Weeks later, the captain, now cured, was possessed by the vast generosity of all those who escape from a great danger. Ah, what a fine young boy! The mariner asked the youth how he could repay him and Montesa confessed that it was his ambition to be a sailor, to travel and flick the ashes of his cigar into the high seas.

Soon afterwards, the grateful captain took the farmboy to distant lands. The first journey was a nightmare: he was put to the test by horrible seasickness off the coast of Canada, and the dreadful cold nearly froze the blood in his veins.

But he soon became accustomed and it was curious to watch him grow, adapting himself to the new life. The native boy grew hardy and strong, with a ruddy complexion. There were many thrills in his new life: trips to the torrid zone, long journeys to Australia, to Africa. From the primitive ship, he moved to a merchant steamer; from this to another; in all, he sailed upon a hundred keels.

As the years passed, and Montesa celebrated his fortieth birthday, there took shape in his mind an idea that had gnawed away within him for some time. His native land. It was like a secret anxiety; neither hunger nor thirst nor pain, but a rare deep feeling, with the flavor of intense sorrow and a vague melancholy. Childhood scenes flickered in his memory and Montesa could soon think of nothing but returning to the island colony. He counted up his savings, which he put in his suitcase; then he signed aboard a ship heading homeward and at last returned to his mountain.

When his old comrades saw him, they thought he was from another world. A robust man, his faced covered with hair, tanned and stout, and so thickly muscled that he could surely demolish any man with a single blow. The campesinos delighted in beholding him and, most of all, in hearing his tales. They soon came to respect him as some super-being, and they rejoiced each time he spoke a foreign tongue; they begged him to repeat that *yes,* that *sapristi,* and that forceful *god damn,* which made them split their sides with laughter.

After he returned, Montesa built a small house. It had a zinc roof, a wooden floor, air-tight walls, cross bars for the windows and locks for the doors.

With the modesty that his scanty capital permitted, he made it into a home, adorning it with a bed, the necessary linen, half a dozen chairs, an equal number of dishes, and the indispensable utensils for preparing a decent meal.

The nest completed, he married. A young maiden from the

valley opened her arms to him, and the curate from the neighboring parish sanctified their union. From that day on, it was to work: she in the domestic beehive; he on the mountain. Juan del Salto hired him, guided him through the apprenticeship of his new job, and he soon became the most trustworthy man on the farm. Up there in the small house, another Montesa was born each year.

More than once Juan del Salto had scolded Montesa for his harsh treatment of the campesinos. One must be condescending and kind, he said, but Montesa had no patience for frivolity. Fine thing if the ship's captain left his whip in the desk drawer! No, *señor,* plenty of whippings; that's how to get the mob moving.

Juan warned him that such sternness was inhuman; he tried to convince Montesa that a ship's deck was one thing and the slopes of the mountain another. But Montesa was severe and bitter; he spit curses at the laborers, as though they were beasts, who responded only to the lash.

The laborers often thought of vengeance. But how? That devil had an anvil in each bicep, a hammer in each fist, and in each leg a fulling mill that could provide the king of all kicks. They resigned themselves before the threat of force, the despotism of his stern will. If someone angrily plotted treachery, he soon trembled over the possibility of his plans being discovered, and feeling those huge hands wrap around his neck with strangulatory rage.

At home, Montesa was another man. His woman, to him, was the best in the region; his children received every indulgence. They all went about dressed and shod. What is that? The little ones running around naked? In no part of the world had he seen such wretchedness. The children must have shoes. They must attend the rural school and learn to read, so that they did not go through what he did, learning the ABC's at such an advanced age that it was harder than tying a knot or gathering in a halyard. In Montesa's house one found order, method, fixed hours, sheets on the beds, firewood in the kitchen. It was a poor, humble house; but it had a head and feet, and it was a place where he, the host, could say without exaggeration: "this is my home."

Such circumstances gave Montesa a superior position among

the people of the mountain and they liked to get into his good graces with their compliments. But during the work day they often heard him yell: "Get up there! Boobs! Idiots!"

That morning, with his habitual acrimony, Montesa dispatched the men to their tasks and when they marched away he mounted a squalid nag and followed behind them.

The women who lived in the small homes near the farm roamed across the esplanade by the buildings. Some headed for the river, carrying on their hips dry striated palm leaves heaped high with dirty clothes to be washed in the current. Others searched for chips of firewood to heat their hearths: three smoke-stained stones beneath a straw shed, open to the four winds, supporting a rusty scorched cauldron.

Other women were returning from Andújar's store with the victuals for lunch: four scraps of food purchased for a few cents or charged towards the work their husbands would perform during the week. Others, seated on doorsteps, breastfed pale infants, or shelled corn, or piled up beans, or crushed coffee beans into thick powder in giant mortars; etched in all of their faces was a strange tinge of sorrow, which made the contrast of their smiles seem even more ostensible.

Suddenly, a diminutive sharp-featured old woman, who was emaciated to a startling degree, appeared on the esplanade.

"Old Marta!" shouted one woman, who sat on a block of wood and peeled potatoes. "Old Marta, come here and tell us what happened on Sunday. We've heard all about it!"

"Shut your mouth," replied the old woman. "You want a laugh at my expense, eh? Instead, lend me a machete so that I can cut a few chips of kindling."

"Here is a machete," said another woman, "but tell us the story; who hit you?"

"Some . . . *idiot*."

"Is it true that they tore the kerchief from your head?"

"I could have torn their eyes out! But listen, child, my grandson has no buttons on his shirt. For your good friend, if you could find me one, even if it is old. Please, I need it."

"All right, Old Marta, here's the button; but let's get on with the story. Is it true that Montesa swept up the game with his feet?"

"It's an abuse, I tell you! I was casually passing by the shore of the brook, and had I not moved quickly they would have trampled me ... Oh yes! I also need a handful of tamarinds. For a physic, understand?"

"But it seems impossible that among so many men no one stood up to Montesa."

"Montesa? Woe is he who looks for a fuss with Montesa! You all know that Deblás is brave, but no indeed! He hid and wouldn't even show his face. And what a kick he gave Gaspar! I'm glad; perhaps now he won't be so mean ... "

"And what did they do to you, Old Marta?"

"Come now, stop annoying me; you have no respect for your elders. *Hombre,* now that I remember, down by the brook I left a few bits of dirty clothes; if one of you could give me a pinch of soap I would be most grateful."

The women laughed. Every morning, the same visit from Marta, scavenging for scraps of food and hoarding discarded trifles, wringling from them the last few drops of use. Begging, always begging, offering as a pretext her decrepit age and those white hairs that hardly inspired veneration. Meanwhile, some hundred *quintales*[1] of coffee that she herself had picked on her plot of earth, and she herself shelled, and she herself spread in the sun to dry, and she herself secretly sold, vanished and was converted into money. No one knew the whereabouts of that money; it left not a trace in clothing, or in the house, or in the hungry look of her grandson. Her greed was sordid, eager, capable of crime. The egg abandoned by a hen in the shadow of the mountain: what a fortune! The sugar or rice dribbled out from a broken sack while it is hauled along the trails: what a find! The bananas given her by neighbors: what a profit!

She lived in a miserable shack close to the river, in the poetic shade of a coffee orchard. Her lone companion was her grand-

---

[1]*quintal*, one hundred pounds.

son; a boy of fourteen so physically underdeveloped that he could barely pass for six. The good grandmother was killing him with hunger: "when one is poor, one must become accustomed to need, because God is everywhere. With a few green vegetables and a bit of salted meat on Sundays, anyone can live and grow fat. The most important thing is to learn how to work and be economical. When the sun shines, one should remove one's shirt and shoes, since they only get in the way. Next, one should care for the little animals, although it means taking food from one's own mouth to give a few crumbs to the poor little hog and the poor little hens. Thus, one learns to be charitable and doesn't spoil the stomach with bad habits."

Her wretched grandchild was living on air, subject to the meager ration doled out by the iniquitous old woman. The people swore that Marta buried her money: the product of her harvests, of the pigs she raised, of the eggs and hens she sold, of the bundles of clothes she washed; a hundred different ways to make a profit, that magically disappeared down some hole in the forest.

One time, Marta suffered a great scare. Night had already fallen and everyone in the hut was prepared for sleep. The hens were perched in the uppermost branch of the nearest tree; the hog had been tethered to one of the hut's weak foundation stakes; the embers of the fire had cooled; and, lastly, as a shield against the intrigues of the outdoors, the giant palm leaf—impenetrable as a sieve—played the role of a door. All was silent: the boy slept in a corner, dreaming of food, while the grandmother dozed, huddled up in a hammock.

Suddenly there were footsteps and the palm leaf rustled. Marta fearfully lifted her head and sniffed about suspiciously.

"Good evening," said a strange voice.

"Who is there?" she asked.

"It is I . . . "

"Who?"

"Open and let me sleep inside."

"And who are you?"

"You don't know me, but I'll do you no harm if you are charitable."

The old woman was desolate. *Dios mío!* Give lodging to a stranger! How could she? Would she have to pay a ransom for her safety? Her treasure was on the mountain; but who could say, if someone clutched her by the throat, that she would not be forced to reveal the hiding place?

The voice continued: "Open and do not fear. Any corner to rest is good enough, and I will be gone at sunrise."

"But I do not know you."

"You had better open, and not force me to break down the door with my fist," he added impatiently.

"All right, all right, I am coming."

By the brightness of the starry sky she saw a man, still young, but with a mean countenance and tattered clothing. The stranger entered in a bound, and the hut tottered like a ship rocked by the waves. Then, groping in the dark, he lay down on the floor next to the grandson, who stirred fitfully on a pile of old rags. Gripped by fear, Marta tried to ingratiate herself with her guest.

"No, I never deny shelter to unfortunates; but since no one bears the proof of honesty written on his face. . . "

"You have nothing to fear from me."

"But who are you? I do not remember having seen you before in the *barrio*, and I know everyone here."

"I have lived in these parts for three months; not in the *barrio*, but on the mountain."

"On the mountain!"

"Yes; I walk with a hundred eyes, on the run from the police. I suppose that you are a good woman and would not sell me. . . "

"Ah! That no. . . "

"I am a fugitive from prison."

Marta was gripped by fear. An escaped convict! A criminal roaming the hills, God knows with what intentions!

"But I won't harm anyone, unless they try to stop me and take me back."

"And why did they put you in prison?"

"That is an old story. One day the rum climbed to my head, I quarreled with another man, and I killed him. I was arrested and condemned to twelve years in prison. At first I was on the point of going mad, but then I decided to wait for my chance. They were taking us out to work on the roads one day and, when no one was looking, I headed for the mountains. I have run the whole way across the *cordillera* until reaching here, where I have a relative. I ate the fruits of the mountains, and bits of *bacalao*[2] given me by kind people I met on the trail. I don't know where I'm headed, nor what will become of me. I have no home and dare not go down to the plain, because I know they're after me. Today I felt sick. My body shivered from the rain, and I felt faint. I came down by that path and saw your cabin. Now, thanks to your charity, here I am, and already I feel warm and recovered. May God repay you, old woman, for your kindness to me!"

Marta listened to the tale with wide open eyes. If that man harbored treacherous intentions he would not surprise her while she slept.

Familiar with every inch of the house, she reached out in the shadows, grasped an old spade handle and pulled it to her side. If he made the least suspicious movement, she would muster up enough strength to crack open his skull with the first blow. She passed the night sleeplessly, while the fugitive snored tranquilly.

Early the next morning, they exchanged courtesies. Marta was grateful to her guest because he had caused no trouble; she generously condescended to share her thick muddy coffee with him. That morning, the grandson managed to get a small bit of breakfast, too. The stranger took his leave, giving thanks:

"I won't forget your charity. If some time you are in need you can depend on me. What is your name?"

"I am called Marta. And you?

Glancing suspiciously about him, he replied, "I am called Deblás."

He disappeared in the forest, carrying with him the heavy burden his presence had imposed upon Marta's fearful spirit.

* * *

That other morning, the women of Juan del Salto's farm had laughed for a long time at the old miser woman's expense,

---

[2]*bacalao,* dried salted codfish, long a food staple in rural Puerto Rico.

supplying her in the meantime with the trifles that she requested in her studiously affable voice. They were accustomed to her visits, and pitied her, although at times they scolded her for her greed and her cruel treatment of the small grandchild.

The joking would have continued had not two horsemen appeared on the trail leading up to the esplanade.

Riding first was Padre Esteban, the parish priest, looking half-clerical and half-secular, with his habit folded up in the saddle, exposing his legs which were sheathed in riding boots. Behind him was Ciro, riding a mule saddled with immense packs that nearly spanned the width of the trail.

Padre Esteban frequently roamed the mountains. He was a man of fifty years, with a lively spirit and energetic temperament. It was a common thing to see him appear unexpectedly in the hills, when some *campesino*—wanting to reconciliate himself with the faith—called the priest to his side.

After traveling about the *barrio* since the previous afternoon, he spent the night in a hut and decided to visit Juan's farm on his return trip.

Juan and he understood each other perfectly. Both loved an argument, and with great facility they would lock horns in arduous, passionate discussion.

Padre Esteban was an open, frank person. Though he was a priest, he was afflicted with none of the mannered solemnity which some of his calling liked to display, as though they were a separate, superior breed of men. Padre Esteban loved good wine; he smoked fine cigars, when he had them; and he understood perfectly that the dark eyes of a beautiful woman can drive a man to certain peccadillos. He was a happy, expansive fellow, but he was also deeply devoted to his faith, and his occasional outbursts of temper proved that he was not so much of a sheep as he might appear. His long, intimate friendship with Juan was the kind that knew the nooks of his friend's house, and the secrets of every member of the family. The padre always arrived with the assurance of one who truly knows the way.

Ciro, Marcelo's younger brother, had been sent to town the previous day. Every week a trustworthy person was sent to perform vital errands for the farm. On his way back early that morning, Ciro met Padre Esteban on the trail and they arrived together.

"Good day," said Juan to the priest a few moments later. "Good day! How fortunate are my eyes to see you as strong and agile as ever in the difficult climb of these mountains."

"*Hombre*, it doesn't go badly. Yesterday afternoon, over there in those dales, I was comforting some poor dying devil who wanted me at his side—a rare thing among these stray sheep—and I performed my divine function in his behalf. But last night it was too late to return, so I slept up there somewhere—in the home of a grasshopper, judging from the crudeness of his dwelling. Still, it was merciful of him to offer me a place to sleep, eh? But what a night, my friend! What a night! I was freezing."

Padre Esteban said he had slept fully dressed, including his boots, to defend himself from the icy filaments of air that slipped through the cracks in the walls. Juan laughed and protested that Padre Esteban should have spent the night in his farmhouse, where there are air-tight walls and blankets that could make even an icicle perspire. But the padre was not a demanding person; evening had fallen, surprising him between two ravines, and there he had passed the night. Now it was a nice day and he had a long trip ahead before reaching his parish; he was urged to sip a good aperitif, as an introduction to an even better luncheon.

As always, the conversation drifted to their favorite themes: life, the affairs of the colony, the people's misery, the strength of social customs, the need for a giant strainer to purify the corrupt ways of the *cordillera*. . .

"And the only purification possible," said the priest in a convinced tone, "the only way to clean up this living charnel house, is the faith. These helots must lift up their heads and see the supreme happiness of another life beyond the blue sky above them. They must believe in God, *hombre*, they must believe in God! But there is no faith here, nor is there hope. These people waste away their lives bit by bit, in exchange for pleasure."

Juan smiled, shaking his head in disagreement. The minds of these people, he said, were painfully concerned with the sickness of their bodies. How can one expect them to be capable of such lofty thoughts?

Padre Estaban listened impatiently. "No, wrong! wrong! Faith is sufficient in itself. Let the church bells resound; let the noise unfold and embrace the horizons; let it reach from the plains to the mountain peaks; let it climb like a gentle wave and enter every home and reach every heart, and let every heart feel humility before God. Let the altar be lit and the candles radiate loving brilliance; let the aroma of incense issue forth; let the faithful feel the powerful magnetism of such a meeting and come to kneel and pray: that is faith. Let God's word reach down and caress the bent heads of the devout; let the sacred mysteries of the church be revealed in waves of eloquence; let the holy laws be sowed among the congregation like blessed seed, and let the people hear and be moved, and pray contritely, and hope for the pardon of their sins: that is faith. And do not doubt it: that is your salvation of the masses and your cure for the world's disorder. In these mountains, filled with pariahs, it would establish a class of people governed and ennobled by work and redemption. But no: the bell peals and it could just as well be the sound of rainfall; the altar is lit and they open their mouths stupidly and follow the smoky spirals of the candles; the priest's words from the pulpit enter one ear and go out the other. One must persist, one must struggle! Faith, and only faith, can save this generation of phantoms, rescuing it from the stagnant pond in which it floats helplessly."

Juan interrupted, trying to convince Padre Esteban that no such deep influence was possible through religion. In order for a man to comprehend the religious feelings born within him, he must first have health and strength. Furthermore, entire civilizations—by exaggerating religion—had succumbed to superstition and wallowed in ignorance. This was an era of analysis and free criticism, Juan said; it was necessary to explore all horizons, because physical phenomena and morals are linked together, like celestial bodies subject to the same gravitational force.

Padre Esteban raised his voice in disagreement. Faith was a potential power like the slingshot poised in a man's hand. Once released, the stone flies swiftly and boldly. Belief was like the slingshot: the feeling was launched across time, vanquishing all obstacles, reaching the horizons of the future.

"No, Padre," said Juan. "Your natural devotion to religious

dogma makes you mistake the cause for what is really the effect. The lack of faith, the indifference that you observe in these people is nothing more than their inability to think. I concede that in the hearts of other peoples profane propaganda can separate the multitudes from religion, and slacken the bonds of faith. But not here; there can be no belief where there are no believers. . ."

"And why are there none? Because their souls have not been developed."

"No. Because their bodies have not been developed. Here, superstitions are as dominant as vice, and—in the final analysis—what are superstitions but morbid thoughts? Don't be fooled, my dear Padre; the causes of this great disaster date back to distant origins. Imagine for yourself an ethnic group that comes to the colony in the days of the conquest, and struggles to adapt itself to the torrid zone. The fears, the encampments in the open, the influences of the new soil, the harshness of the new climate, the strange foods; they could not have prospered physically. Then came the cross-breedings. So many mixtures! A cross between Caucasians and aborigines determined the population of these woods. The women of the conquerors also raised their newborn children in the new zone; but these were a minority, because the European woman was late in coming to the paradise found in the seas. The aborigine woman was the pasture, her savage grace the only genetic choice, the only fecund cloister where the new generation was formed. That mixture was prolific, but at such a price! The sturdy native of the forest yielded physical strength; the sprightly man who set foot upon the soil of the Occident yielded vigor and force. From this lot, the born composite emerged physically inferior, and was abandoned to the flow of the centuries. The aborigine race was unequal to the collision and succumbed, disappearing forever from the face of the earth. The offspring, the half-breed son, was begotten amidst misfortune and suspicion, in the spacious bridal chamber of the forest, under the imposition of the stronger. The woman was a machine. Love—and spiritual harmony—took no part in the impregnation. One being fell under the epileptic ardor of another, amidst the grandeur of a land filled with splendors, in the lush shadows of the woods, under the galvanism of a fiery sun. And there, from that surrender, rose up a new race whose offspring would populate the Canaan of the fifteenth century, the most beautiful region on earth. Then, time did the rest. New layers of life were produced, each weaker, each less like the original. It was a horrible current, heading fatally to death, a flood of life condemned to extinction by its own ferment!

Juan rose and continued to speak, passionately and eloquently.

The priest, meanwhile, stirred impatiently in his chair or paced about the room; at times he looked serious, on occasion he would smile with disdain. What bluster! Where would it all end if, in order to learn what ails a man, you must ask his grandparents, who are already eaten by the worms? That was an unrealistic way to reason. It was just like the riddle; who came first, the chicken or the egg? Come now, the priest said, it is not so difficult. Education, culture, preaching; good example: that's the way to tame the beast in man.

"They must not be abandoned," the priest continued. "It is important that they be guided in some way."

"Yes," said Juan, "but the method must be humane, and cannot avoid the physical problems."

"Much searching must be done to find the medicine that works the miracle."

"Not so much, although the cure must be gradual."

"But it will have to be started someday, I suppose."

"Yes, if it is ever to be completed."

"How terrible it is, to wait centuries for the solution to problems!"

"In the life of nations, one century is a minute. Perseverance and time conquer the world. If the problem is ever to be solved, waves of new life must come, torrents of vigor from abroad, abundancies of ethnic mixtures, the breath and vitality which are lacking here, the atmosphere of sincere, honorable liberty that is not now enjoyed. The nourishment will come in many ways: compulsory education, health vaccines, enforced hygiene, and other defenses against the forces of nature; military service, which converts weak recruits into robust veterans; the encouragement of hunting, which eliminates softness and rewards agility; clothing to awaken the shame of nudity; the encouragement of alternate crops that allow a healthy, varied diet; stimuli to build cheap, clean and sensible housing; and, above all, there must come the merciful hand that snatches away from the people the slow poison, the miserable enemy of their health, of their peace, of their redemption. . . alcohol!"

"And the church, *hombre*, where do you leave room for the church?"

"The church will come, with culture, to those hearts that are able to feel it. First comes health, then the belief in whom one wishes to believe."

"No! First is belief, then the salvation of the body and of material things. . ."

"In nature, all is important, all is transcendent."

"But one must depart from somewhere, and religion is. . ."

"Nothing is first, nor last. Take an absolute sphere in your hand: completely round, true? Could you fix the point where the sphere begins and where it ends? Impossible! Well, then, my thesis is like that sphere: wherever you put your finger can be a point of departure. All is primary, nothing is last!"

At that moment, they were told that lunch was served. Still chatting, the two friends headed towards the dining room where the dishes—already on the table—steamed appetizingly. They were now seated, and Padre Esteban still philosophized:

"All these ideas of yours are prettily immoral. First is first. The faith, there is the cure. There is the medicine. . ."

"Look, Padre," Juan interrupted, uncovering a platter and revealing a great hunk of meat. "Look: here is one of the medicines that poor patient needs."

Abandoning themselves to the luncheon, they ate and laughed with the jollity of two schoolmates.

Chapter Four

Several *campesinos* were seated upon a bed of moss by the riverside, playing cards. They were in a small wood behind Andújar's store: a hidden place, free from the gazes of passersby on the road.

Deblás, shuffling a soiled deck of cards, dealt the cards upon the soft earth, arranged the bets, uncovered the cards, paid the lucky ones and collected from the losers. They were betting *ochavos*, with a limit of one *peseta*, and the bank brimmed with a heap of coins that was further magnified by the players' anxiety.

Deblás, a fugitive from the police, had found a good hideaway in the region. His cousin Andújar protected him. Several times Andújar had misled the forest police, throwing them off the track.

On certain occasions, a cousin like Deblás could be useful to a man like Andújar. True, he was obliged to support him with money and food; but such an expense was preferable to having a relative in prison or, perhaps, having him freed by an enemy.

Deblás was a rare bird, the type with no roost of his own, who flies from one place to another, ever alert for prey. His situation with the police prevented him from working on the farms, unless his duties were not of the sort included on the weekly payroll; and the landowners, knowing the convict's history, avoided giving him work for fear of becoming involved with the law.

The fugitive subsisted on Andújar's favors, on the friendship of a few *campesinos,* on the tolerance of all, and on the profits of the game which he established every Sunday without fail.

He was in charge that day at the river bank. With his thin, shriveled body he looked like a parched man sucking the money from the others drop by drop. His fingers, wide and flat at the ends, gathered in the coins like a broom sweeping up dust, and his hands seemed guided by a secret magnet. The cards could not fall or scatter: they were fastened to those lithe hands which, with every muscular contraction, imprinted them with a distinct form.

Round about were the bettors and, further away, those who watched without gambling. All told, twenty or thirty rustics sweated over the fortunes of the game.

Among them was Ciro, with his knavish face and greedy expression. If he lost, he roared coarse epithets and then laughed to conceal his annoyance, damning his bad luck. At times he shifted his posture, as though he were changing his battle plan. He would become very serious, like someone who has at last discovered the key to an enigma and has united his five senses to check the truth of his find.

But now and then he neglected to bet, and gazed beyond the circle of players and spectators. He seemed to be waiting for something. His eyes met with the snarl of shrubs that blocked the way and, lifting his head, he managed to see the back wall of Andújar's store atop the ravine, with its haphazard surface of cedar planks dirtied and faded by rain and time.

Gaspar's giant, ignoble head stood out in the front row. He crouched amidst the drunken melee, showing his tuft of thick, tangled gray hairs; his depressed forehead; his pronounced cheekbones; his great bony eye sockets set wide apart; his broad nose, with one nostril larger than the other; his scant, bristly mustache; his ears, with the lobes adhered to the skin of his face and, dominating all, his massive snout-like jaw.

Calculating his hand, straining to guess what the others had, he bet along with a lucky one, then ran counter to the one who was losing. If some dispute arose, he egged the banker onward; if there was an argument, he barked viciously at those who had interrupted the game. He shouted enormous oaths that were like stones angrily hurled to disturb the silence of the woods. To him, they were all a bunch of imbeciles, always annoying the real players . . . a bunch of *know-nothings* . . .

When he drew a poor card, he exploded. Luck was a *woman of the streets,* who gave or denied with irritating fickleness. May lightning cleave her in two! He was a gross, cruel man; happy over another's grief, lazy in his work, vengeful over the slightest offense, selfish for pleasure but cowardly before danger, swaying between anger and laughter, with outbursts of uncontrollable violence each time the fortunes of the game brought him a profit or a loss.

Marcelo, who was among the spectators, glanced about dolefully. The timid look cast from his pale countenance was like a yellowed leaf fallen from a dying tree.

He didn't play: it seemed dangerous. A man could become involved in a quarrel or some unpleasantry for the silliest reason. Marcelo, a perpetual fugitive from danger, couldn't risk himself in the shifting situations of the game. He felt sure that he would lose, and he feared that if he won they would think him a cheat. So he resigned himself to watching. He smiled when the others burst into laughter, and if their spirits soured he retreated, separating himself from the group.

In the meantime, Andújar and his assistant were busy in the store.

The *campesinos* were shopping and settling their accounts. Since it was Sunday, the accounts—scribbled upon sheets of paper—showed the amounts and dates for each person.

The store glistened in the midday light, showing its greasy counter and filth-caked threshold. The spirit of nausea itself would have collapsed in a faint if confronted with such a sight. The shelves bulged with provisions, trinkets and cloth goods so plain that they seem to have been expressly weaved to cover the flesh of galley slaves.

On the edge of the counter there was a scale, ready to fall off at the slightest nudge. At one end of the counter there were innumerable bottles containing drinks; on the other end, pieces of dried beef, crackers and bread. There were two rooms behind the counter: one served as storage space for casks, pack saddles and work tools; the other, where Andújar slept, had a cot, two chairs and a huge trunk. This was the nocturnal lair for the octopus who clung to the back of the region with greedy tentacles.

Andújar had arrived there some years before. He appeared one day in the *barrio* with his only assets the clothes that covered him and his thirst for riches at any cost.

In that same place there once lived a seventy-year old man and a girl of twenty: an extravagant old bachelor not yet resigned to losing his good appetite, and a young girl desirous of a wealthy husband. The old man owned a few hectares of land extending from the hill to the river, and he also possessed a rustic farmhouse with palm leaf walls and a straw roof: enough to harvest fifteen or twenty *fanegas*[1] of coffee, which provided sufficient income for the barren home.

Andújar asked them for shelter, it was granted, and he strode across the threshold never to leave.

First, he knew how to inspire the pity of the old man, who conceded him generous treatment; then he burst out in a flurry of work, helping his host with the field labors. He became a valuable aide and, on humid days, when the old man coughed or quietly soothed the cruel rebellions of hidden vices, Andújar was indispensable.

When the old man was unable to work, Andújar bore the entire burden. He took charge of the farm and—with shrewd treachery—also of the bridal chamber. The girl, in her role as nurse to the invalid, encountered the furtive prize of a robust youth, and thus they continued until the old man bid *adiós* to life.

Then Andújar unfurled his wings. There was neither a will nor an heir. The farm was ownerless. In that epoch, the colony had neither property lists nor mortgage title offices: each person possessed because he possessed. A simple piece of paper and a witness sufficed to prove ownership of land. The "widowed" mistress had no right to anything, and Andújar spied an open road to his ambition.

Since it did not suit his interest to get rid of the girl, he tried to dupe her: of *course* the farm was hers. Furthermore, it was necessary to increase its production to make it profitable. So he continued to be her "man."

Within a year, Andújar wrought miracles: there was a wooden house with three *cabañas* encircling it, and the farm had doubled

[1]*fanega*, a grain measure, about 1.6 bushels.

in value. The "widow," seeing herself become richer, was delighted and the bond between them remained close.

But Andújar grew tired of her and dealt the finishing blow. One day, with admirable barefacedness, he dismissed her and put her trunk out on the road. Adrift in a sea of confusion and affection, she found her only relief in a good cry. She wept, but the house was closed to her. Andújar, in turn, generously bribed a throng of witnesses and initiated a writ of possession. The outcome was that Andújar became the rightful owner of the farm, which he said he had verbally purchased from the old man. To authenticate this, he produced a filthy, faded bill of sale he had found while rummaging through the deceased's effects, a receipt which had been granted by the previous owner.

The girl disappeared after the plunder. How could she fight for a property which was not hers? How could she prove that Andújar was an impostor? Andújar glowed in his new dominion: his plump body puffed with pride and his look was intense and sagacious. Later he established a store: a pinhole of fraud through which the money of the *barrio* would drain away.

The store extended like vines scaling a wall. Next he built three structures: one held six driers, wide troughs with wooden wheels which were kept beneath the floor of the house and served for drying coffee in the sun; another was a warehouse for the crops; the third was a type of shed to shelter the threshing machine and the serrated cylinders for crushing the coffee beans.

Andújar's businesses flourished. Multiple interests crowded together in his head like the seeds of a pomegranate. In the store, a pound of lead on one side of the scale equaled twelve ounces of food on the other side. The measuring stick was an accomplice of the scale: the regency or muslin was stretched like the limbs of a circus clown, and nine-tenths of a *vara* of cloth always corresponded to a full *vara* on the stick. Thus, all was profit: the provisions and cloth goods were bought in the lowlands at discount prices and then shrunken and sold dearly on the mountain. When they sold beans or chickpeas by the pound, Andújar and the clerk filled the container to the brim, but they always skimmed a hand along the top with consummate skill, trimming the heap by a few ounces.

Business flared out in other directions. Andújar bought unshelled coffee at the cheapest price, processed it himself, and realized an even larger profit. Other times, *campesinos* in urgent need sold him their unharvested coffee and then there was no limit on the price. On some occasions he paid for one *fanega* and reaped ten in the harvest.

To certain freeholders who offered good guarantees, he supplied advances payable at harvest time. The advances were measured by the same scale and *vara,* in goods or in money, supposedly without interest. He did not understand this business of "interest," and it annoyed him to get involved in complex bookkeeping. No, no interest: if he handed over twenty *pesos* cash, they owed him thirty *pesos* worth of coffee measured by his scale. That was all.

They sometimes brought him sacks of unshelled coffee to be processed in his machine. The machine resembled an equestrian circus, and the rammer a runaway horse on the track. There was a secret sluice in the bottom of the thick wooden ring: when the ring was filled and the rammer revolving, coffee beans slowly escaped through the hatch, never to be seen again by their rightful owner. Later, the clerk would crawl beneath the machine and gather up the secret spoils in a sack.

Sometimes, in exchange for provisions, Andújar bought small pieces of bordering property. On other occasions, he furtively changed boundary markers and made himself owner of a few more *varas* of the mountain. Deblás often helped him in this business.

The victims either never discovered the transgression or were dazzled by the verbosity of the shopkeeper, who seemed to be working miracles before their naive eyes. All was profit. He was hungry, blind, possessed by a burning nightmare of success.

But that was not enough: he descended to contemptuous trifles. In the store he would buy stale bread and sell it as new, diluting it with rum and neutralizing the taste with pepper; now and then he would fatten up an old ox, bought for a pittance, and sell it as tender meat, at outrageous prices. In his coffee transactions, he did not return the sacks used to hold the merchandise. He took a percentage of the winnings from the card players by the river bank. He always paid a less than a just tax sum, because the classification of his business in the municipal treasury was errone-ous, concealing its true worth. In tune with these trifles, his stock was almost always of the worst quality, with spoiled meats, grossly diluted liquors, and cloth materials deteriorated by time.

More than once, Andújar had to cope with suspicious laborers. When he was unable to bully them into submission, he affected great disdain. All right, it is just the same with me, there will be no deal. For what there is to gain, it is better to forget it. Yes, better not to worry about the matter. And to prove his indifference, he would treat the stubborn laborer to a stiff drink, a tactic which often brought results. The alcohol would begin to romp about in the fellow's veins, he would feel as though he were reborn to a second life, in which things looked different. Then, under the influence of that ticklish joy, the *campesino* softened and the apparently impossible business was settled after a few gratuitous drinks. Andújar knew the people's weakness, and lost no oppor-tunities.

In the past week he had finished a transaction that cost him some bitter quarrels. Small thing: the hollow talk of a whip-persnapper who didn't appreciate favors.

It concerned a small landowner who, for lack of other recourse, came to the store. He had a good farm and he was a reliable man. The matter was settled in this way: Andújar would give him eight hundred *pesos* in small portions of cash or goods, whenever they were needed. As collateral, the farm was in Andújar's hands. To get it back, the laborer was obliged to pay eight hundred *pesos*, and two hundred more in the form of a lease, by the end of one year.

With the money due, the debtor proudly appeared, eager to pay. Then Andújar declared that, having received one thousand *pesos* that day—the total of the debt—there remained eight hundred more pending.

"What?" said the man, astonished. "I received a loan of eight hundred *pesos* and I promised to pay a thousand after one year. Here they are, we're even."

"No, not even. You still owe me eight hundred *pesos*, and you must pay me before I return the farm."

"But did you not lend me eight hundred *pesos*?"

"Yes."

"Am I not paying you the thousand I promised?"

"Yes . . ."

"Well, what more?"

"You are calculating *your* way. Listen, one thousand *pesos* from the mortgage, and eight hundred worth of goods that you received on account, according to my books and the receipts you gave me, are one thousand, eight hundred *pesos*. Now do you understand?"

"But how can that be?" argued the laborer, lost in a labyrinth of confusion.

"It's very simple. Just think about it."

"No, no, it's impossible. Devil! What account are you talking about?"

"The one and only. Look, have you received eight hundred *pesos*?"

"Yes, and not a cent more."

"You promised to pay me one thousand in a year?"

"Yes."

"How much are you paying me today?"

"A thousand!"

"How much have I given you on account?"

"Eight hundred."

"So you are paying me the sum of the account, plus two hundred *pesos* toward buying back your farm; now you owe me eight hundred *pesos*, and I won't return the farm until you pay me."

The laborer was dumbfounded. What kind of law was that, receiving eight hundred, and having to pay back a thousand eight hundred! It was a fraud! The argument raged for two hours, but it was no use. Andújar refused to return the farm. The debtor went to town, hoping the municipal officials would help. The documents were studied, but Andújar had spun his web carefully. The deed of re-sale simply said that the property had been sold for a thousand *pesos*, which were noted as received; that it had been leased for a year at two hundred *pesos*, and that, with the year over and the lease paid, the purchaser was obligated to return the farm. But the laborer had also signed a series of receipts for small sums which added up to eight hundred *pesos* and Andújar presented these as debts owed to him. Neither the deed referred to the drawing account nor did the account refer to the deed. They were two things completely apart. Two debts, but just one fraud.

The unsuspecting *campesino* was at least granted one right: having received the thousand *pesos*, Andújar was forced to return the farm. But the other eight hundred debt remained, and how many anxieties there would be to wipe it clean! How many tribulations to settle it, bit by bit! This good bit of business had been terminated in recent days; the last *fanegas* of coffee had been delivered, liquidating the debt. Eight hundred *pesos* converted in two years to a thousand eight hundred! All was profit.

That Sunday, Andújar, eager as ever, devoted himself to selling and scheming. The clerk, a strapping youth of the *barrio*, worked according to the pace set by the clientele. Both of them bustled about behind the counter like squirrels enclosed in revolving cages. Andújar sweated copiously, wiping away the perspiration with his shirtsleeve. At times, drops fell into the packages of purchased tidbits, as if to ennoble the people's food with the seal of labor. The mountain folk were not very demanding: one fly more or less floating in the liquid meant little; hands more or less clean were still able hands, capable of slicing a roll and holding a handkerchief when one had a cold. Cleanliness was a bother, a hindrance. In the long run, everything goes in the mouth, and the worms will eat us all. Only the rich are permitted the luxury of being finicky.

At that moment, the sun divided the day. The air was ablaze with vibrant heat; filaments of light penetrated the depths of the forest. The June heat was intense. The fiery tropics scattered the life force from the leaves of the trees to the deep roots. The tropics, galvanizing the most beautiful place on earth, embellishing it with splendors and converting it into a gem that adorns the bosom of the world. Light slipped through the tree branches, warming the mountain, glistening upon the grass and beds of fallen leaves. Each pebble was like a burnished mirror, reflecting the sun. The brightness was overwhelming, making the eyes squint, producing lethargy, while the luxury of color and the stifling heat of the air made the forest shade welcome.

In front of the store, a goodly number of *campesinos* amused themselves. Several women laughed gaily over the sharp witticisms of the men.

Old Marta was there, scavenging as always. The pickings were better on Sundays, because the purchases were larger, and pockets were filled with the week's earnings.

Also there was Aurelia, the desolate widow of Ginés, kicked out of her hut by Galante. Her black dress, almost red from age, contrasted with her pale countenance. There were rings beneath the eyes of the beautiful countrygirl, her features were tense, and her chest sunken. Sorrow had wrought disasters, grotesquely bending her tall slender body, withering her once mellow breasts.

Mingled among the gossipers were the *Flacas*[2]: three sisters nicknamed thus for their extreme lankiness. They were high-spirited party lovers who organized their own dances and were most generous with the bold young men. They bubbled with joviality and when they burst into laughter it seemed that their skin would crack open and expose their bones. Many other women enlivened the group: some pretty, others ugly, others genteel, others sullen and shy, and all of them, with their colorless, languid miens, seemed enveloped by a pale diffuse light.

Several small children were tossing coins. Standing behind lines traced in the earth, they tried to land *ochavos* in the holes a few feet away. Elsewhere, a few battling cocks that were tethered to small posts by fiber ropes blurted out their high-pitched cry. They were hideous: the feathers on their necks and tails had been

2*Flaca,* meaning thin, or skinny.

removed and in their ridiculous nudity they were odd, repugnant creatures.

An occasional horseman traveled along the road in front of the store. As they moved off in the distance they were obliged to detour from the trail because planks of lumber blocked the way; lumber which was being carried to the farms for construction work, but had been abandoned there on Saturday until work resumed next Monday.

The mountain people stirred about in front of Andújar's store. A *campesino* scratched out notes on a small crude bandore which, if played skillfully, produced sad melodies. It was the native *tiple*,[3] stroked vigorously to emit basic harmonies of sweet simplicity and exquisite rhythm. Several *campesinos* grouped round about the guitarist and there was no lack among them of someone who would hum the musical air in a low voice. Occasionally, a voice was heard reciting *décimas*[4] in time with the instrument's monotonous tempo. A rondolet of four verses was repeated after an equal number of *décimas,* which were admirably sonorous and cadent, but lyricized with thoughts of folly. The songs were like melancholy psalms, almost always involving embryos of ideas inspired by love.

Thus passed the burning hours of the Sunday afternoon.

The women were all excited about the next dance in Vegaplana.

"It will be a party of parties," said the first born of the Flacas.

"And who's giving it, eh?" asked another woman.

"I don't know."

"Someone from the other coast," added a third. "He came here to sell horses, and he's sold them very well, I believe."

"So now he spends his money on dances."

"God only knows why he gets mixed up in such an affair."

"For my part, I wouldn't miss it."

"Nor I."

[3]*tiple,* a type of small guitar.
[4]*décima,* a ten-line stanza set to music.

"Nor I."

"Pancha Melao was in my house the day before yesterday and she told me that everyone is all excited, that even people from the lowlands are coming."

The women continued to chat about the party; they would dance until sunrise, and there would be plenty to eat and drink.

They dwelled for a long time on the question of dress; one must put up a good appearance, so the seamstresses of the *barrio* had a great task ahead. Andújar was striking while the iron was hot, doing a booming trade in cloth material and colored ribbons. After all, one must have fun, and take advantage of the horse thief's invitation.

Silvina materialized from amidst the trees. Her delicate countenance harbored the enchantment of her dark eyes. Her face reflected anguish and vexation. It also reflected her wild impulses, those delirious excesses which overcame her when Gaspar was not present, making her bite her fists and curse her black fate. Reflected, too, were the restless nights spent pacing the floor of the shack, the sleepless hours, until she surrendered to slumber at dawn. There was also a vagueness to her expression, suggesting lapses of memory. It was a winsome, attractive face, with features as changeable as the young girl's character.

Barefoot, she showed her tiny delicate feet, not yet toughened by the harsh terrain. Her worn little dress did not have a superfluous fold: it was hardly enough to contain her, and since the chemise barely reached her knees, one could see against the light the contours of her legs, fashioned in the gentle lathe of voluptuousness, robust from running along the trails.

Silvina entered the store, then left with a package in her hand and joined the group of gossiping women.

They asked if she were going to the dance. How could she know? She couldn't be sure. If Gaspar had a fancy to go, whether or not she wanted to, he would take her along; if he made up his mind to the contrary, her only choice was going to bed after sundown. She envied the liberty that others enjoyed. Above all, she envied the Flacas who—with neither husbands nor known lovers—always did as they pleased. But she—*ay!*—she had to suffer the insults of that brute Gaspar; to see his fists raised over her head and suffer his outbursts of bestial anger. She didn't enjoy herself at parties. Gaspar took her to a carousal for Three Kings Day, and when he lost control of himself from too much drink, she left the dance in tears. She still recalled how he brutally pushed her all the way uphill to their house. And why? Because he demanded that before each dance he be consulted to see if he approved of her partner. That is why she preferred to curl up in some corner of the shack.

"What makes me angriest," she added, "is that he enjoys himself. He dances, he eats, he drinks, and . . ."

"And one little thing more, true, dear?" said Old Marta, caressing the young girl's hair. "One little thing more that disgusts you . . ."

The women laughed at Marta's malicious hint, but Silvina answered:

"Bah! He's not even good for that . . ."

Just then, they heard sounds. The card players had ended their game by the river. Deblás and several others had raked in everyone's money, as well as next week's wages. Gaspar, who had won, was jovial and witty. *Ea!* Everyone to the store for a drink, he was paying. The group of *campesinos* joined the contingent stirring about in front of the store.

Gaspar saw Silvina and with his habitual gruffness he asked; "What are you doing here?"

"I came to buy some things for Leandra."

"Well, now you have them. Get going, *now.*"

She moved away at once, but as she reached the trail she heard Gaspar say:

"Oh, Silvina, give those things to your mother and come back."

Ciro stared intensely at Silvina. How much he cared for her! But she was so elusive and feared the old man so much that his longing for her—a hundred times dormant and a hundred times awakened—had never been satisfied.

As Silvina left, Ciro disappeared into the mountain wood, behind her.

Marcelo, who was alone, glanced about inside the store and

yawned wearily. He entered the little woodland behind the shed, stretched out on the ground and took a nap.

Soon, he heard voices. Deblás and Gaspar were chatting inside the shed, next to the threshing machine. After a few drinks they had retired there, to a shady spot, where they sat upon a carriage pole and spoke of private matters.

Marcelo was indifferent at first, but soon he was overwhelmed with curiosity.

"What I figure," said Deblás, "is that you want to back out."

"Me, frightened? You don't know me . . ."

"Then why won't you make up your mind?"

"I am decided. I've told you a hundred times. But I won't rush into things . . ."

"Come now Gaspar, don't deny it, you're afraid."

"I tell you no, *hombre*! Damn, you are hard-headed!"

"Then why so many doubts? It's a good business and a sure thing. Lots of money, and only one person to deal with."

"But ghosts are walking the mountain now. Didn't you see them yesterday? You had to hide so they wouldn't spot you. Let some time pass, *hombre,* let them leave and forget our *barrio.* Then . . ."

"If one thinks of all the problems, nothing ever gets done. And to you everything is a problem. Also, you've managed to mix Silvina up in the business and I don't like it."

"But that's the best part of it. She has to be there to help us. Tomorrow, if things go badly, she'll keep the secret because she, too, is involved. Otherwise, any little thing she learns, how can I be sure she won't tell? Also, the other fellow is strong, and we may need three to . . ."

Marcelo heard everything from the shady grove. He felt chilled, as though he were one of the inventors of the tenebrous plot. Such was his luck! Trouble followed him! Even to this place where he had stretched out for a peaceful nap.

He wanted to get up and flee, so as not to learn any more; but his first movement rustled some dry leaves and he feared being discovered. Only the thin foliage of a few plants separated him from Deblás and Gaspar; if he moved they would know that he had heard everything. He feared that they would direct their wrath at him. No, better to remain invisible, to stay quiet.

He remained immobile as the words slipped through the foliage and danced about him.

"Since you insist that Silvina help us, so be it," said Deblás. "Now let's speak in detail of the plan. What do you think of my way of doing it?"

"It seems all right to me, except that I would change something."

"What is that?"

"Are you sure that he's a heavy sleeper?"

"Like a rock. Once I promised to wake him very early, because he was going on a trip; well, I nearly had to knock the door down."

"That doesn't mean he's not a cautious man."

"True. He keeps a revolver on the chair next to his bed. Have you ever noticed it? From the counter you can see into the room, and the revolver is always on the chair."

"If he has time to reach for his weapon . . ."

"You must be awake to use a gun, and he doesn't wake up so easily. He snores terribly. Many times I've stood by the wall and heard him grunting like a pig. It will be easy to tell when is the best time to act."

"I wouldn't want to hurt him."

"Then how can we get anything done?"

"Look, we take a rope and a big handkerchief with us; the three of us bind him up and gag him. Then let Silvina guard him with a dagger, so he doesn't move about."

"But he'll recognize us, and the next day we'll all be in jail."

"That's true!" said Gaspar, with consternation.

No, they mustn't be recognized. Gaspar, the braggart, the self-styled hero, felt a terrible fear deep within him. They were planning to rob Andújar, to strip him of several hundred *pesos* that they suspected were locked in his big trunk; they were planning to attack a robust man who would defend his interests and his life; a man whom they were going to kill. This was serious. Gaspar was afraid. If they could only avoid bloodshed! He was a he-man, not a coward, he thought to himself. But it was wise to avoid a big commotion,and make the finishing stroke a silent one, so that it would be bruited about less by the people. Deblás insisted: a dead man neither talks nor gets in the way. Drawing blood was the only way. But who, Gaspar wanted to know, would be entrusted with the "cutting"? Deblás refused. How could he be expected to finish off his own cousin? He said that Gaspar—who was no relative of Andújar's—should plunge the knife in.

Gaspar resisted. What if the victim fired his revolver? In such a case, the person with a knife poised would surely be the one to receive the bullet. No, it couldn't be, he said; things were not well thought out.

Deblás was on the brink of violence. What kind of man was Gaspar, to be frightened by a simple little stabbing? They argued at length, but couldn't agree.

Suddenly, Gaspar had an idea. The two of them, who were stronger, would subdue Andújar, and the actual stabbing—which requires little strength—would be Silvina's job.

"Are you sure she'll do it?"

"She does as I say."

"Hmmm. I doubt that she'll obey you in this case."

"I tell you yes, *hombre*. She'll help us. Leave it to me."

"*Caray!* But don't you think that's too much for a woman?"

"I tell you Silvina will obey me. If not, I'll break her in pieces . . ."

The problem was solved, and they began a thorough study of the plan.

At ten in the evening of the night chosen, they would meet near the Palma Cortada cliff. Then, one of them would reconnoiter the area. The clerk was no problem, because everyone knew that he didn't sleep in the store. When they were sure that Andújar was asleep, they would force one of the rear doors, tie up the sleeping man, and then the knife. Next, sweep up the money and anything else of value into the smallest package possible, and everyone home. Time elapsed: half an hour. The next day, they would innocently join the great clamor lamenting the despicable crime. If necessary, Deblás would excape to the *cordillera*. All was ready: only the date had to be chosen. The full moon was now nearing, and complete darkness was necessary.

They decided to act at midnight, the first day of the new moon.

The two comrades fell silent. The project left them recondite, suspicious. The afternoon heat lulled their limbs and a drowsy lassitude prevailed in the atmosphere. Gaspar lay back among some packsaddles and Deblás stretched out upon the ground.

Close by was the threshing machine, resting beneath the roof of the shed. A pile of rubbish was stored in a nook. In one corner was an enormous wooden mortar, roughly hewn from a single tree trunk. It supported the great wooden pestle which rested against its inner rim as delicately as if it were a teaspoon in a golden goblet.

As the two men moved to their resting places, Marcelo skidded flat on his back down the side of the gorge; he reached the river, walked along its bank, returned to the store, sat down at the entrance, and stared at Andújar with compassion.

Meanwhile, another drama was developing on the crest of the hill.

Silvina had obeyed Gaspar: she waded the river, followed the trail and headed towards Leandra's shack. Ciro, without being seen, began to run uphill. He must take advantage of the occasion, he decided: Gaspar was drinking in the store, Leandra was busy with her chores at home, and between them was the dense forest, a silent witness.

Climbing in leaps, he could see Silvina following the zig-zags of the trail with the grace of a young fawn. He knew it would be hard to overtake her, and imprudent to shout, but she would return. Gaspar had ordered her to. He decided to hide behind some tree and wait.

Growing there was a plantain plant. The splendid leaves traced graceful curves from the trunk to a point just short of the ground, forming a green swaying roof that canopied the earth below. Nearby, fruit trees rose to giant proportions, dwarfing the plantain grove. A multitude of wasps hovered about, building a honeycomb that hung from a hidden branch. A few spiders weaved nearly invisible threads from limb to limb. Glinting in the sun, they formed a delicate network of gold filaments. In the web, a spider scuttered about in solitude and—with maternal love— defended her replete oviparous sacs from the attack of other insects. Up above, the chattering leaves grazed against each other, the young caressing, and the dry ones falling the length of the trunks in a swoon. Dense, thorny brambles of *agave* and *magüey* blocked the path, menacing passersby with their piercing spines.

Further on, *mimosa púdicas*[5] shriveled under the sun's ardor: they folded their small sprigs, compressed their sensitive leafage, and waited for the cool evening to once more unfurl the pageantry of their regalia.

Amidst all this sounded the voice of the woods: that wordless voice of a hundred throbbing noises. The forest was filled with mystery, encircled by sublime solitude, in the midst of a multitude of frenzied beings.

Ciro didn't have to wait long; minutes later he saw Silvina descending the path. His hands were clammy, his heartbeat quickened. He watched her cut the distance between them with each step, as though she were coming to fall in his arms. Finally, Ciro jumped out and blocked her way.

She stopped, startled, and when she recognized him she was gripped by profound emotion. He was there, in the wild solitude of the mountain, close to her; the man she loved and idolized!

"Silvina," said Ciro.

"No, let me pass; they're waiting for me."

"This time . . . I promise you that it will be."

"Impossible. What you want can never be."

"Yes, it can. Here we have our chance."

"I tell you no. Remember that I belong to another man . . ."

"No, you're mine, because I love you, and you love me. Have you forgotten already? You were ready to run away with me before that damned . . ."

"Yes, and they made me marry him. But what can we do? There is no way out."

"There is: love me."

"You're crazy!"

"Forget about him."

"Do you know what you're saying?"

[5]*mimosa púdicas,* a plant that is sensitive to light or touch.

"Forget him for a minute . . ."

"No, no; he would kill me."

"He'll never know."

"I die of fear just thinking about it. That beast would tear my head off; especially if it were you, because he bears a grudge against you."

"Bah! He'll kill no one. You were going to be my woman; you loved me once and you promised me everything. Then, whatever happened, happened. A hundred times I've wanted to come close to you, but you always run . . ."

"For fear of him . . ."

". . . a hundred times I've looked for a chance, but you always escape. It can't be, it's not just. Even if I must fight with the *devil,* I want you to keep your promise."

"But it's not my fault. When Leandra found out we were in love, she said you weren't a man of respect, that you couldn't support me. Since then, I haven't had a happy day. When they married me to Gaspar, everything became impossible. I don't want to cause you harm by pleasing you. That man is terrible, he could *cut* . . ."

"Many times I've wanted to reach for my knife and free you from his power."

"God free us! I love you, but . . ."

"Some love! It's a lie. If you loved me you would forget about everything. For example, now that we're all alone, here in this cool shade, you would prove it to me."

Silvina, near tears, swore her intense love for Ciro. Yes, she loved him, she thought of him always. By day, by night, at all times. But, *alas!* she was a wretched slave. Other girls of the *barrio* did as they pleased, but not she. Always a hundred spying eyes! No, it was impossible!

"You don't love me; it's all talk," Ciro insisted.

"But I do. Look, to prove it to you, I'll confess a secret. Some nights, when Gaspar is about to make me sick, I think of you. I hate him, but thinking of you, when he holds me, I imagine that it's you."

"Ah, Silvina! Don't say such things . . ."

Then, Ciro was seized by an impulse. It would be! He took hold of the young girl and they struggled. He dragged her, bit by bit, towards the foliage. He surrounded her, he kissed her, he embraced her; but she resisted.

"Get away . . . get away . . ."

They fell upon a bed of leaves and continued to struggle. He didn't speak: he was blind, delirious, resolved to win. She sobbed, as rapture subdued her, and at the same time she imagined Gaspar's giant fist poised over her head.

"Let me go," she pleaded.

The fallen leaves rustled and the branches shook as they rolled against the plantain stalks; a cheerful sun ray descended from above as though to celebrate the occasion; the youths, together then apart, squirmed among the dead leaves; he close to triumph, and she, still resisting, feeling on her bare flesh the tingling brush stroke of the sun, and moaning languidly.

"No . . . no . . ."

Then boisterous sounds shook the air: words, laughter, cackles. Ciro bolted up fearfully. Silvina arose in a leap and was free of him.

* * *

The sounds came closer along the path, passed them by and diminished in the distance: *campesinos* on their way to Andújar's store.

Recovered from the surprise, Ciro became enraged when he realized that his plans were ruined. Silvina—listening to the voices and still very frightened—stood a few steps away, sweating, aflame, but wanting to escape. The young man wanted to come closer, but it was useless. Silvina darted away towards the river, to obey Gaspar's order.

Ciro wrathfully flexed his hands; he stepped out of the thicket and onto the path. Upon spying the now distant group of *campesinos* he angrily exclaimed:

"May lightning strike them dead!"

When Silvina reached the store, Gaspar and Deblás had left the shed. A group of *campesinos* were listening to the monotonous sing-song of a *glosador*,[6] chanting his incoherent *décimas* amidst a chorus of horselaughs and jests.

"Here I am, what do you want?" Silvina said to Gaspar.

"Oh, nothing, just stay near in case I need you."

Gaspar always abused his power. She had to follow him everywhere and always be within view of his stern glance, always ready to humor his most capricious whim. At his side, she always felt the compunction of a virgin about to concede the *derechos de pernada*[7] to the master of her fief. She could not fathom the origin of that power. When she was deeply annoyed and swore to rebel, she felt uneasy and fearful, as though by just thinking about it, Gaspar would learn of her disobedience. A glance, a gesture, a grimace by Gaspar submerged her in a sea of desolation. She yielded always, protesting inwardly, but lacking the strength or boldness to resist.

She had heeded his order that afternoon. Still nervous and panting after her encounter in the plantain grove, she had remained obedient to Gaspar.

Ciro arrived soon after. He was irritable, violent, eager to vent his anger upon anyone . . .

He entered the store, where several youths were drinking. He sat upon the counter in a leap and drank with them. Then he saw Marcelo squatting aloof on the doorstep, gaping at the branches of a tree with a stupefied expression.

"And what are you doing there, idiot?" said Ciro uglily.

Surprised, Marcelo turned his head, looked at his brother and grinned. He was accustomed to such jests. Ciro, who always wanted to act like a brave man, often insulted him.

"Come here," said Ciro.

"What do you want?"

"Haven't you had your afternoon drink, yet?"

Marcelo grimaced. Such a question: everyone knew that he didn't drink. But Ciro persisted:

[6]*glosador,* a glossarist, or musical story teller.
[7]*derechos de pernada,* a feudal Spanish law that allows the lord of a fief to sleep with his peasant girls on the eve of their wedding day.

"I want you to try a glass, come on."

"No . . . no."

"The boy has served it. Don't tell me 'no,' because I'm in a bad mood. Don't be such a coward: be like the *other* men. Come here!"

A ridiculous scene followed. Marcelo was resolutely opposed, but Ciro was pledged to pouring some rum down his brother's gullet. The *campesinos* intervened. Some urged Marcelo to be a man, others applauded his temperance. There were stinging jests. The majority was against Marcelo. Not to drink was stupid. What does one little glass matter? It's good for the health. It warms you up when it enters the gullet, and then makes your body as strong as an *ausubo*[8] beam. Marcelo was proving his cowardice—a 25-year-old boy! And Ciro, his younger brother, was more a man than he.

The matter became a full-fledged dispute, and soon Ciro regarded it as a question of self-esteem to overcome his brother's resistance.

Meanwhile, Marcelo defended himself. It was no one's business what he did—he was a free man. They should leave him in peace! Liquor burned his throat, made him cough, sickened him. If they wanted a good time, why didn't they buy a monkey? He wasn't there to entertain them. For nothing in the world would he drink!

The joking intensified. Ciro grabbed him by the arm and pulled him close. What would everyone there think? He could not tolerate the fact that even the women were laughing at his own brother. He must drink . . .

Then the youngest of the Flacas entered the store, snatched the glass from Ciro and drained it in a gulp.

"Look," she exclaimed to Marcelo, "this is how the men do it. You're just an old *lady* . . ."

"Bravo! Bravo!" shouted the spectators.

Marcelo turned green with indignant rage. They were mocking him, making him the butt of their jokes. All right, he would glut himself with rum and prove that he was the equal of any man.

He ordered a glass of rum and drank it without hesitation.

---

[8]*ausubo,* an extremely strong, durable wood.

The *campesinos* applauded Marcelo's decision with a great outburst of laughter and, amongst a tumult of stinging jests, they all left the store.

Marcelo remained still for a moment. He felt the burning friction of the drink which was like a claw scraping his insides as it descended to his stomach. Then he fell serious and became very pale.

Seeing that they had left him alone, he withdrew a few steps and hid his face, as the tears poured out. He felt morose. He didn't enjoy drinking. As he sat down and put his head in his hands, he felt a strange languor, a burning in his eyes, and his body was drenched with perspiration.

A few minutes passed, and he lifted his head. What was happening to him? That was not the same world as before. Such a bright afternoon! Such green trees! How gay the fields looked! His body felt inflated with well-being and strength. The disagreeable taste had gone away, the feeling of faintness had disappeared, the deep sorrow was vanishing bit by bit. Without realizing what he was doing, Marcelo joined the group, and let loose a happy laugh that seemed to recall the memories of a hundred years of pleasure.

Suspecting the origin of his rare joviality, the *campesinos* celebrated this change in Marcelo. From that moment he threw himself uncontrollably into the stream of the conversation. He argued prolixly, and lost his patience over the most insignificant contradiction.

They had taken him for a coward and now he would prove the contrary. Let one of them dare to start something and he would see how quickly he was knocked silly with a punch. They were all a lot of crack-brains, big talkers, but afraid to face up to him. Ciro was his brother, but if he got in his way he, too, would get a kick. He yelled this at the top of his lungs.

Thus he leaped from theme to theme, while the others laughed. He spoke of Andújar: a bandit, yes, *señor*, a bandit! He was bleeding the country people. But Andújar had better not fool with him, or he would be stretched out with one punch.

He snatched the machete from someone's hand and slashed it

menacingly in the air. He was like a time bomb: one jolt, one bit of friction, the slightest contradiction, and he would explode.

Marcelo went back into the store, raised the machete and hacked it into the counter. Andújar, upset, wanted to throw him out, but the young man's eyes were gleaming in such a way that the shopkeeper did not act.

Finally, several of Marcelo's friends managed to get him outside where Ciro took him by the arm and led him to their hut.

En route, Marcelo rained blows upon his brother and, when they reached the far side of the river, he stopped suddenly, raised a forefinger to his temple as though trying to recall something important, and said to his brother with labored words:

"That woman: she's not for you. Do you hear?"

"What woman?"

"Look, she's not for you, understand? I saw you today when you followed her . . . she's not for you!"

And when he reached the hut he fell inert, overpowered by the imbecilic stupor of the alcohol.

Chapter Five

The moon was full the night of the dance in Vegaplana, which was located one kilometer away.

In many homes, where people were usually fast asleep by early evening, smoky straw lamps or sputtering tallow candles were still lit.

The great pale mob shook off its lethargy and prepared for pleasure: a painful pleasure like a sick man smiling, a smile that seemed more like a grimace on the face of an invalid.

The girls adorned themselves with red or yellow linen dresses and gaily colored ribbons; many wore flowers in their straight black tresses, and others twisted their locks into buns fastened on the crown of the head with hairpins.

Wardrobe was a simpler question among the men: a white shirt, ordinary drill pants and a starch-stiffened white jacket. This and a wide-brimmed straw sombrero, unblocked and without lining, completed the finery.

And in their hands, the machete: the classic weapon, with its curved blade and its handle ebonized from use; the neverforgotten object—for work, for support, and a fierce avenger and defender in moments of danger.

Since it was an extraordinary occasion, they wore shoes: the young boys could barely find footwear wide enough for their feet, which were swollen and calloused by the harsh soil; the girls, almost all of whom had diminutive feet, nevertheless felt annoyed by the unaccustomed pressure of those yellow leather tyrants. Many people carried the shoes under their arm and donned them at the entrance to the dance; thus, the journey was more comfortable, and there was less wear and tear on the shoes.

In every part of the mountain, wherever there was a home, one could sense the wave of excitement set into motion by anticipation of the dance.

Everyone in Leandra's hut was ready. Gaspar was humming out in the yard; Leandra, wearing clean clothes, was effervescent and the ruffles beneath her skirt rustled loudly when she moved about.

Her enormous breasts were gathered together above her waist, which was more tightly girdled than usual, making the bust appear misleadingly large and mellow.

Silvina was dressed very, very simply. Her graceful, narrow-waisted form exuded youth. She was beautiful, her large black eyes and long lustrous lashes. Her slim, firm body glittered with enchantment, displaying fine contours in her back, her arms and her soft neck, which tempted kisses. She moved with elegance, with an innate gentility, like a woman aware of her beauty, who takes pleasure in displaying it.

Pequeñín was also in the retinue. He couldn't be left alone in the hut, so he would be put to sleep—when he would sleep—in some nook of the dance hall, or in a neighboring house.

If Galante was going to visit the hut that night, it was important that he find the door open, thought Leandra. So she swung the palm leaf shut, but did not bind it with the rattan stem that she customarily used. They sallied forth, but when they reached the river bank, Gaspar stopped.

"Now," he said, "keep going. I still have an *errand* to take care of."

"You expect us to go alone?" Leandra asked.

"No, woman, there are plenty of people on the trail! What are you afraid of?"

"For my part, I'd rather go alone," Silvina said.

"But there are so many abusive people!" Leandra asserted.

"*Ea!* Move on. Plenty of people are going. Walk slowly, I'll catch up right away."

The women set out on the trail and began the trek to Vega-plana, a settlement located in the lowest part of the *barrio*. Gaspar slipped slowly into the woods.

Meanwhile, the night flowed serenely onward. Such a sky, such splendor!

It seemed that the angel of night was bathing herself in tepid lights. Not one shipwrecked cloud floated across that ocean of brilliance; not a single smudge of vapor spotted the ringlets of the full moon; not one star disputed the magnificent sovereignty of the moon, which reigned in the supreme pomp of the heavens, soaring in the void, tracing a wide poetic path. From a colossal distance, she was death, reflecting life, like a statue still bursting with herculean strength. The sky accepted the lights tenderly, with the calm of a giant caressed. Grays joined timidly with the pale blue, blending into an ashy brilliance which the earth reflected back towards the gentle watcher of the night.

The earth reposed, swathed in the copious unraveling of its revolutions. The forests high above tempered the luminous rays, tingeing them shades darker; the corpulent trees drank in the light, disgorging dreadful shadows; the tangle of the woods formed stern green canvases spread over the hills; and on the summits scalloped terrain and jagged peaks resembled sickles and arrow heads that would shatter the moon were it to fall.

In its craggy bed, the river weaved its way among large boulders, gaining impetus at each dip, forming brilliant cascades, sounding, ever sounding, harmonious in the backwaters, boiling and ferocious in the rock deltas, clamoring and colliding at the curves, roaring like a landslide at the falls.

Thus, the moonlit night displayed its vestments, with tiny dreamworld spirits hovering everywhere, spreading phantasmagorias of romantic love. Nature offered a grandiose frame for the tableau of human conflict: a magnificent stage for the restless men who skulked about below.

Gaspar furtively retraced his steps for a few meters and then followed an oblique path up the mountain. He slipped from shadow to shadow, eluding the moon's brightness.

Climbing a good distance through a grove of trees, he finally peered between the immobile trunks and spied a hut canopied by vegetation. It was Old Marta's orchard. He stopped, sat upon a rock, and stared at the house, where someone holding a dim light moved about inside.

Marta was preparing for bed. Sunday had been a grand day. Four dozen pieces of clothing washed, four hens and two dozen eggs sold and—the real triumph!—she had found a buyer for a squalid cow, with impoverished udders. From these sources, she pocketed four *pesos*. A good day's work. Marta was content, jubilant; the air felt keener in her lungs, the light shone brighter.

Hers was a silent, reserved joy, hidden from the observation of others.

Because of this, she was concerned about the buyer of the cow, who had been very indiscreet. Haggling so loudly over a confidential matter! Several *campesinos* overheard the transaction, and Gaspar had been quite impressed by the news.

Gaspar had spent the whole day engrossed in thought. For a long time he had been tempted to spy upon the old woman. How much money did she have buried! What risk was there? It would be simple to find out, and then . . . Gaspar couldn't repress a violent desire to steal her hoard. He tried to rationalize his doubts. Who was she? Just a miser, killing her poor grandson with hunger. Such an atrocity deserved the most terrible punishment one could mete out to a miser: snatch away her treasure. Thus, Gaspar regarded himself as an avenger, a judge.

One day he wondered: why hasn't Deblás yet thought of such a maneuver? Who knows if he isn't slyly bleeding her bit by bit, without her even being aware? Gaspar decided to do it alone, and not share the booty with anyone.

But where was her treasure hidden? Marta was crafty, and she would take every precaution to maintain her secret.

Nevertheless, by following her every night, perhaps he could glimpse her hiding place. Thus, when he heard that the old woman had just come into a considerable sum, he figured that she would be sneaking about the mountain that night, after her grandson went to sleep. He was right.

After pacing restlessly about in the hut, Marta barred the door and extinguished the light. All was ready: the light out, the grandson asleep, and the old woman curled up in her hammock, thinking.

No one would ever get the best of her. The cow gave no milk, but it was fat and well worth the low price for which she sold it.

No matter what, she thought, she must hide her little pile of money. But such a bright moon! On nights like these, people of means were in danger. She looked with annoyance at the moon rays that filtered through the cracks in the wall of her hut. Why must there be so much light? The moon should sleep, like people. God must know what he is doing, but she could not fathom why—after a full day of the sun's glare—the sky should still be like a bonfire. It was wise to wait for a dark night to put away her money, but would it not be more dangerous to keep it in the house?

Furthermore, she couldn't carry the sack of money around with her, when she went down to the river, or to the store, or scavenged about the *barrio*. It was wisest to put away her savings that very night, while everyone was at the dance.

After waiting for some time, she crouched to pass beneath the eaves of the roof and left the hut.

The moon swathed her in brightness. The old woman circled her home two or three times, looking suspiciously in all directions. She didn't fear known thieves, but was more concerned about those hypocrites who pretended to be saints and were capable of anything. Yes, she had often caught the sly ones glancing suspiciously at her. Better to trust a lad like Deblás than those fakers; he might be as evil as they come, but since the night of their encounter he had behaved towards her like a grateful guest, constantly reassuring her that for nothing in the world would he cause her trouble. Proceeding almost on all fours, Marta peered about. Nothing; only the night, draped in tranquility.

Then, treading cautiously, she entered the woods.

Gaspar—who hadn't missed a single one of her movements— sighed joyfully. At last! He hadn't been mistaken. The Methusaleh of the orchard was going to put her hands on the treasure that night.

He straightened up slowly and followed Marta. The shadow of the woods enveloped them both. Gaspar, above, moved forward in a crouch; Marta, below, on the lowest part of the slope, glided slowly along, looking in all directions, zigzagging as though to confuse anyone who might be watching.

Soon she reached a clearing. In the center of a small rocky

plain, there rose the gigantic trunk of a ceiba tree. Gaspar, hiding in a nearby thicket, saw her approach the tree and sit down next to it.

A few minutes later, the old woman took a turn around the tree; she raised her head and fixed a stern glance upon the trunk. The moonlight fell serenely upon her aged countenance. The rays of light silvered the sharp-pointed nose and chin, the wrinkled lips, the beady eyes buried in the depths of their sockets, the rugose pendulous skin of her neck and the long messy locks of tangled gray hair on her head.

When Marta felt sure she was alone, she bent over, her knees upon the grass, cupped her hands like small shovels, and scraped at the foot of the tree. An instant later, there was a hole. Gaspar strained to see the details of the scene, which were darkened by the shadow of the tree.

Marta took a package from her pocket, opened it and let fall a heap of money. A faint metallic sound proclaimed that they were coins.

The miser looked about once more. Alone, still alone. Hurriedly she filled the hole, leveled off the ground with her hand and piled a few stones there to conceal the recent digging.

The old woman sighed, as though relieved of a great burden. Now let them come to rob her. Some job they would have trying to sniff out her cache! Still suspicious, she hobbled slowly back to the hut.

Gaspar hesitated for an instant. Calm, be calm. First, let the old woman go to sleep. He followed her cautiously and watched as she entered her house. He waited. The silence of the hut enlivened his spirits. Marta must be asleep. The time had come.

Struggling to contain the great pleasure of his triumph, he returned to the ceiba tree. There was the gnarled trunk, looking like a face wrinkled by ill humor. Its branches, swimming in space, floated overhead, and the leaves hovered together like a flock of green butterflies whose wings had been bound together.

Like Marta, Gaspar scraped at the earth and uncovered the mouth of an earthen jar. Jesus Christ, what a pile! He felt dizzy, and if at that moment someone had disputed his claim to the treasure, they would have first had to cut him to pieces. It was all his. But what he was doing was dangerous, so it was wise to finish quickly.

Myriad ideas crowded his mind. Should he grab it all? Should he take only a part and return another night? Yes, that would be better. Taking everything would cause too much of a fuss. Marta would wail horribly, and a scandal would be inevitable. No: little by little and one gets further. He wondered: how much could there be?

He plunged a hand into the jar and wriggled his fingers. Bah, it wasn't so much! The jar was very small. But it was said that the old witch had lots of money; perhaps she had several hideouts and kept her money divided in portions. Whoever found one would find the rest.

Gaspar extracted a fistful of silver and copper coins. He groped about in the jar, but there was no gold. Undoubtedly Marta had gold, but not there. Gaspar calculated: among the various silver and copper coins—*pesetas, vellónes* and *ochavos*—there must be some two hundred *pesos*. Not as much as he first imagined. He swore not to stop until he found the other deposits. He kept a generous handful of coins; ten or twelve *pesos* was enough. With that, he could sport about in Vegaplana, sleep without concern all day Monday and live the good life the rest of the week. In time he would return for another helping . . .

Gaspar refilled the hole, leaving it as though no profane hand had ever defiled Marta's fortune. Then he returned to the river, crossed the causeway and—with a smile on his face—set out on the march to Vegaplana.

The great mob was dancing gaily there. The hall bubbled like muddy water thrown upon live coals.

The dance was being given in a farmhouse larger than most, but of the same haphazard construction: four sieve-like walls and a roof that shuddered when a gust of wind swept by. Three or four lamps burned in the hall, spreading—instead of light—shadows that enveloped everything. Inside, the roof showed its surface of palm leaves and crude beams that crossed from one side of the hall to the other. The ceiling absorbed the humble sparkle of the lamps which strained to brighten the surroundings. The lamps were fashioned from small flasks with a tin tube fitted to their mouths; inside the tube, an absorbent wick burned the fuel in the container. Black, oily smoke issued forth from the lamps, filling the hall with a stifling odor.

"Another turn, another turn!" said a robust youth who towed an old woman around in time to the music.

The others chorused his appeal. The song had finished and the dancers wanted an encore. The musicians, obliging agreeably after receiving permission from the director—the *maestro* of the dance—once more undertook the *contradanza,* and the couples, drenched with sweat, again surrendered themselves to the vertigo of the rhythm.

Leandra relaxed upon a wooden bench, together with other *campesinos* who had not found a dance partner. Handkerchiefs and fans fluttered from their hands as they made small talk about the host's generosity and the excellence of the drinks. One little woman was critical of the dresses worn by the dancers.

"I would walk about in a *petticoat* before wearing a dress like that! She looks as wide as a *verdolaga*![1] And look, look at Filomena. How her belly shows already. And now she acts so silly and innocent-looking."

"They say she's getting married."

"That I must see .. .."

"No, *hombre,* it's said that Moncho will take her."

"Surely . . . he'll keep taking her little by little."

Gossiping in low voices, the women muffled their laughter over some of the funny-looking couples, or over those who were blind to criticism and had become too enthusiastic in the voluptuous rocking of the *contradanza.*

Now and then there passed from hand to hand the lavish rustic drinking cup: the polished *higüera* shell, which served to satisfy the thirst of all. It was submerged at every instant into a pot of *agualoja,* a fermentation of sugar, ginger and anise. All quaffed

[1]*verdolaga,* the purslane, a wide-leaved plant.

the sweetish drink with relish, and returned it in the form of perspiration.

The couples revolved around the hall like the links of a chain pump. They would whirl around a few times, then glide to the left or right, then he or she would retreat, moving backwards. In the latter case, it seemed as though the male was a hunter pursuing the futigive woman.

The men, encircling the women's waists with their right arms and locking the grip with the left, were timid at first, then more intense, then so firm that the girl could not extricate herself without falling out of step.

The women let themselves be led in the gentle swaying. They rested the left forearm upon the partner's right arm, giving him the other arm, and wrapped together in that embrace they submitted to the tender lazy movement of the dance.

Bodies grazed against each other as the couples collided or as arm touched arm; the women's waists were stained at the back, where young men's damp hands left their traces; and throughout they moved their feet in a tiny space, as though trying to dance on a pinpoint.

The billowing wave of humanity stirred incessantly, knee striking knee, each couple sharing the same breath, feeling at every instant collisions of tender delicacy and the friction of short hair tingling against foreheads. creating currents of restless love—of desires mortified by the nearness of the unattainable object that tantalized them—the warm soft desire of a life filled with anxiety for pleasure and happiness.

When the *contradanza* began, its rhythm filled the hall. There were three instruments, a big guitar, the *cuatro*; a smaller one, the *triple*; and a dissonant object called the *güiro*.

The grotesque *güiro* was the memorial of a primitive tribe, salvaged from the calamities of time. A dissonant object made from the hollowed dried fruit of the *marimbo*, it was generally curved like a scimitar with a grooved surface on top, forming narrow parallel lines. It had narrow ends and a wide belly, in the middle of which was a hole to allow exit for the sounds. A copper wire, or any other sharp-pointed object, scraped across the grooves of the *güiro*, produced the shrill creak of rusty metal, or the noise of sand being trampled on a hard surface.

From that lofty trio of instruments emanated the rustic musical airs, sweet romantic melodies that dealt with themes of primitive simplicity. They were Quechuan airs astride the crest of evolution, caressed by the sentimentalism of Andalucía.

The net effect of these two influences was peculiar and original. A calm or tremulous note would sound, and others immediately surged forth to revolve about the first; together they progressed methodically to a point higher than the gamut, and then the tune subsided to the primitive note. This created a sad, somnolent monotony, like the song of a lover mourning the disdain of his beloved.

At times there was a variation: the *triple* became animated, the notes somersaulted on the pentagram, creating a vigorous allegro tempo; the measure, always cadent, intensified; the anxiety of the moment sprung forth in impulsive gusts from the instruments; but the excitement was short-lived, receding once more to the previous monotony, like an harmonic wave.

The music exerted a peculiar fascination over the people. When he was at sea, Montesa whistled the native melody a thousand times. Hearing it, the creoles felt a vague melancholy. Their hearts grew heavy and in their memories a light rekindled the past, etching in sharp relief the dormant poems of infancy. In the colony, music was soothing, endearing and charming, caressing with the smoothness of its rhythms; but away from home it was touching, almost moving one to pity, presenting visions of the native soil, enticing one to return, attracting with cherished memories, swelling one with pride for having been born there.

The music was also ennervatingly carnal. It was like a gust that nudges one into motion, a stimulus which compels two beings to possess each other without possession, a gentle touch that awakens worlds of sensations, a rapture governed by convention, a hypocritical means of throwing one's self into the arms of bestiality, without ultimate pleasure or scandal.

The sounds permeated the air and were heard from afar, like a dirge, the painful lament of a dying people who sink deeper and deeper into abjection while they smile and sing.

The gaiety mounted as the night progressed, and tongues bathed in drinks of anisette and rum. When the rice pudding satisfied their appetites, laughs, cackles and shouts gushed forth.

The harsh wing-flappings of vulgarity hammered against the walls, rebounding to the floor which was stained black by chewing tobacco. Reigning above all was that grossness which curses and shouts to celebrate a joke, as both men and women abased themselves in the brutal torpor of the rude gathering.

Finally, Gaspar's giant head loomed at one of the doors.

At that moment, Silvina was dancing with a young goodlooking laborer. Upon making a turn, she saw Gaspar. What luck! Had he arrived a few minutes earlier, he would have found her in Ciro's arms.

Passing in front of the door, the couple stopped and Silvina directed a questioning glance at Gaspar. He nodded his consent and Silvina spun away with the young man.

Gaspar launched forth also. Along the way he had tarried in several tiny inns and consumed a goodly dose of rum. With the liquor sloshing about inside him, and Marta's money tucked deep in his pocket, he was in a good mood. Yes, he would enjoy himself; without any quarrels or scrapes, of course. Whoever wanted to fight, out he goes. There were people of respect here, and it was important that they be allowed to relax. Spewing forth a flood of vulgar talk and lectures which no one had asked for, he lost himself in the whirl of couples, colliding here, stumbling there, and putrefying the air everywhere with his drunken breath.

Gaspar's good mood reached its apogee. The laborer dancing with Silvina spied Ciro dancing with his fiancée. She extricated herself from Ciro's arms and took hold of her gallant, leaving Silvina and Ciro alone in the center of the dance floor.

An imbecilic uproar celebrated the event. And everyone proclaimed the logic of the two "jilted" ones joining together in a dance.

Silvina was apprehensive, but she stole a glance towards Gaspar

and saw that he, too, was grinning and joining the others in the
chorus urging them together. Then she felt herself seized by Ciro,
abandoned herself in his arms and was lost with him in the
tumult. They had hardly begun to dance when Ciro lowered his
face to the young girl's ear and whispered:

"Tonight . . . yes?"

"Tonight . . . what?" she answered gaily, feeling intensely happy
over being allowed to dance with the young man.

"I tell you, tonight I'll risk it."

"Are you starting again with that madness?"

"I won't give up. I love you. I've decided to try, even though we
both get into trouble. Tonight he'll be drunker than a still and
he'll fall into bed like a stone. Wait for me . . ."

"Do you think that I live alone?"

"What do I care?"

"But Leandra is there. And Galante will surely be there, too.
And then Gaspar . . ."

"I don't care. Galante and Leandra sleep in the back room. You
and that animal are in the other."

"Don't even think about it, do you hear?? Don't even *think* . . ."

"I'll be there!"

"No, it's impossible. Forget it."

"Look, I'm going. No matter what, I'm going. If you wait for
me, nothing should go wrong; but if you fight me and make noise
and they awaken, I won't turn my back. I promise you. I'll be
carrying my *mocho,*[2] and I'll stand up to the whole *barrio.*"

"But how will you get in?" she whispered

"I don't know. But stay awake and wait for me."

"This is insane! Oh God, I hope there's no trouble!"

They spoke of nothing else throughout the dance. Silvina was
panic-stricken, but he was determined. How could she stop him?
She feared such a bold venture, but a secret gladness made her
wish that the scheme could work.

"My God! If they hear you, what will become of us? Especially
me!"

---

[2]*mocho,* slang for machete.

"Sound sleepers hear nothing; don't be so frightened. I've prowled about outside the house many times and thought of this, but you never knew. Now you do, and things are different. Whether it pleases you or not, if we're caught, we're caught together."

She still doubted that Ciro would dare do such a thing. She decided that arguing would not change his mind. It was better, she felt, to let him have his way. Finally, the dance was over and Silvina hurried to Gaspar's side.

The atmosphere of the dance hall was like a giant cloud, saturated with dust, tobacco smoke and human effluvium. A few old women nodded their heads drowsily, while the young couples persisted in prolonging the joyous hours, and the children—who had been cast into the corners—slept contentedly.

With the moon nearly faded from the sky, the dance was over. Gaspar, Leandra, Silvina, the Flacas and several other *campesinos* returned in a group to their mountain.

When she stepped outside, Silvina, still flushed from the excitement, felt the cool splash of the early morning air in her face. Her eyes burned, she felt sleepy, listless, in low spirits.

She walked a few paces and suddenly stopped. A vague inexplicable aura seemed to surround her. She felt bewildered. Fixing her glance on a point in space, and taking a few quick steps, she grasped hold of a tree and embraced the trunk. Then she lost her senses. Everything vanished, and she tottered dizzily.

The others came to her aid. They seated her upon the grass and tried to revive her.

The spell passed quickly. She opened her eyes and looked about with astonishment.

"What's happened to me?" she asked.

"Nothing, it was nothing."

"But why am I here on the grass?"

"Because you nearly fell down."

"I felt fine, then the world suddenly left me. I fainted, didn't I?"

"Come now," said Gaspar, "it's all over. You women are all crazy. You were jumping around all night and then you went out

into the night air. Of course you felt a little faint, but you're all
right now. Come along . . ."

The group continued the march and Silvina followed; she felt
crushed, burdened by a great sadness, and held back her tears.
How strange it was! Why had she felt that way? But by the time
they reached the hut her fears had vanished and she felt more
tranquil.

When they opened the door, a whiff of human odor came from
inside, and they heard the loud breathing of a sleeping man.
Leandra imposed silence. No noise. Galante was there, in the
rickety bed. They all entered the dwelling, and soon the silence
was interrupted only by Gaspar's coarse snoring.

Leandra and Galante shared the bed in the largest room and
Pequeñín was wrapped in some rags on the floor. In the other
room, Gaspar and Silvina were in their bridal bed: a yellow mat
covered with rags and a few sacks for pillows.

Thinking of Ciro, Silvina disrobed slowly. Holy God! Would he
dare to come? She longed to abandon herself to the adventure,
but anguish and indecision gripped her. She stretched out at her
tyrant's side, thinking.

Gaspar, not bothering to undress, had fallen inert, as though he
were an enchanted prince condemned to sleep for a century. He
lay next to the wall, and she was about half a yard away.

Darkness blackened every detail of the hut. Through a few thin
cracks in the wall, one could see the brightness outdoors, and
down below, one yard away, was the grayish-brown earth, visible
through the crevice-ridden palm plank floor.

All was quiet, except for the sounds of birds and insects.

Half an hour later, Silvina sat up, frightened. She had heard a
strange noise; a sound of footsteps outside.

It was Ciro. He had followed them from Vegaplana. He waited
in the woods until he judged that all were asleep, and then he
cautiously approached the shack, probing for a way to enter.

Silvina listened, her frightened heart galloping. Ciro crawled
beneath the house. He knew that Gaspar and Silvina occupied the
smaller room, but he wasn't sure where the bed was located. He
shoved his machete through a crack between the floorboards. The

weapon struck against something; undoubtedly it was the mat. He thrust the machete further to the left, but the same obstacle stopped him. He continued probing until he reached the front wall and then returned to where he had begun, searching once more, moving to his right.

On the third try, the blade penetrated completely. He measured a space perhaps half a yard in width and calculated that he needed to lift four planks. Feeling his way to the end of one board, where it touched the wall, he tried pushing it. The boards were tied together with strong vines. He cut the knot holding one board and it gave way, creaking slightly. Ciro lifted it a few inches, pushed it slantwise and let it rest upon the adjoining board, In the same way he cut the knot of a second board and, in a few moments, Ciro's bust appeared inside the shack, as though he had emerged through a trapdoor.

Silvina didn't miss a single detail. Such daring, such boldness! She was immensely afraid, but at the same time she felt ecstatically happy.

There was the beloved man who would expose himself to the greatest risks for her. And in the shadows of the little room, seated upon the mat with Gaspar at her side, admiration for Ciro surged up from deep within her; she felt he was worthy a hundred times over of the prize he had so doggedly pursued.

But if they were caught! What would happen? Then, resolutely, she crawled towards the hole which Ciro had made in the floor.

"For the love of God . . . be careful!"

"Silvina, Silvina my darling!"

They embraced, he with his feet on the earth, and she huddled close to him; their lips met and they kissed gently, afraid to make a sound.

In subdued voices, they exchanged endearments which were twisted by fear into incoherent babblings. He was eager, impatient, aware of the dangers of being surprised in another man's home, where he might suddenly fall victim to the stroke of a machete. She was intoxicated with passion. Yes, the story must have an ending.

"Wait," she whispered into Ciro's ear.

"What?"

"I want to be sure that *he* is fast asleep. Don't come up yet .... I'll tell you . . ."

She crawled back to Gaspar who was snoring like the bellows of an iron forge. She came close and watched him for a while. Could he be awake, waiting to surprise them?"

She looked again. He was sleeping. But she wanted proof. She reached out and touched him; she nudged him gently, calling to him in a low voice, as though fearing that she might awaken him.

"Gaspar . . . Gaspar!" When he didn't respond, she continued, "Gaspar, *please* Gaspar."

He lay there like a mass of spoiled beef discarded by the slaughterhouse.

She shook him more forcefully, but in vain. Then she breathed with pleasure. They were safe! She returned to Ciro and, in a low, deliciously affectionate voice, said:

"Come."

But at that moment they heard a guttural murmur in the next room.

Galante heard Silvina calling to Gaspar. At first, he was indifferent. Then, that *please* made him lift his head. He heard the girl's insistent voice and smiled. Poor little thing. After a lively night she couldn't sleep, and that brute Gaspar had doubtlessly gone to sleep, indifferent to the demands of his young woman.

He called to Leandra. She, who was sleeping belly up, awoke groggily. He said something and pushed her. Awake at last, Leandra understood. She got up, and as her feet touched the floor the entire hut creaked.

Silvina froze with fright and Ciro, who had begun to climb up through the narrow opening, stopped.

"What was I telling you . . . see?" she asked.

"No, it's nothing."

"Go away, go away!"

Footsteps sounded. Leandra felt her way in the dark to Silvina's room.

Ciro measured the risk. If Silvina was willing, any occasion was better than this one. To stay there would mean getting into trouble foolishly, without success. As Silvina retreated to Gaspar's side, Ciro shrank back into the hole and fled, disappearing into the woods.

Leandra came up to Silvina's side, leaned over and took her by the hand.

Filled with deathly dread, Silvina understood.

She pretended to be asleep. But Leandra pulled at her forcefully. Ah, it was all impossible. After being on the brink of happiness, she was back in reality. No, she wouldn't go . . . she was wretched enough without consenting once more to such a despicable thing.

But Leandra shook her rudely.

"Silvina, day is breaking. Get up . . . gather some firewood to make the coffee . . ."

"I can't . . . I'm dead tired . . ."

"Silvina . . . don't you understand? Come, come . . ."

She knew that her mother's words were a pretext, a tatter of civility. And she resisted.

But Leandra shook her roughly, made her rise, and led her to the other room. Meanwhile, Silvina was thinking that her resistance would awaken Gaspar, that they would light a lamp, and they would see the hole in the floor, which she had to close before sunrise. She thought, finally, of her immense abandonment, her loneliness in the midst of these people, who were resolved to tear her heart to pieces, to twist her soul . . .

Then, in the darkness, a man's arm encircled her waist.

Leandra went down to the shed, gathered a few chips of wood and kindled them; they sputtered with an unsteady flame. She put the water to boil for breakfast and sat cross-legged in front of the hearth, waiting for it to bubble. In the serene sky, the splendors of the dawn began to unfurl the first colors of the day, so gentle, so innocent, so pure.

Chapter Six

The thin crescent of the new moon was greeted by torrential rains.

The sky—crystal clear before—was milky and turbid, filled with grotesque clouds, like winged hairy monsters.

Juan del Salto, confined by the weather, was at his desk amidst a sea of paper. He reached into one of the pigeonholes and extracted a bundle wrapped in a rubber band: his son's letters.

Juan and Jacobo del Salto wrote to each other once or twice a month. Jacobo, twenty-four years old, was in his final semester of law studies in the capital of Spain.

Juan recalled that as a boy Jacobo was lively, genteel, intelligent and of sound judgment. Little by little, in the course of the years, he noticed in his letters how the influence of the great European cultural center was affecting his son. Juan was pleased; he had faith in his beloved son's future, a future that was solidly based on the fortune that he was amassing for him, as well as the brilliance of a cultivated spirit and his superior intelligence. He removed the most recent letter from the bundle and began to reread it, tenderly.

In that letter, as always, the first words were those of filial worship. Jacobo eagerly awaited the happy reunion in his father's arms. His was an intense boy's affection, like a ray of sun reflected in a mirror.

Then came the native soil: in all his letters he lavished affection upon this other love. He remembered something of the colony; vague images, spaced far apart without connection; the palms, the vast reaches of cane fields, the undulating rivers, the interior of his father's house on sunny days. Apart from this, his homeland was etched in fantasy: he imagined more than he knew in fact. He saw it through the prism of his romantic soul. A genteel land, more magnificent than any other. Nature, intoning hymns of eternal poetry; the earth and its inexhaustible riches; the people, enjoying such good fortune. From afar, he saw it all, embellished by his illusions.

He imagined an ideal homeland, and all his desires and aspirations went out to her.

When Juan answered the letters, he prudently tempered those idealisms. Although his son was away, and already a man, Juan regarded his mission as a father still unfinished. He must prepare Jacobo for the disappointments of reality, and with consummate tact, without wounding his optimism, he sent him brief accounts of the colony, entrusting him with the maturity to form his own convictions. Jacobo's replies revealed a gradual change in attitude. First, surprise; next, doubt; then, disenchantment. Juan's written word was absolute proof for Jacobo, who believed in him with an infinite faith; but he struggled before abandoning his illusions.

"Don't think," he wrote in his last letter, "that I've come to believe my land is a biblical paradise. I know all too well that life is a struggle everywhere. But I can't conceal from you the sorrow that your words have caused me.

"You tell me that you rejoice over my boundless love for our land, but I should not forget that, together with its beauty, there are also swells which overrun its beaches and floods that ravage its fields.

"I understand that you want me to keep contact with reality. It's true then, is it not, that the reality is neither as perfect nor as placid as I visualize it? All right. I must not be so deluded to expect that a land could be free from such ravages of nature, but I believe that you mention these merely as symbols.

"I must be be frank: to me, our country is the best on earth, and my compatriots are my brothers. You are pleased with my enthusiasm, but you tell me of storms and floods. Yes, I see it clearly. My brothers are adrift in the storm of a difficult rebirth. What is it that they want? A free country redeemed by conviction or blood, a country that would equal the heroics of others that shook off the yokes that humbled them. My brothers would like that, but they doubt themselves; they fear defeat, they are frightened by disaster. They would like to tighten the bonds with the original homeland, the homeland in which I now dwell, so loving, so kind, so wonderful; but whose good intentions are destroyed by the greed of evil Spaniards. These are the torments of which you speak. They, too, are Humanity; they, too, are subject to the general laws of social evolution, the eternally progressive laws of all living things and of all peoples. I presume this, I know it . . .

"Incidentally, I heed with true devotion what you tell me of patriotism: *the good that one should do for his own country must not be founded upon lies, nor deceit, nor the adulation of the multitudes. After God, the loftiest grandeur is the truth.* These words of yours, which I underscore, impress me deeply; I must never forget them. The truth, yes the truth, not the lying of serfs and beggars, for sale at the price of flattery, fear or revenue. The truth, I consider it to be the most Christian deed of virtue and honor!

"I also want to mention three paragraphs in your letter which struck me with the impact of cold water.

"First paragraph . . . *that way, like the bird which sees a garden reflected in a mirror, you would fly and collide rudely with the glass.* You mean that in the mirror of my illusions, I see vague phantoms; that if I don't temper my optimism I run the danger of colliding with the mirror. How sad! Could it be that sentiment cannot create reality if it doesn't exist? Could it be that all our countrymen think as you and I?

"Second paragraph . . . *just as stirring the air with a fan will never split mountains, fits of lyrical passion will not solve arduous problems.* Those words caused me to tear up an 'Ode to the Patria' which I had written. In the ode, I sang the glories of my country, basing it upon its natural opulence and upon the romanticism of a great cloud of loving sentiment. I tore it up, convinced that it was like the breeze of a fan, spending its force in the void of futility.

"Third paragraph . . . . *since Humanity owns the world, as it grows it must become worthy of the splendor of its creation. Many societies succumb apoplectically to theories without ever having the good fortune to put a single one of their philosophical speculations into practice . . . Nations are like individuals: one achieves more when he plans to plant a tiny tree, and does it, than he who proposes to raise an entire forest and falls asleep in the furrows. Reality! Here you have the great lever. We should concern ourselves with what already exists, in order to achieve what should be. By only singing of what we would like it to be, we accomplish nothing . . .* I sense a severe criticism in these words, and since I know how much you love our land, that criticism is immensely important to me.

"Please continue explaining to me the results of your observations. I notice that you are not explicit on certain points. What giant, sick 'stomach' is it that you refer to? What morbid depression is it that passes by heredity from one generation to another?"

Juan enjoyed rereading it all, and a benevolent smile brightened his countenance.

His son had imagination and wit. He loved everything with childlike candor, but at the same time he was a thinker, who was beginning the great journey along life's rugged trail. Juan loved him infinitely, as though Jacobo were made of fragile Bohemian crystal.

Thus passed the hours of that nostalgic day. Now and then he peered out the window at the sky, filled with dropsical clouds which collided at the impulse of hostile winds, replete with dark shadows that hastened the coming of night and made a long dusk of the day.

The trees, lashed by the rain, were tearful. Their leaves and branches glistened wetly and shed huge drops of water. It was a day made painful by forced leisure, by the suspension of work and loss of time in the fields.

The weather vexed Juan. It was the end of June, and the coffee beans could be ruined by the rain and wind. The crop appeared exuberantly pregnant, but it had the kind of indolent look which promised a slow ripening. It had been a rainy year, too rainy.

Occupied by these thoughts, Juan approached the window. The heights of Gaspar's farm were veiled by a nimbus of clouds, a milk-colored curtain that descended to the woods.

It stopped raining on Juan's farm. A current of air whisked away the clouds as a smoker would dismiss the hazy spirals from around his head. Despite the scourge of rainfall, the coffee groves

and banana plantings were standing happily erect. Juan, with a
look of resignation, scanned the landscape which abounded with
life and nostalgia.

Suddenly there were the sounds of a quarrel and he recognized
Montesa's voice.

Juan looked out from the balcony on the other side of the
house. He saw Montesa amidst a group of *campesinos* who were
huddled beneath the eaves of the machine house roof, to escape
from the rain. The foreman was buffeting and pushing them
furiously. When one of them answered back, Montesa wrathfully
crossed his back with a whip. The *campesinos* yelled angrily, while
the foreman prepared to strike again.

"Montesa! Enough! Come here immediately."

With the meekness of a schoolboy, Montesa came up to the
house.

"What have I told you a hundred times?" asked Juan.

"*Señor* . . ."

"How many times must I tell you, before you obey me?"

"It's just that . . ."

"Just that nothing. What you've done is barbaric."

"The reason was that . . ."

"Whatever the reason, whatever that man did . . ."

"But hear me, *don* Juan. The whole day is lost with this rain.
This morning they left the mountain; it stopped raining and I
made them go back. After lunch the same thing happened, and
only an hour ago they ran off for the third time. The shower
passed and I ordered them to the mountain again. They refused,
but I made them respect me, and most of the workers were willing
to continue. It has rained so much, the grass is up to our ankles,
and we mustn't neglect it. When they were all going back to work,
Inés Marcante, that worthless idiot who asks permission from one
foot to move the other, objected. He made some smart remarks
and was a bad influence upon the others. When I saw that they
weren't obeying my order, I told him to keep quiet. He didn't and
I pushed him. He called me a foul name, and I gave it to him
good . . . that was all."

"I won't argue whether or not your order was just. The truth is that with this weather the plantations are flooded, and the men are in danger of becoming sick. They are human beings, like you and me!"

"Some bunch they are!"

"But supposing your order were reasonable, to raise your hand to a man is repugnant; I won't stand for it on my farm. I've told you this a hundred times."

"And how do I make them listen to me?"

"If someone disobeys you, fire him; if he doesn't do his best, fine him; if he threatens you, go to the sheriff."

"Surely, you've told me this many times, but . . ."

"But what?"

"It never works. I know from experience. Hit them until it hurts, and they bend like corn silk. Even the boldest ones turn humble. There's no other way to get a day's work out of them."

"There is . . . with conviction and persuasion."

Montesa smiled incredulously.

"Violence is degrading. If you treat your men like that you'll turn them into idiots or madmen, and in both cases you'll be hated."

"Oh, if I had my way!"

"If you did, you'd be a real tyrant."

"But I don't know these people, *don* Juan."

"For that very reason you should be lenient. Do you regard them as irresponsible? Well, if you abuse them, if you oppress them and fail to respect their rights, you establish no difference between their unsound way of doing things and your sensible way."

"So long as that mob isn't held with a firm hand . . ."

"That's enough! Tyranny produces nothing but hatred and ignorance, and a tyrant will sink in the very mire which he creates. I've told you, this is the last time I'll tolerate such disgraces."

Montesa exited mournfully. Bah! Some system, with all that pampering. *Don* Juan was a real gentleman, and judged the others as he would himself. But those donkeys needed a strong stick. If only they had some idea of the word "duty"! One could not depend on them. They began a task and abandoned it, they promised to arrive at a certain time and they never came, they never even notified the boss. Without proper shelter, barefoot, with no plan in life, they were like beasts screaming and begging for the whip. In a bad mood, Montesa thought no more about resuming work that day.

Marcelo was among the group of *campesinos*. With his anemic look, his vague gaze, his mouth half open and his chest sunken, he occupied—as always—a place removed from the uproar.

He had suffered greatly in the last few days; he felt weak and shaky, his pace was unsteady, and he was practically useless for work.

Since the Sunday they had forced him to drink, he was even more melancholic. After Ciro led him to their shack he had slept deeply for twelve hours. The next day, when he awoke, the memories lashed him with remorse. He felt badly about his misbehavior. What had he done! He should have struggled, rather than yield to the goading of the idlers in the store. When Ciro departed for work, he had left the door ajar, and the sun dazzled Marcelo. His head felt as though it were hollow and a roisterous goblin was dancing inside. It was a sultry day: a golden cloud of dust particles descending from the sun forced his eyes shut.

Depressed, he slumped down on the door sill and once again the memories marched by. That entire Sunday was reborn, with all its alternatives and mixed emotions. His heart felt leaden. Ah, never again! He wouldn't drink again, even though they ripped him to pieces with their ridicule.

Suddenly he felt pierced by the memory of Andújar, Gaspar, Deblás, and the dialogue he overheard in the shed. Holy God! He remembered that while lying behind the shed he had wondered: should he keep silent? Should he tell Andújar of the danger that he was in? He had promised himself at the time to say nothing; after all, it was none of his business. But, if they killed Andújar? Wouldn't it be a crime to stay silent if he had the power to spare the man? He recalled how, after hesitating for some time, he had thought of Juan del Salto's words: *the complicity of silence*. And he remembered that he had finally decided to thwart the terrible plot. Then, before deciding upon a course of action, came his struggle with the *campesinos* and his drunken spree.

But now he was alone and undisturbed: he had to decide. He sat thinking, worried. The obvious thing to do was to hurry down the mountain to the city, and tell the judge everything. *Señor Judge, they are planning to kill a man in my barrio* . . . Yes, right to the point. But where is the proof? *Señor Judge, I myself heard two men discussing the crime* . . . But did he have witnesses? Then, for sure, there would be police and a great hubbub. Gaspar and Deblás would be taken prisoner; who knows if he himself might not be arrested! Gaspar and Deblás would, of course, deny everything. *Señor Judge, this man Marcelo has a grudge against us, he's lying* . . . How could he prove his accusation? Without proof, everyone would be set free, and the two killers would be upon him. No, he couldn't do it that way!

Discarding the idea of going to the police, he thought of Juan del Salto. He would go to his farm and tell him of the plot. Yes, Juan del Salto was the man. What would he decide to do? God knows! After the first shock would come the indignation he had displayed when told of the stone murder perpetrated by Galante. Then, undoubtedly, there would be a message to the judge. Always the judge, with his battalions of clerks, policemen and failers! *Señor Judge, Marcelo has told me about this, that and the other* . . . And here, too, Marcelo would be seized, forced to publicly accuse them, and run the risk of their revenge. He, too, would go to jail, where disease kills even the strongest, where prisoners destroy themselves, wallowing in repugnant vices, and wounding each other with pieces of glass or weapons smuggled into the big yard.

Marcelo was overwhelmed by dismay and bitterness; tears welled up in his eyes. To be trapped in jail! To become involved in a trial! It didn't occur to him that he wasn't responsible; he felt that, having overheard the murder plot, he had committed some offense. He had no faith in the power of honor, of courageously declaring the truth, serene in his innocence.

Finally, he thought of Andújar and he felt relieved. Yes, that was the answer. Tell the victim, who could then elude the danger.

Andújar would take precautions, he would create some means of defense to keep himself clear of traps. And he, Marcelo, would satisfy his conscience and thwart a crime, without having to show his face. Andújar was Deblás' cousin, he had hidden him and kept him alive with money and clothing. It was not possible that he would openly accuse him; he would seek a quieter means of defense. As a last resort, he would wait for the night chosen by the assassins, and kill them in self defense. Marcelo's presence would not be necessary. So he could tell Andújar of the conspiracy and make him promise that he would be left in the background, safe from the retaliation of the two would-be killers.

Marcelo spent a great part of the day thinking about the problem. Then he felt a gnawing hunger in his stomach and left his hut, disappearing in the woods.

Beginning with that Monday, he hesitated each day. He trusted that until the first day of the new moon there was nothing to fear.

Each time he pondered the problem, he wondered: should he keep quiet and let it happen? should he talk, and prevent the crime? Assuming the latter, there were three choices: the judge, Juan del Salto, Andújar. And night would fall with the puzzle still unsolved. He favored Andújar, who was more of his kind, who was on closer personal terms with the *campesinos* and demanded less respect and formality. But still he hesitated. He must be patient; soon the moment would arrive; when Andújar was alone, and he could speak to him without arousing suspicion.

Thus, on the day of the heavy rain, when he took cover beneath the eaves on Juan del Salto's farm, nothing had yet been done. Several times, while in the store, he had been tempted to get it over with, but he controlled himself. No, not yet . . .

When Montesa punched Marcante, Marcelo moved away timidly. He had nothing to do with the quarrel, he was ready to obey; let them put the others in line. When the row was over, he stayed there, an absurd expression on his face, contemplating some vague spot in the heavens.

Despite the heavy rain, the atmosphere was heavy and the mass of blackish clouds flowed by like a legion of runaway chargers. A great roar rose up from the river as though a hundred giant engines were whipping the waters.

Suddenly the alarm sounded. Juan del Salto, Montesa, all the *campesinos* scurried downhill to the cliff overhanging the river bank. The river! The river! It was swollen and descending furiously from the sierra.

A colossal mass of water had broken its dike, and was rolling through the rocky basin with great force. The torrent threw itself headlong, howling like an enraged cur, screaming with the wrath of a chained jackal, twisting like a gigantic serpent. The air shuddered from the din, and its joltings were like angry snarls, unleashing a centuries-old hatred. The muddy red waters buffeted the slopes, creating enormous alluvia that widened the river bed; they tumbled frothily down the slopes or whirled in a labyrinth of concentric circles; they undermined rocks, leaping upward like jets until they dislodged them.

The torrent looked gory, as though the *cordillera* had been stabbed and were bleeding into the river, into that angry channel where death raced by, filling the mountain with roars and hurling its voluminous force against all obstacles; a red-countenanced death rushing down from the *cordillera* and sweeping up everything in its path.

A crowd of *campesinos* on both shores let out prolonged shouts to broadcast the alarm. Occasionally, the lugubrious sound of a *bocina* warned of the danger: it was a large seashell which magnified the human voice, giving off a grandiose echo, like a thunderous edict from the gods.

The *campesinos* stirred about with fright and curiosity. It's climbing, it's climbing! They followed the progressively violent advances of the flood, and backed away from the shore as huge chunks of earth broke off and slid into the river; they pointed with awe-struck fear at the violence which menaced them. Death was swooping down from the summits and laying waste the land.

The waters uprooted tree trunks and great leafy branches; huge rocks somersaulted by as though set in motion by the kick of a colossus; fragments of riverside homes were snatched away by the mighty current. The red water was flecked with gray-colored objects. At times, a tiny island of thicket holding stones and clods of dirt in its roots would appear at the height of the river, frozen there for an instant. But soon it would slip by and disappear in the distance. It's climbing, it's climbing! The *campesinos* were troubled over the fate of their compatriots who lived up above, in the mountaintop cabins, or down below, in the tiny houses of the valley.

There was a hideous shriek. A goat had been tied to a tree on a flat piece of land which jutted out from the river bank. No one suspected at first that the waters would climb that high, but suddenly a new spurt of the tide flooded the small peninsula. The goat's owner, a fourteen-year-old boy, saw that the current was going to sweep away his treasure, perhaps his only fortune! Without measuring the risk, the boy plunged into the water, reached the goat, cut the rope, and the animal splashed up to dry land unscathed. The boy stumbled, fell to his knees, rose shakily, fell again, and was finally swept away.

A cry of terror shot forth from the onlookers. The boy, tumbling about in the water, managed to seize a tree branch which leaned over the river and dipped its foliage into the water. The situation was critical: the tree could collapse and the exhausted boy would disappear forever.

Then, something beautiful and thrilling happened. Juan del Salto felt wonder, not surprise. He had witnessed similar things many times before. Inés Marcante, the one who had been whipped by Montesa earlier in the day, dived into the water from the left shore, Almost simultaneously, six more *campesinos* dived in. The liquid monster parted, allowing a few shreds of Humanity, ennobled by heroism, to penetrate its depths.

No one spoke. The boy clung to the branches of the tree; the *campesinos* struggled boldly on the surface, while the bellowing torrent churned about them. The tree, by some caprice of nature, was rooted from the side of the bank; it was impossible to get ashore from the tree without the aid of a rope or a long pole. The boy was in immense danger.

Two of the seven swimmers were close to drowning and were forced to return to shore. Four of the others fought to cross the river. Only one, Inés Marcante—more dexterous, more agile, luckier—reached the tree, grasped the boy in one arm, and perched him atop the thickest branch. Then he, too, got on, dragged the child along the trunk, and waited for help. Later, back on dry land, he stretched out shivering with cold. The other rescuers finally got out of the water and the consternation of the people gave way to a cry of victory.

Juan's chest swelled with joy. That had been a ray of light cast upon the blackness of his pessimism, a flower blossoming among nettle, a gem found in a swamp.

The river, meanwhile, continued its mad race, coating the shores with foam and destroying the crops nearby. Juan, followed by Montesa, made a tour and took note of the damage. The waters had swept away several coffee trees and demolished a few of the levees.

As night fell, the *campesinos* dispersed. Some were unable to cross the river and return home. But no one was in want of coffee; the congregation burst with hospitality and soon the palm floors of the huts were covered with sleeping strangers and their charitable hosts.

Juan returned home in a pensive mood. When he reached the house, he said to Montesa:

"All right, now what do you think of Inés Marcante and his friends?"

Montesa removed his *sombrero,* scratched the back of his head, hesitated a moment and said:

"Well . . . they . . . why those devils nearly made me cry."

An hour later, the night was dense. The river, though slackening in its fury, still roared with menace, while shadows hooded everything. There was not one star, not one smudge of cloud; only some distant thunder booming its elastic report. It was a gloomy night: the sky, black; the earth, black; the void, black also, as though all were in mourning over the sun's absence. Humidity rose up from the earth; the spongy land, sated by rain, was disgorging it in invisible, rich clouds.

Nature rested from the disasters of the day, elaborating in her hidden breasts the exquisite marvels of her maternal labor.

Chapter Seven

Marcelo felt relieved. Andújar now shared the great secret which had burdened him so greatly.

He had finally mustered enough courage to speak. It was at midday; the store was deserted, and the clerk was busy loading a pack mule.

From the back door Marcelo called to the shopkeeper and, after a thousand circumlocutions, came to the point.

"Word of honor?"

"Yes."

"Your word of honor that you won't involve me?"

"Yes, *hombre*."

"On your mother?"

"On my mother!"

"You will never say that I told you?"

"No! Will you get on with it? I'll keep your secret, but tell me, *caramba*! I'm bursting with curiosity.

Then without omitting a detail, Marcelo spilled the entire story.

Andújar paled. Rob him, kill him! Beasts! He had sheltered that fugitive, his rascal of a cousin, freeing him a hundred times from the persecution of the rural police, only now to be made victim of such a despicable plot. He wondered whether Marcelo was telling the truth. But why should he lie? Marcelo was a poor young fellow, incapable of such trickery.

In all the time he had lived in the region, never had he feared anything; it was a good land, free from menace. A few petty thefts now and then, but that was all.

But Andújar's prosperity had undoubtedly aroused his kinsman's envy, and he was dragging that barbarian Gaspar into the plot.

One must not be too trusting; his house was almost bare of safeguards: thin wooden walls, doors fastened shut with weak

128

crossbars or locks identical to everyone else's. Nothing was simpler than smashing a window or removing a door. Ah, how lucky he was to have a loyal friend like Marcelo!

During those days, Andújar had been preoccupied with important business that distracted him from his routine.

The rich landlord Galante had made him a tempting offer. It was not some trifling business on the mountain—let the coffee trees keep spilling forth gold—the smart thing was to strike out on some venture in the lowlands.

Galante laid before Andújar a vast plan that involved food provisions and finance, proposing that they establish a house of commerce by the sea to be called "Andújar and Galante."

The shopkeeper was very impressed by the plan; a certain tickle of ambition joggled about inside him, stretching farther than he had ever before dreamed, filling him with pride. Business on a grand scale; raking in the fruits, stowing them in the holds of ships, launching them across the sea, and then waiting for the flow of riches from the exchange, from the agencies, from the commissions, from a multitude of sources. Alert men should expand, reach out for the horizons. Leave the mountain to the underlings of commerce, the apprentices, the poor bedeviled pennypinchers.

Another affair also caused him some thought. Close to the store was a small bit of land that belonged to Old Marta. Why not buy it? People swore she had hard cash buried there. He himself had observed how the old woman's earnings evaporated with no sign of their use. He was convinced that the purchase of the orchard was a smart move. However, when he dared to propose the transaction Marta was hostile, stubborn. He must be patient. Perhaps someday he could convince her. Wait and be ready: that was the secret.

His mood was shaken when he received the awful news from Marcelo. He thanked the youth with a vigorous handshake and marked his account in the store "paid": forty or fifty *centavos* worth of *salazones*.[1]

---

[1]*salazones,* a type of salted fish.

He spent a long time thinking how he could defend himself against the brutal attack. He didn't like the idea of getting involved with the law: if he stirred up the waters too much some of his own old maneuvers might float to the surface.

Most important was to safeguard the money he kept in the big chest, and save his own skin.

He had several thousand in a friend's strongbox in town. When his money accumulated, he took it there immediately and the horde kept in the chest fluctuated between eight hundred and a thousand *pesos*. It was now full: one thousand five hundred in silver and gold.

So it was urgent to withdraw the money from danger. It was a simple matter: he had a good horse, and he would equip it with packsaddles and steal away without anyone knowing.

But, what about the store? They would smash their way in and rob ... bah! Some haul, bothering with all those cheap trifles! Barrels of *bacalao,* sacks of rice, baskets of potatoes, pieces of ordinary cloth, and the pile of trinkets that dazzled the mountainfolk. Let them steal it! The day after the one set for the assault, he would return to his house and if they had stooped to robbing him he would know immediately how to find the stolen goods: any cheap little store in the region, which he could search with absolute freedom. That is, if they had been foolish enough to serve as accomplices to the crime by buying the loot. what the thieves really wanted was money—*onzas* of gold—if they found nothing they would probably sneak off, and try again.

Andújar shaped his plan. Tomorrow was the first day of the new moon. At seven, after the clerk departed, he would bundle up his wealth and disappear with the first shadows. Then ... let the world go to blazes! Anyway, the danger would be short-lived, since Galante's plan would require that he move away.

Freed from the burden of his secret, Marcelo shuttered himself in his cabin, resolved not to venture out until the tempest subsided. That night he had a torturous, suffocating nightmare: he dreamed that he was bound to a tree next to a torrent of blood, with bodiless heads floating past, and that the level was climbing bit by bit; when it reached his waist, and he was in the depths of suffering, he woke up feeling fatigued as though he had just completed a long journey.

The same afternoon that Marcelo spoke with Andújar, with the sun already behind the mountains, Gaspar and Silvina found themselves alone in Leandra's hut. Leandra had gone down to the store, taking Pequeñín along to bathe him in the river, which was pleasant and calm after the recent flood.

Gaspar was seated on the stone in front of the house which served as a step. He entertained himself by slashing his machete into the earth or severing in two the small lizards that passed within his reach. He would smilingly contemplate the agony of the poor creatures, whose sundered halves shook convulsively.

Silvina sat at the threshold, her hands buried in the folds of her skirt, gazing at the landscape.

Gaspar was usually quite sullen, but he had been rather affectionate of late. He gave Silvina some red stockings and a glass bead necklace, paid for from his frequent dippings into Old Marta's buried earthen jar.

But Silvina knew what Gaspar's facade meant: he wanted to ask something very important of her. She accepted the magnificent presents without hesitation, and when Gaspar called her *mi negra*[2] she became frightened and disconcerted. Such unusual affection must have a catch to it, and she—inured to misery—felt uneasiness instead of joy; especially when she recalled the terrible business of which her husband spoke so often.

"We should realize," Gaspar said, continuing a thought, "that here in the country we're dying of hunger. All our lives, dragging ourselves up these hills; some fun! We have no children, but we must find a better life. We should be landlords, eh? Not here, of course; only a bat can survive around here. Over in the lowlands, or on the other coast, or even farther, in a country they say is about two days' voyage by sea. Do you know where? In the country where they say the slaves escape to. You know how we can do it: I'm up to my neck in a business affair which will make me

---

[2] *mi negra*, literally "my dark one," but used as a term of endearment, to mean "my darling."

enough to settle down far from these parts. I think that *he,* over *there,* ought to have more than three thousand *pesos.*"

"Who?" she said in a frightened tone.

"'Andújar . . .'"

Silvina was dismayed. He hadn't abandoned the terrible scheme!

"Well yes, girl; we must shake off our sadness and seek our fortune. With our share, we'll be in the chips. Well, say something, woman."

"I've already told you plenty. Honest people . . ."

"*Barajo*! You must be newly born, girl."

Seeing her burst into tears, he added: "Is this how you're going to help me? I won't turn back, you hear? Cry or not, it makes no difference. Shut up! Listen, it's the easiest thing in the world. Without any risk, in no time at all, we can be rich."

Silvina sobbed, thinking to herself: no! They were trying to force her into a crime. Why didn't they leave her alone? Why drag her along?

"Deblás and I," Gaspar continued, "have everything arranged.'" He'll take a look about the store early; when the fellow is asleep he'll come to meet us at Palmacortada, over there, next to the cliff. Then we'll go down to the store. The easiest part is next. We tie the bandit up, break the lock on the trunk and divide what money there is in half. The next day, we stay calm, and after two or three days: *feet, what are you made for?*

Silvina trembled. Gaspar's cold-blooded narrative was dreadful. She felt like dying, to free herself of her anguish. "As for you, it's the same whether you like it or not. I want you to come with us, and that's that . . ."

"But how can I—your woman by the Church, a good woman who has never stolen—be expected to be part of such an outrage? How could I even dare do such a thing? How could a poor, unhappy . . ."

"Bah! Look, don't be an old woman . . ."

"I should try to save you from this temptation, from this madness . . ."

"God help you!"

". . . and I should tell, instead of keeping it a secret, so that you'll control yourself . . ."

Gaspar leaped up, seized Silvina's hands and squeezed them violently.

"That's exactly why I want you to come; so that you're involved, too; so that you don't sing . . ."

"*Ay*! You're hurting me! Let go!"

". . . so that you'll have to keep quiet . . ."

"Let me go!"

". . . so that you won't sell me out . . ."

"*Ay*!"

"I pity you if you disobey!"

"Gaspar, Gaspar! You're breaking my bones!"

"I could take your neck and twist if off, traitor! I give the orders; you keep quiet and do as I say . . ."

Silvina finally managed to wriggle loose. She was quivering with fear. Holy God, he was capable of killing her! She had to do something; life couldn't go on like this. But to whom could she turn? She cried and cried with infinite bitterness, feeling alone in the world.

Gaspar pulled a knife from the leather sheath attached to his belt.

"Here," he said, "take this knife in your hand."

"For the love of God, Gaspar!"

"Take it in your hand . . . like that. Now I'll take your hand in mine, like this. If you dare to disobey me, your own hand, pushed by mine, will shove this point through your heart. Go now, tell everyone about your husband's plan. Go, I dare you!"

Silvina's soul was tortured; her face was bathed in tears, her arms limp at her sides. She cried for a long time, until nightfall, when Leandra returned and paid her no mind, since she saw her cry every day, and Gaspar laid himself down upon the rag bed and began to snore, gargling the air.

Later, alone by the door, she thought of Ciro, the lone stroke of blue in her bitterness. Ciro loved her; it was he who awakened her first passions, who enchained her in the feeling of first love. But all was useless; misfortune had placed a barrier between them.

When the first outrages destroyed Silvina's innocence, Ciro had ignored everything. Later, when she was forced into a repugnant contract marriage, Ciro continued loving her, imploring her a hundred times to follow him, free from care. She loved him, but—alas!—Gaspar was always in the way. Many young girls of the region surrendered themselves without marriage, ceding one day to passion, the other to caprice, choosing a new mate from the mob of seducers whenever circumstances demanded. She observed how many married young *campesinas* paid little attention to the marital knot and considered themselves free; when discord arose they abandoned the husband and submitted to another lover, while the legitimate mate went looking for another devoted woman to replace the fugitive. The breaches, the mendings, were enacted without rancor or grief, like the most natural thing in the world, causing shame or dishonor to no one. Silvina recalled the stories of other homes and felt tempted to imitate their conduct. She wanted to run away, take flight. Leandra's shack was not her home, the cozy nook of her dreams. There she found only grief, tyranny, brutality and hunger. Why not escape with Ciro, her beloved, who after so much ill fortune deserved the prize of possessing her?

But then, the terrible phantom rose up before her. A few moments ago he had proposed a terrible thing. Ciro was almost surely prowling about close by, constantly searching for his chance, even more resolved and ardent since the night he broke through the floor, waiting for her, always waiting . . . Why should she stay? She was alone; everyone in the shack was asleep; outside, the invisible arms of the night beckoned to her; the chance was tempting, irresistible. Why did she hesitate, pining with cowardice?

A distant, stronger will held her. Run away! She felt rebellion welling up within her. But no, Gaspar would kill her. He would track her down, seize her and pierce her with a glance from his domineering eyes. She lacked the strength for such a bold act.

Then she entered the shack, placed the palm leaf over the hollow of the doorway and stretched out on her part of the mat, in the superb bridal chamber that had afforded her only misery and disgust.

The next day the store was closed early. The clerk usually called Andújar at dawn; he would then open up and work was resumed. The shopkeeper fidgeted restlessly all day, thinking about his escape. By leaving at dark, he would be unable to return until quite late in the morning, so he gave the key for one of the doors to the youth, ordering him to open at the normal hour and await his return. He invented some urgent affairs in the city, telling the lie when the store was closed, and the yawning clerk had no more on his mind than sleeping off the greasy fatigue of the day's toil.

Soon, Andújar was alone. To the right of the store was a stable where his horse slept on a bed of straw. He quickly haltered the animal, equipped it with pack saddles, carefully placed the two well-wrapped packages inside, slipped the revolver in his belt and locked the door to his room; he put the key in his jacket pocket, and in a leap was atop the mount, placing a sharp machete behind one leg.

In the meantime, he mulled over his decision. He had good friends in town; he would take lodging in the home of the most discreet, go for a stroll, sup in some inexpensive place, and return to the mountain early in the morning. His money—for which he would be granted a receipt—would be safe.

Satisfied, he gave the animal its rein and, since it was already nighttime the rider and his mount soon vanished in the shadows.

Gaspar had spent the whole day searching for a natural excuse that would permit him to leave the hut with Silvina in the early hours of the evening, without arousing Leandra's suspicion.

The idea of a visit occurred to him; a courtesy call to the godfather of any of the mountainfolk. But to visit on the eve of a work day? No, this was too unusual. Then he considered inventing an excursion to town. No good either. At ten in the evening, he must be by Palmacortada, waiting for his accomplice; the business would take an hour, more or less. How could he, in truth, travel on foot to the city, leaving at six in the afternoon, and return by midnight? The maneuver would seem suspicious, and Gaspar wanted to proceed with the greatest caution. What to do, then?

For a moment he thought the problem was resolved: they would spend the night at Galante's farm because an important matter demanded Gaspar's attention. No good. After the attack, why the devil go to someone else's house, if the wise thing was to hide? Why not feign a simple stroll in the woods? They would set out at dusk, complaining of the heat; they would walk about for a while and then come back to retire for the night. Gaspar favored this plan, despite the fact that he habitually went to bed early, and everyone knew it.

A chance event—one quite common in the life of the *campesinos*—resolved the problem.

A young boy, the son of a laborer whom everyone knew, had died in Vegaplana. Ah, what a shame! How could one ignore the propriety of at least a brief visit to the mourners? They would leave early; but they would pray only from eleven to twelve, because Gaspar didn't like the customary all-night vigil.

Thus, everything was credible. From six to nine at the wake; at ten, in Palmacortada; then . . . to the other place; and in bed by twelve. If, just out of curiosity someone asked what they did between the time they left Vegaplana and midnight? Why,the most innocent of all diversions: an enjoyable dip in the river. At six, Gaspar left the hut and Silvina was behind him.

The new moon peeked through a misty veil of low clouds, looking like an Oriental plume adorning the turban of the twilight.

At nine, all was silent and deserted; only the river sent up its eternal murmur from the depths of the gorge.

A timorous breeze riffled through the foliage. The woodland surrounding the store and the sheds obscured all details. Everything was blurred together: the houses, tree trunks, the stable, the grove of trees by the cliff. A faint light fell upon the transit-hardened road, and a few burnished stones glimmered dully.

Suddenly, a shadow emerged from the woods. It was Deblás.

He looked about and then slowly approached the store. He

rested his hands on the thin wall and stood still, listening. He pressed his cheeks against the wooden boards, straining to hear the slightest sound. Nothing: not even the buzz of a mosquito.

Andújar was usually snoring by this time. Why such silence? Could he have gone out?

Deblás took a complete turn around the house; he tried all the doors, he stopped to listen by the front porch, and quietly returned to the door leading to Andujar's room. Nothing. All was silent.

Again he listened, hoping to hear Andujar's breathing. In vain. Finally, he saw something that surprised him. On the left frame of the door was an enormous nail from which there usually hung a halter connected to a rope which reached to the ground. Obviously the shopkeeper was not there.

Deblás went to the stable, leaned over the feeding trough and peered in at the spot where the nag slept. She wasn't in there.

The bird had flown. Deblás tumbled into a sea of confusion. He knew that the shopkeeper went on occasional nighttime sorties, pursuing some cheap adventure, and finishing at an early hour.

But it was incredible that he should leave the money behind in the trunk. So his absence also meant the absence of the money. He took another walk around the store; he couldn't convince himself that his great project had failed. Greatly vexed, he wondered: what to do now?

Why had Andújar gone out? Did he guess what awaited him? Who knows? Could Gaspar have been indiscreet? Ah, Silvina! Perhaps that beast of a woman was to blame. But how could she, so frightened of her mate, have dared to ruin it for them? And if Andújar knew something, why hadn't he enlisted some people to help catch them in a trap? Above all, he would have expressed his loathing for Deblás, his own cousin, who was betraying him. No, Andújar must have gone out by sheer chance, and the business had to be postponed.

Again he wondered: and the money? Could Andújar have taken his savings with him? At night, along lonely roads, all by himself? For a man of Andújar's suspicious nature, such a reversal of character was most unlikely. But how to explain the improbability that he would go out and leave the money unguarded? In any event, one thing was certain: Andújar wasn't there. Now they had to find out if the money had also evaporated.

Deblás speculated that the shopkeeper had to leave suddenly, and left the money behind. In that case, he would return soon.

There was no time to lose, if he wished to eliminate all doubt. He pulled out a crowbar, shoved it through the slit between the door and the wall, and gradually worked it up towards the lock.

Then a thought stopped him. Should he tell the others, who were waiting for him at Palmacortada? What for? With Andújar gone, he could do it by himself. But their pact? He wavered, imagining Gaspar becoming impatient, coming to see what has happened, and catching him in the act of treachery. On the other hand, why should so many people be involved?

At last, he decided to tell them that the plan should be postponed for a better time. Believing him, they would agree upon a future date; in the meantime, he would return. If there was no money, there would always be another night. If it was there, the entire slice would be his. Even though Gaspar later learned of the trick, he would never complain to anyone. Bah! He was a coward, and it would be easy to settle accounts with him. Furthermore, he could always hide in the *cordillera*.

He found them quickly. In a cluster of royal palms, there was one whose cleft trunk marked the disaster of a lightning bolt. Gaspar and Silvina were at the foot of this trunk.

It was a rugged site. The palms stood close to the irregular edge of the cliff, a chasm in whose depths flowed a tributary rill of the river, which descended leap by leap from the distant *sierras*.

"No luck," Deblás exclaimed as he approached.

"What?"

"Nothing can be done tonight."

"But . . . what's happened?"

"Something we didn't expect: the bird flew away."

"What?"

"Andújar isn't there. He's grown feathers and taken the money with him. Our business must be postponed."

Silvina, who had been silent and mopish, breathed with relief.

"All right," insisted Gaspar, "how do you explain it?"

"A coincidence. The man's trunk was full, it was running over, and since he's so distrustful he must have left with the money. There's no use following him. You're to blame, you know. If you hadn't hemmed and hawed so, and we'd have done something last week, we would have gotten there in time. You wanted to think it over so much . . . now you see the result."

"I'm not convinced. Do you think he left just by chance?"

When he said this, he directed a fierce look at Silvina.

"Why else, *hombre?*"

"A warning . . ."

"I doubt it. He left with his money, and he'll return soon. If he had known something, he would have stayed to catch us in a trap. But don't be impatient: we mustn't think about it now. We'll soon see when the time is right to go back to our tricks."

After a few instants of reflection, Gaspar added: "since no one is at the store, we almost owe it to ourselves to search it."

"Sure! And while we fill our pockets with potatoes and stale bread, he comes to entertain us."

"True . . . but how could he have left the store alone? It's strange that he didn't leave the clerk to mind it."

"I tell you there's no one, and there's no money. Andújar prefers locking everything up to letting some young boy stay inside. He trusts a key more than a man."

Silvina felt calmer now. What luck! The infamous deed was postponed, and there was always a measure of hope that things would change by then.

"Now then, everyone home, and until we meet again," Deblás added.

"Don't go; wait. Let's think this over. Why not go down there and take a look around?"

"No, we might wind up having breakfast in jail."

"Listen, if he's taken the money to the lowlands, he probably won't return until morning. If he comes back right away, it's a sign that he's left it behind."

"So."

"Let's try something . . . a look around . . ."

"You try; look around by yourself, I'm going to sleep."

"Ah, no! Not alone."

"Don't count on me."

"But, *hombre* . . ."

"I'm not so crackbrained that I'd get mixed up in such a foolish trick."

"Listen . . ."

"It won't work."

"But look . . ."

"I tell you it won't work."

"It won't work, Gaspar," Silvina dared to murmur. Enraged, he slapped her, saying:

"What do you know about it? Shut up or I'll cut your tongue out!"

"Come now, are you going to quarrel with your woman? Good night."

"Listen . . ."

"No, *adiós.* Until tomorrow. We'll talk it over slowly and get things settled."

"Listen, *hombre.*"

"Good night."

Deblás vanished in the woods while Gaspar flexed his fists in rage, muttering curses. Then he pushed Silvina, who fell seated in the thicket.

'Sit down," he said, seating himself also.

Crossing his legs, with his elbows on his knees and his forehead in his hands, he set to thinking.

The night flowed by like a ghost wrapped in an ashen tunic. The starry sky was aburst with brilliance. Each star radiated a shaft of light, first timid, then intense, then timid once more; blinking and quenching the ardor of its glow, as though it were horrified by human strife and wanted to close its eyes. The immense blue-tinged sky was tranquil, pure, serene. The mountain peaks tumbled over their huge bases, extinguishing the dim lights on the faded landscape. The cluster of palms stood in discord; one trunk erect, another oblique, one tall and slender, another bent over, as if it wished to put its fruits brimming with cooling liquor within the reach of man. And always the eternal concert. A gust of wind whistling as it stirs the trees; the tireless lament of the river, forming whirlpools and polishing rugged stones; the grand insect sonata of winged violins, of shrill cicadas; and standing out from the chorus the chant of the little toad of the brooks and gullies, ever repeating its monotonous *co-quí! co-quí!*

Finally, Gaspar spoke:

"No matter what Deblás says, this thing has reached down to my marrow. It's a nuisance ... a complete nuisance! So much thinking, so much planning, to arrive at *nothing*! It won't work for now.. For now! Well, *when*? I tell you, the money is there! I'm not satisfied. But why has Andújar gone off? Could he know something? Was it a coincidence? Some girl? Who knows if he isn't around here somewhere, chasing after someone else's woman? And why was Deblás so disagreeable? Has he turned coward? Him, such a braggart! So many obstacles, and me so *prepared,* so hungry to put my hands on that bundle. Bah! Deblás frets over nothing. And he was in such a hurry! Well, just wait and see how it will turn out that the store was untended and the money was there."

Wrinkling his brow, he looked up at the sky, calling into play the extraordinary instinct of the *campesinos,* who, with only slight error, could tell time by merely observing the stars.

"If I would dare," he continued. "If we tried! The store is still left alone; Deblás is sleeping up there in his hideaway; we have about an hour and a half until midnight. We can look about, open a door, break the lock on the trunk, and if there's no cash, at least we'd be convinced of the truth, and have a few drinks. It's so easy! Of course, we must move quickly. If he appears and catches us touching even an *orange,* paf! Feet up from a bullet. Yes, I believe we should try; if not, what are we going to do here, with our mouths hanging open? We can't go home until twelve or one; we'd have to wait two hours out here in the open, in the dew ... some fun, eh?"

Silvina, who had been tranquil for an instant, felt distressed once more. Gaspar scratched his head, as though he were asking the messy tangle of hair to resolve his doubts.

"Truthfully, this would be a great stroke," he continued. "Let's leave that rascal out of it and do it ourselves. If there is no money, there will surely be something worth taking. Even if Andújar left at dark and hasn't gone far, he can't be back until at least midnight. If he's gone to the lowlands, then there's nothing to worry about . . ."

He continued thinking. Silvina stared at her companion, who was barely visible in the shadows. She was terrified, trembling, waiting from one moment to the next for his decision.

Much time passed. Suddenly, Gaspar bolted upright.

"Come on!"

"For the love of God, Gaspar! What are you going to do?"

"Get moving."

"Gaspar . . ."

"Shut up!'"

"But don't push me, *hombre* . . . I'll fall down the hill!"

"Let's go . . ."

"Have mercy on me! Look, some other day . . . it won't work tonight, there are many dangers . . . The money isn't there . . . Deblás had his reasons for not wanting to go. Believe him: forget it for now . . ."

"Come on, come on."

"Gaspar, for your mother, for whatever you love most, please forget it."

"Walk, walk!"

"Oh, at least let me go home. Why must I go along? I'll only be in the way . . ."

"If you don't shut up, you know what to expect. I'm mad, I would kill the *devil* if he got in my way. Keep going and stop fooling around. If you bother me, I'll throw you over the cliff.

And they began the descent down the mountainside.

Meanwhile, Deblás hadn't wasted time. Leaving his accomplices at Palmacortada, he returned to the store.

He paused once more to listen, and again slipped the crowbar between the crack in the door. He worked it upwards towards the lock. Then, squeezing his hands into the narrow space, he pulled hard, the lock snapped, and the door gave way.

With the first problem overcome, Deblás went into the store. A hot heavy odor of food enveloped him.

Once inside, he struck a match and barred the door with a piece of wood found nearby.

He lighted a tallow candle that was propped inside a bottle atop a chair next to the cot. When there was light, he looked about him. Alone at last!

Next to the chair was a chest, a giant coffer, older than it was strong. Lifting the light, he took note of his surroundings, searched the room with the packsaddles, and passed like a phantom between the cupboards and the counter.

He checked everything: it was important to proceed with the greatest caution, and for the biggest profit. He remembered Gaspar's dilemma: *if Andújar took the money, it was unlikely that he would return until morning: if the money is there, he'll return soon.* The important thing was to eliminate all doubt. If the money was in the chest he must hurry and get away with it quickly; if not, Andújar wouldn't return until the following day, giving him time to painstakingly search the store and strip it of everything worth taking.

He turned to the coffer, shoved the crowbar into the crack below the lid and lifted the brass strip that covered it.

With little effort, he snapped one latch, then the other; at last Deblás saw the hollow of the coffer before his eyes. A disorderly pile of clothing was stuffed inside; in the bottom was an empty wooden box, once used for storing crackers; only a few *ochavos,* fallen unobserved, blackened the white paper lining like grotesque moles. The treasure was gone!

In a fit of rage Deblás hurled the crowbar to the floor, and it bounced beneath the cot. He stood erect, clenched his fists and cursed aloud, as he looked down angrily at the empty bowels of the chest. Ah, that miserable cousin of his had played a mean trick upon him!

Then he walked about the store. Bah! Junk! Only the devil

could carry off such bulky things and later transport them without
arousing suspicion.

There was a sausage atop a filthy shelf. Deblás took a piece in
his mouth, and then a great mouthful of bread and cheese.

He kept searching. Nothing he saw appealed to him: fabrics,
bundles of ribbons, cheap shoes, sewing thread, copper buttons.
Some pickings! He continued to eat cheese, bread, sausage, ham
. . . He nervously gobbled great mouthfuls, which he swallowed
almost without chewing. He yearned for an appetite of ten years
of prior fasting, so that he could take advantage, consume the
greatest amount possible, and annoy his cousin, punishing him for
having carried away the coveted treasure.

He searched everywhere, passing from one side of the counter
to the other, climbing atop it, reaching for high objects, crouching
down to rummage below. Since all the doors and windows were
closed, the temperature was extremely high; Deblás felt soaked
with sweat, suffocated by the scarcity of air.

Searching and eating, he finished off a can of preserves, prying
into all the provisions, turning the store upside down. He felt
thirsty. He poured himself a rum and drained it in a gulp. He
opened the cash box: not one *céntimo*. Only a counterfeit *peseta* on
the counter, nailed there as a warning against trust.

Thirsty again, he scooped a cupful of water from an earthen jar
beneath the counter. He quickly spit it out in disgust; it was filthy
and warm. He opened a bottle of beer and drank it down.

Continuing the search, he stuffed a few trifles into his pockets:
a pocketknife, a leather belt, and two or three handkerchiefs.

He spent an hour searching and drinking. Finally, after a
generous amount of *aguardiente,* he returned to Andújar's room.
His filled pockets were so bulky he had to change the position of
his dagger, which he carried sheathed at his belt.

Ready to leave now, he placed the light upon the chair, flicked
away some sweat with the back of his right thumb, and began to
lift the crossbar.

But something detained him. High up on the wall, next to the
cot, there was a shelf: from afar, Deblás saw a multitude of things
heaped upon it.

He wanted to look it over. He climbed atop the cot with one foot on each side, his legs spread wide, he began the search. Nothing: empty boxes, fragments of old string, piles of wrapping paper.

Standing there like Colossus, Deblás felt a strange vertigo, an extreme heaviness in his head, an irresistible drowsiness. He fell to his knees on the cot, and then sat down on the edge. What was happening to him? Since it was late, already midnight, and he had been drinking, it was not unusual.

He contemplated the cot and punched the pillow. Ah! His cousin was a scoundrel, a cheap crook who owed his fortune to thievery. He would never forgive him for tonight. Such a pity! Everything so well prepared, every detail of the plan so carefully arranged! And that was his cot, where he slept like a hog, after counting the cash box's daily harvest a hundred times. There he weaved his cunning plans; there he snored like a moldy bellows; and there he would have remained—nailed fast by a dagger—had it not been for his accursed luck!

He rested his elbow on the pillow and gave out with a great yawn. Such a pity that his plans should crumble when he was so close to success. But he would catch him some other night. In the morning, Andújar would return, looking so ruddy, so plump, so sturdy . . .

Deblás felt an indomitable drowsiness overcome him. His limbs lapsed, and soon it was not his elbow—but his head—that rested on the pillow.

There, on his back, he gazed up at the rough-hewn ceiling. He mustn't lie idle, or he could doze off. During his fugitive days on the *cordillera* he had learned to sleep with one eye, keeping watch with the other; and always, at sunrise, the first cock's crow would awaken him. It must be midnight; he could sleep there a while, and get away early.

Usurping Andújar's bed could cost him dearly. He might fall asleep, and some mess he would be in, snoring there with the sun already up! No, he must leave, get away . . .

But sleep gradually overpowered him. Commands to flee issued forth from his head, but his body didn't obey. Reason and alcohol were locked in a hand-to-hand struggle. Finally, he lost his grip and was no longer master of himself. He fell into a deep sleep.

Mouth up, arms spread wide, Deblás lay there immobile. The tallow candle, about to consume itself, dripped jaundice yellow filaments upon the bottle's greenish surface. The wick blazed with red-hot intensity, and a tiny column of smoke wafted up from the flame, tracing short-lived spirals. The rays of light filled the room with hideous shadows, and the lambent flow reflected dimly on the scale in the next room.

Soon, there was no more tallow. The small candle tilted in the mouth of the bottle and fell inside. For an instant, it glistened with the brilliance of a glowworm; then it died,, leaving the room in complete darkness.

Then two bodies emerged from the coffee grove that canopied the gorge. It was Gaspar, dragging Silvina behind him.

Although Gaspar was sure that the store was empty, he wanted to be prudent. He pressed his ear against the rear wall: not the slightest sound.

With his knife, he began to force the door leading to Andújar's room, but Deblás had barred it. Still dragging Silvina, he circled the building, testing the strength of the doors. They all held fast.

On their roundabout course they reached the door whose key Andújar had given to the clerk. It was on the porch facing the road, and had no crossbar inside.

Gaspar managed to slip his knife inside the crack and work the lever up to the lock. He inserted a stone in the juncture and thus kept the two leaves of the door apart. He pulled hard and the door—splintering like firewood chips—jarred open. The warm air inside, smelling of foodstuffs, bathed their faces. They entered.

Gaspar closed the door and paused: not a sound. He struck a match, lifted the hinged board at one end of the counter, and they went into the back room.

Gaspar found some tallow candles in a compartment that once served to store cereals. He lit one and wedged it into the mouth of the bottle.

Immediately he thought of the chest: he must force it open wide and examine every inch of it.

He knew that his knife would never do the job. Beneath the

counter, he spied an iron pickax, the kind used for digging holes in the plantings. That would do. He placed the light upon the counter and lifted the pick from the floor.

"Just follow me," he said to Silvina. "I'll make the lid fly off the trunk with this thing. But we'd better be ready for anything. Here, *you* hold the knife."

"Me? No!"

"No arguments! I don't want to lose time. I'll shove the pick in and we'll both push until the lid gives way. When I tell you, follow me, understand? Cheer up! Maybe we're close to the mon . . ."

An unexpected noise—Deblás' loud breathing—cut him short.

Surprised, Gaspar ducked beneath the counter and tugged at Silvina's dress, forcing her to kneel at his side. He whispered:

"We're lost! Andújar is there . . . he's there! Deblás has tricked us!"

Silvina's heart was like an iron hammer raining blows upon an anvil. She was mute with terror, helpless.

Gaspar now knew that he had to cope with Andújar, a strong, determined opponent. At any moment a death-dealing pellet from his resolver could whistle by. He must escape . . .

But not another sound was heard. Undoubtedly the shop-keeper was still asleep. Planning his escape, Gaspar saw that they could slip along beneath the counter, and be out on the road in two bounds. But, alas! If Andújar was there, the money must be there also. With an effort, with a bit of calm, perhaps they could manage to get the money. Yes, courage, spirit!

Gaspar rebelled against his cowardice. Risk it, he told himself. He rose, jerking Silvina erect with him; he checked to see that she still had the knife in her hand; he got a firm grip on the pickax, peered into the darkened room and whispered into Silvina's ear:

"Go on, but be careful. Don't give him time to shoot . . . Kill him with one blow, go ahead!"

He pushed her by the waist. Horrified, barely conscious, without the strength to resist, she ceded. They entered Andújar's bedroom: she first, armed with a knife; he pushing her from behind, armed with the pick.

They approached the cot together and distinguished a body

stretched out in the darkness. One more move and it would all be over . . .

Silvina felt an intense chill; her mind went blank. She stood frozen, her arms limp, staring at what seemed to be a luminescent spot on the wall.

Harried and trembling, Gaspar urged her again:

"Now . . . give it to him now!"

But Silvina could not, and her head lolled backwards.

"Kill him, damn it! Kill him!"

It happened quickly. Gaspar reached out, gripped Silvina's right hand in his, and raised it high. But Silvina staggered, shrieked, and fell backwards, her arms spread wide.

Gaspar felt a lightning flash of fear. He thought that the young girl had fallen wounded by Andújar's doing, and that the invisible weapon would soon be directed against him. The instinct of preservation tensed his limbs, and he impulsively lifted the pickax. He discharged a terrible blow upon the sleeping body.

There was a muffled groan and a torrent of blood issued forth from Deblás' body, percolating through the bed, inundating the room, leaping out in red fibers, drenching Silvina's face and clothing like warm rain as she lay on the floor.

Gaspar took in everything with a glance: Silvina, immobile, apparently dead; the money chest wide open, miserably empty, without a *céntimo*; on the cot, a dead man's body. All at once: a single gesture prompting a hundred surprises.

Gaspar fought to control the trembling in his legs as he went to the counter and returned to the room, holding the light.

He brought the light closer to the bed, recognized the victim, and drew back with astonishment. The light fell from his hand as he bellowed in a horrified tone:

"Damnations of Hell! I've killed Deblás!"

Standing there in the darkness, he felt panic. Two murders . . . two corpses! In a bound he was at the door which opened towards the outside; with a blow he made the crossbar fly and it crashed noisily upon the floor; with a push he opened the door and—like a wild beast that spots an escape route from its pursuers—he darted out into the field, descended the ravine, bounded across the river, clambered up the hill and plunged into the woods, possessed by a longing to flee, drenched with sweat, bareheaded, his eyes dread-stricken and his mouth uttering horrible curses at the sky, at the earth, at Hell and at God.

The cool evening breeze floated through the open doorway into the store, vanquishing the foul odor of nearly spoiled food.

A few minutes passed. Silvina's body shuddered convulsively. A short breath sucked air into her lungs; her tightly clutched fists, fingers digging into her palms, yielded rigidity; her head, tense before, commenced to stir from side to side

Finally, she inhaled, and a prolonged sigh dispersed the tension in her pain-racked body.

Silvina lifted her head and raised herself up on one hand. Where was she? Why did she feel such unbearable pain?

She wanted to remember, but could not. She looked about, trying to shake off the dullness of her senses. She tried to fill her vacant mind with the light of memory; she reached out, struck against the cot, grasped it by the edge and, using it for support, got to her feet.

Suddenly, like a bursting cloud, a tumult of memories spread through her mind. As though by the glare of a lightning bolt, she saw, she remembered, she knew everything . . .

"Mercy!" she exclaimed with a penetrating shriek, as she bolted out the door.

Reason, swayed by terror, concocted visions. The blood-stained body she had just seen was chasing her, to strangle her, and she ran as though propelled by a sling.

She stumbled at the ravine: though fear gave her wings, the crisis sapped her strength. She wanted to get away, to disappear. In the river, when she was already close to the far shore, she fell. She rose and continued to run.

She glanced back and tree trunks appeared to be shaped in the bloody man's image. Yes, he was chasing her, to seize her by the neck, to kill her. "Mercy!" she cried, and kept running.

As she climbed the steep rocky hill, she fell with every step. But she ran and ran; she leaped from mound to mound, colliding with trees, slipping on the stones.

When she stumbled, she loosened stones that rolled down the slope and frightened her with their lugubrious rumbles.

Finally, she reached the path. Ah, it was easier there! She followed it, woozy from the vertigo of her flight.

By a bend in the trail, she fell again. As she got up she looked back and saw the dead man. Yes, it was him, horrible, red-tinged, with one arm extended to seize her.

The new wave of panic gave her more energy and she took off with the speed of a greyhound. Up . . . up! Atop the hill was the shack and safety, the company of people, merciful nooks where cowards can hide. Up, up! If she were going to die, let it not be out in the open, at the hands of the vision that pursued her . . .

Painting, disjointed, she climbed the slope, losing strength with each step.

When she heard someone call her, she thought she would die: "Silvina!"

She leaped, and the voice repeated:

"'Silvina . . . Silvina!"

Then she heard the unmistakable sound of footsteps; swift, living footsteps climbing uphill.

"Silvina . . . Silvina!"

In her desolation, she obeyed no other master than her fear. She continued to run.

Whoever was calling her had gained ground. Since the path snaked up the mountain, her pursuer—taking advantage of one of the bends—bounded through the thicket and as Silvina ran along the path, he managed to arrive first at one of the curves. Swooning with fright, Silvina saw the fearful shadow in front of her.

"Mercy . . . Mercy!" she said, raising her hands as though to defend herself.

"Silvina, wait, don't you know me?"

It was Ciro, who had seen her go out with Gaspar and head towards Vegaplana, who was looking for a propitious occasion, and always gambled on the likelihood of finding her.

Silvina was shocked, breathless, faint. She still didn't realize exactly what had happened. The youth stepped forward and she retreated.

"It's me . . . it's me . . ."

At last, Silvina saw the light. It was Ciro, the man she loved, the only merciful person in her life!

He squeezed her in his arms. At last, the moment he'd dreamed of! Thinking only of her anguish, she embraced him also, pressing tightly against his body, hanging from his neck with joy. What good fortune! Her defender, her protector. As calm slowly displaced terror, it appeared to her that between the store—with its lugubrious scene, its pool of blood, its mutilated corpse—and Ciro—with his vibrant embraces and thirsty kisses—there interceded a wall, very thick and very high, as large as a mountain, insurmountable by fear, closed to the hideous memories of the past.

She embraced Ciro as a castaway would clutch for floating timber. She squeezed him tightly, tremulously.

Ciro guided her off the path, and in the woods they sat down upon the severed trunk of a banana plant.

He rejoiced over his good fortune, but as he bestowed abundant caresses upon Silvina he noticed clear signs of panic in her confused expression.

"But what is it? You keep trembling and looking about, as though you're worried. Do you fear that he'll come? He can't see us here . . ."

"Ah! I . . ."

"Calm down, woman. You're with me. Just thinking about him makes you afraid, true?"

"Yes, . . . I don't know . . ."

"Where is Gaspar?"

"Ah! I don't know . . ."

"Where have you left him?"

"Over . . . that way . . ."

"But what's the matter? You're shivering . . ."

"Nothing . . . it's just that . . ."

"Ah! Now I see. That animal, that pig, he's hit you, and you're running away from him. Yes, he's pushed you in the river and you fell, because you're all wet . . ."

Touching the young girl's clothing, which was drenched in Deblás' blood, Ciro couldn't distinguish the color of that wetness.

"Yes, he must have hit you. But don't worry, *vieja*, I'm here. Now there's nothing left for you to do but run away with me. Let him scream, let him rage: come with me and don't fear. Pig! Pig! Raising his hand to a poor woman! But tonight he won't have his way."

"Ah, Ciro, don't ever leave me!"

"Nothing could separate me from you. Forget that man. If he chases you, I'll defend you. I'll kill him if I must.

"I'm so afraid . . ."

"Bah!"

"I'm afraid, terribly afraid . . ."

"My darling, forget your fears. We should rejoice over the good fortune that brings us together. Ah, how lucky I am. Tonight, you hear? *A night of nights.*"

Ciro's talk became tender, but she—preoccupied with her terrors—only half listened to his murmurs.

They felt two different emotions. He was in the real world, in the world overflowing with desire. She was in the world of dread, peopled by phantoms. He did not fear, he loved; she did not love, she feared; and as love grew large and sheltered terror, terror shriveled in the arms of love, without understanding it, without feeling it, resigning itself with gratitude, for the greatest of kindnesses.

She thought no more of fleeing from Ciro, as she had on other occasions. Now he was her refuge.

He dwelt in his longings, his raptures, the intoxication produced by the warm touch of his beloved. He thirsted for caresses, hungered for kisses, yearned to shudder in rages of passion.

With a supreme embrace, Ciro kissed Silvina's mouth.

Tenuous was the blue of the river; voluble were the gusts of the breeze. With marvelous harmony, nature spread its enchantments throughout the solitary landscape.

Tenderly, lovingly Ciro pursued the long desired goal. Silvina did not joyfully succumb to passion; she was a fearful victim, huddling in her protector's embrace, poor flesh hiding tremulously in the arms of a courageous defender.

Meanwhile, all about them there stirred the winged notes of the nocturnal psalm, with their strident voices, their subtle sibilations, their gloomy hoots; and rising above the chorus was the two-syllable chant of the little marsh toad, sorrowfully modulating its eternal *co-quí!* . . . *co-quí!* . . . *co-quí!*

Chapter Eight

At two in the afternoon the next day, the Court of Justice established in the store was engaged in the first summary proceedings.

Consternation had spread quickly through the region.

Soon, everyone knew that Andújar's store had been entered, robbed, filled with blood, and a dead man was found inside. The story raced from mouth to mouth and by now was so exaggerated that persons in distant parts heard that the store had been sacked, Andújar was found riddled with stab wounds, and that there were more than ten dead.

All the *campesinos* felt chilled, as though a gust of polar air had circulated among them; some were shocked by the savagery of the wicked act; others feared that they might be suspected, and others were rattled by the ostentatious presence of the police.

Once the first moments of surprise had passed, many went deep into the woods; others only dared to exchange timid comments in low voices.

This was the mute, frightened crowd with which justice had to cope; from this mob of evasive, sightless souls the truth would have to emerge.

Hours after the crime, at four in the morning, two *campesinos* had passed by the front of the store. By chance, they tarried near the door, whose lock had been smashed by Gaspar, and as one of them leaned his hand against the door it swung open.

That alarmed them and they drew away uneasily, so as not to become involved with the law.

On the road, they crossed paths with the clerk, who recognized them. He reached the store and noticed that the door was ajar and the lock broken.

He retreated fearfully down a nearby path to awaken the

154

second *comisario,* a type of deputy who lived in the *barrio* and used to help Gaspar.

Once he was informed of the case, the two of them left for the store and by the light of the dawn they became aware of the gruesome event; upon the counter, in an almost unintelligible scrawl, the second *comisario* laboriously wrote a message to the authorities in town, which was quickly delivered by one of the first *campesinos* who crowded together at the scene.

Close to town, the messenger encountered Andújar, who was on his way back to the mountain. Andújar was perplexed. What had happened? Who had been killed?

He hesitated. Should he continue? Should he turn back? If his house had been the scene of the crime, it was natural for him to go there, especially since the messenger had seen him; his not returning would appear suspicious. As he walked, he promised himself to try not to become very involved in the matter; he wanted no reckoning with the police, nor did he care to get involved in the bother of coming and going to court.

At midday, the judge, the scrivener, Doctor Pintado, a clerk and several policemen arrived at the mountain.

The formalities of the law were fulfilled with exquisite zeal: a primary inquiry; the *fe de libores,*[1] calling fruitlessly to the dead man; a topographic layout of the scene; the task of identifying the victim; the gathering of fragments of evidence, etcetera.

All the *campesinos* crowded around the store were asked to try and identify the corpse.

Deblás' body was hideously mutilated; the pick had entered the left cheek and—since his head was tilted back on the pillow when the blow hit—it penetrated to the base of the skull and tore the brain to bits.

Despite his deformation, all the *campesinos* recognized Deblás, but they remained silent.

"Do you know that man?" the judge said to Andújar, staring fixedly at him.

---

[1] *fe de libores,* an old Spanish legal custom, requiring that the corpse be called by name several times before being pronounced officially dead.

The shopkeeper paused for a long time and then calmly replied:

"I don't know him."

"Take a careful look."

"No, *señor,* I don't know him."

"Is it possible that there's a person from your region that you don't know?"

"I know everyone around here . . . but I don't know this man. He could be from another *barrio,* or he could be new here. Since his face is smashed in, he's so disfigured!"

"How's that?"

"I mean . . . he's all mangled."

A ray of doubt flashed in the judge's mind. An old astute criminologist, he wondered about the true meaning of the phrase: *he's so disfigured.*

He summoned a policeman and told him something in a whisper.

Then he turned to the clerk and repeated the question:

"Do you know that man?"

The youth, who had time to speak with Andújar before the judge arrived, responded firmly:

"I don't know him."

"Neither by his features, nor his body, nor his clothing?"

"Never in my life have I seen him."

"Don't you find him disfigured?"

"Yes .. . . I mean, I don't know . . . since I didn't know him before."

The question was repeated to twenty-five or thirty witnesses.

"I don't know him . . ."

"I don't know him . . ."

No one in the crowd knew the dead man.

Ciro was in the group. He had risen late, and while he was en route to Juan del Salto's farm he had learned of the crime and came out of curiosity.

He hadn't the remotest idea of what had happened; it never occurred to him to link the details of his adventure the previous evening with this outrage.

Called forward by the judge, he recognized Deblás, but like the others answered:

"I don't know him."

"Look carefully. Don't you find some detail in his face, his body, or his clothing that would lead you to think who that man was?"

"None."

"You've never seen him in the region?"

"Never."

"He resembles no one from this *barrio*?"

"No, *señor*, no one . . ."

The judge stared at Ciro. He had noticed something suspicious . . .

He made him come closer, and took a harder look. Ciro was wearing pants and a jacket of a rough fabric, and a cotton undershirt, all of which were worn and frayed.

"What are these stains? the judge asked suddenly, pointing to some brick-colored spots on the young man's shirt and pants.

Ciro, quickly checking himself over, was dumbfounded.

"Can you tell me what kind of stains they are?"

"I . . ."

"Those are blood stains . . ."

"Blood!"

"Yes . . . where did you get them?"

"But . . ."

"Don't beat around the bush! How did you get those stains?"

The world grew dark for Ciro. Stains, bloodstains! How could he explain what he himself didn't know?

"I don't know . . . this isn't blood . . . I'm mixed up . . . I don't know what it is . . ."

"Calm yourself. We have time to clear up this question."

Giving another confidential order, the judge continued his work.

The depositions relating to the first news of the crime were begun. The young clerk was asked:

"At what time did you come to the store?"

"Between four-thirty and five in the morning."

"You were alone?"

"Yes."

"No one saw you?"

"No one."

"The second *comisario* has declared that while he was writing his message to the authorities you told him of having met two men on the road . . ."

The youth hesitated, looked about, stooped over, pinched a crease in his trousers, and scratched his leg. The judge, noticing the witness' every gesture, persisted:

"Do you know them?"

"Well . . . yes . . . I know them."

"What are their names?"

"Since it was still nighttime . . ."

"Since it was still not clear daylight, you knew them, but didn't see their names . . . is that it?" the judge asked, wrinkling his brow. "Come now, answer the question. Who are those men?"

"All right . . . I'll tell. But, the truth is, I'm not sure who they were. It appeared to me that . . ."

"What did it appear to you?"

". . . that it was Tomás Vilosa and Rosendo Rioja."

Another confidential order was transmitted to the police officers.

A thorough search was made of the site: two doors violently opened, the locks smashed; the lid of the counter raised; scraps of food scattered about; empty glasses that smelled of beer and *aguardiente;* indications that all the boxes, shelves and cupboards had been searched; in the room, an open chest surrounded by blood-spattered clothing; a wooden crossbar in the center of the room; a pickax with blood along several inches of its point, also thrown on the floor; a rough-handled dagger, its blade completely clean of any stains, found on the floor near the pool of blood; a crowbar beneath the bed, bloodied on its top side; amidst the mess there was a section of clean floor that corresponded perfectly to the shape of the crowbar, which proved that it fell to the floor before the victim's blood did; a dirty straw *sombrero,* unblocked and unlined, with the vertex of the crown fuzzy and torn, having served, from all appearances, to shade a very large head; another filthy straw *sombrero* found on the floor, also behind the cot, and, finally, other objects of small or large significance, such as empty bottles which apparently served as candleholders, the halter on the nail outside, and several other things that were culled and noted down.

When the judge held up the torn *sombrero,* everyone there recognized it. Gaspar's name sounded in the depths of their consciences . . . but they all kept silent, and the reiterated questions of the judge and the scrivener brought only denials.

"I don't know . . ."

"I don't know . . ."

"I don't know . . ."

When Ciro saw the hat, he thought that Gaspar had been the assassin. There was no doubt. The youth recalled Silvina's anguish, the terror by which she seemed possessed . . . Ah, what a mystery! What a terrible mystery! But he wouldn't rush to any conclusions; he would think it over carefully before "singing," and above all he would sacrifice anything before implicating Silvina.

Not once did he entertain the thought that she might be involved. No, she was innocent; the guilty one, the murderer, was Gaspar.

Then Gaspar's *sombrero* was tried on the cadaver for size. It danced on his head. The judge persisted. Perhaps the victim wore an extra large *sombrero.* But he saw that the difference in size was conspicuous. On the other hand, when a similar test was made with the *sombrero* found behind the cot, there was no doubt: it was the victim's *sombrero.*

The corpse was searched. They found a sharp dagger concealed behind his belt, and his pockets were full of objects which Andújar claimed belonged to him.

A record was taken of everything. A plan of the scene was drawn, the vicinity was searched, the formalities of the law were discharged to the letter.

The judicial party returned to town that afternoon. Aside from what had already been done, the preliminary hearing convinced the judge to take a few precautions.

Taken in custody, and returning with the retinue, were Andújar, the store clerk, Ciro, Tomás Vilosa, and Rosendo Rioja.

A long list of the neighbors' names was made, and with an arsenal of preliminary proceedings and bits of evidence, after closing and sealing the store entrance and sending ahead an escort of laborers to carry the corpse on a litter, the interpreters of the law returned to town.

During the trip, the judge was pensive. Such a rare case! An incomprehensible crime! Why were two doors shattered? If one served to enter, and the other to leave, why were the locks broken on both? To open a door from the inside, it suffices to lift the latch and remove the crossbar so that the lock gives way. Why were those two locks smashed? It seemed probable that there were several assailants, who worked as a gang. Andújar's ambiguous attitude; his departure the previous afternoon, still not fully explained; his lack of concern over the possible theft; the clerk's hesitations and indecision before answering questions; his furtive glances at Andújar each time he was examined by the judge; the coincidence of the clerk's encounter with those two men on the road; and, finally, the stains, the indubitable blood stains on Ciro's clothing; all these things made the judge suspect that it had been the work of a gang.

But why on earth would Andújar rob himself? What had been the motive for the crime? To kill the man found in the cot? Perhaps it was an ambush, to dispose of an enemy for reasons of revenge. No, inconceivable. The dead man's pockets were filled with objects from the store. So he, too, was an intruder. Then why had he been murdered? A struggle over the spoils? Doubtful. The dead man had a dagger in his belt; another dagger was found on the floor, clean of any stains. Had there been a struggle, he would have defended himself, the weapon would have been found outside of its sheath, and perhaps the other dagger would have been bloodied.

The one unavoidable fact was that the pickax had been the death weapon. Here was another doubt. Was the victim on his feet when dealt the blow, and then dragged to the cot? Was he struck while lying down? The autopsy would tell.

The judge stretched his wits: what a maze! Undoubtedly some facts were missing.

The case was conducted with great zeal. Half the region was sworn in, information was gleaned about those arrested, comparisons were made, several scents were pursued ...

After many days of involvement, the judge had still not unraveled the tangle. He was alone, completely alone; he could only guess ...

In the meantime, the mountain people grew calmer. The truth was suspected ... At times, in passing, they looked askance at the murderer, but no one spoke, no one wanted to become implicated.

Gaspar was silent and grave. He did not drink, seldom spoke, worked assiduously, and locked himself in his hut very early.

He had suffered several great frights after that grisly evening. During the fateful hour, fleeing cross-country through the woods, he reached Leandra's hut and sat down on the floor, gasping for breath. What had become of Silvina? Could Andújar have killed her?

He recalled the night of the dance in Vegaplana, when the girl lost her senses. Ah, who knows! Perhaps she had fainted at the very moment that, under his direction, she was about to deal the death blow. In that case, she would be back soon. It was everyone for himself.

Most important now was to erase all clues ... He waited for a long time without knowing what to do, uncertain of Silvina's fate.

Finally, the young girl emerged from a coffee grove, having just left Ciro nearby.

She felt calmer; it had been difficult to tear herself away from Ciro. He wanted her to run away with him. But she, hesitant, ever dominated by Gaspar's tyrranical influence, declined such a rebellious idea; she postponed it for some remote opportunity, and escaped, promising Ciro that she would go away with him some other time.

When Gaspar saw her approaching, he motioned her to keep silent: this was no time for talk. In a whisper, he told her the result of their expedition.

Still shuddering with fright, she wanted to enter the house, but Gaspar didn't let her. In the store, he had seen her blood-stained dress. First, with a few tugs, he ripped her dress off; then, in the shed, he stripped her completely.

The night breeze gamboled on that nakedness, cooling the poor girl's still vibrant ardors. He made her wash, and as she went into the hut—trying to obey Gaspar's order not to make noise—he dug a hole behind a nearby tree and buried the pile of bloody clothing.

Then, to sleep; to squeeze her eyelids tightly together, so that the dreadful images of the past should not frighten off her slumber.

Cruelly tormented by her emotions, Silvina was stupefied, almost insensible. As she stretched out in her nook, however, the memory of what had happened in the store contorted her face with a bitter sob; but immediately the remembrance of Ciro's loving raptures erased the sob, and drew a smile on her face. Smiling, she fell asleep.

Gaspar had not lived in peace since that night. He felt that he must run away, but how? Thanks to the accursed *sombrero,* he knew that many people suspected him, and that he was at their mercy, exposed to their accusations.

His anxiety grew when Galante called him aside and with no explanation said:

"Be careful, very careful . . . keep your eyes open."

Surely he was surrounded by great danger. If they arrested him, who could guarantee Silvina's silence? She, too, would go to jail, she would call a spade a spade, and he would be fixed forever. The only answer was to run, far, very far. But his thoughts always concluded with: how to escape?

During one of his moments of concentration he seemed to come upon a solution: Old Marta. Since the night of the dance, he had raided the old miser woman's treasure three or four times, always bleeding it of small sums. Why not apply the finishing stroke?

He trembled over the prospect of another exploit as luckless as the last. But though he strained to dissuade himself, he finally became convinced that he was completely helpless without money. A few *pesos* could put an end to his troubles.

Silvina frequently cried by herself, without realizing why. Was it the past, with its remorse? Was it her wretched, degrading life? The sad lot of Ciro, who was innocent, but locked up in a jail cell?

She often thought how simple it would be to reverse the situation: explain the origin of the blood stains on Ciro's clothing, and free him, putting her husband in his place.

She knew that she was doing wrong. She ought to tell all . . . but what would become of her if she talked? She, too, was an accomplice: she had taken part in the illegal entry, she had run away, stained with still-warm blood. They would arrest her and sentence her for being equally guilty. How could she explain that Gaspar had driven her to the crime? Who would believe that she had assisted in the attack, despite her own wishes and instincts?

In her ignorance, she found no words to express such contrary feelings. If they arrested her, Ciro would go free, and she, once more, would be dragged along by that accursed man, who would drive her into prison for life . . . she trembled with dread, and kept silent.

When Gaspar told her of his escape plan, she felt an instant's joy. She elevated her soul to God and prayed fervently that the plan should be successful. Alone, alone without him! She could die happy, after enjoying one minute of that solitude.

Leandra, as ever, gave her flaccid breast to Pequeñín and did the wash on the wide flat stone by the river.

Those days she was distrustful, stealthily regarding Gaspar's changed ways, observing Silvina. She suspected some connection with the atrocity in the store.

The night of the crime, she had heard strange sounds: the return from an "all-night wake," at which Gaspar and Silvina did not spend the night; odd noises in the shed; muffled breathing; Silvina arising the next day wearing the blouse she had taken off before starting out for Vegaplana, and neither the blouse she had worn nor the dark-colored dress she had put on for the nocturnal condolence call were ever seen again ... A cluster of small, dubious details. Gaspar, seemingly calm, solicitous, pensive, withdrawn from all commotions.

She suspected, but she kept quiet. The *sombrero* was the final touch: nowhere in the house could she find her son-in-law's *sombrero*; and now he was wearing a clean new one, with the brim intentionally bent. Yes, she was positive that Gaspar had been the aggressor. But what to do? Quite candidly, nothing. She had kept quiet so many times in her life, she had held her tongue so many times! Once more meant little. It was no concern of hers. . . .

Montesa these days was as vociferous as a thunderclap. Now see where softness gets you! A loose rein on these people was like putting a pack of wolves in a broken cage! He launched terrible oaths that seemed to condense in the atmosphere, take the form of rockets, and burst against the huts and the woods. No, those are not people. If they're not whipped like black slaves, they go from bad to worse.

In the field labors, he was more despotic and temperamental than ever. The most honorable workers, those best known for their virtues, merited severe rebukes; slackers were fired on the spot.

"Out of my sight, you worthless no accounts!"

The foreman felt indignant when he saw the unworked soil, the precious earth waiting to be tilled, while the mountain rabble wasted their time on idiotic pleasures. He excepted no one, and made no distinctions between the good and the bad. To him they were all alike. But at the core of such gross injustice there was a cry of honor, of stubborn dignity that was offended by the misconduct of the others.

Since Montesa's life was limited to his hearth after working hours, he knew little of the rumors circulating through the *barrio*. The crime had impressed him, but he was not concerned about details.

Marcelo confined himself like a ferret to the summit of Galante's farm. What days, what nights of anguish in his hovel! What pain, what immense fright when he heard of the crime and of Ciro's imprisonment! His poor brother was in danger, but where did the stains come from? Could his brother be capable of such a crime? Could Gaspar and Deblás have involved him in that horror? He could not believe it. He stayed in the hut for many days, subsisting on some cold victuals, unable to work, overcome by a sickly lassitude.

Apart from his terror, he was indifferent. He aspired to nothing, he wanted nothing; only to live free from fear, even though he could eat no more than a banana or some wild fruits of the forest.

In his solitude, he imagined himself plagued by dangers. They were like tiny imps, hovering about him and harassing him with pricking insistence.

One day he was near collapse, when the deputy notified him that the judge wanted him to testify. Testify! He who wished to forget everything and suffer no more!

The youth's emaciated figure inspired the judge's pity. The veins in his neck pulsated, and his languid gaze reflected suffering.

Since Ciro was considered the central figure in the case, he was treated with great care. He was obliged to explain, minute by minute, his activity the night of the crime.

Ciro lied. Should he tell of his encounter with Silvina, his rounds since the early hours of the evening, his return to the hut after four in the morning? Never. He didn't want to even remotely implicate the girl.

Thus, he answered that on the night of the crime he had gone to bed at eight in the evening.

The judge called Marcelo forward, to confirm or refute Ciro's statement.

"Hear me," the judge said. "Your testimony is of vital importance. Do you understand?"

"Me?" answered Ciro, stultified.

"Since you are the suspect's brother, the law excuses you from testifying. Do you wish to exercise that right?"

"They told me I must come. . . ."

"Yes, of course. But now I'm advising you that you are at liberty to go as you came, or to offer your testimony. What is your choice?"

"As for me . . ."

"What?"

"I haven't done anything to anybody."

"That has nothing to do with it. Will you testify or not?"

"I . . . whatever you say . . ."

Seeing that he was indecisive, the judge asked:

"Well now, tell us what you know."

He began to ask about important points that needed clarification. Unprepared beforehand, Marcelo was sincere throughout the interrogation. Ciro often stayed out all night; many times he didn't sleep in the hut.

"On the night of the crime," the judge asked, "your brother retired very late, true?"

Marcelo understood the importance of his reply, and he realized why they had called him. The judge's gaze and the interested looks of the spectators confirmed that importance. It occurred to him that if he told the truth, Ciro would be unable to account for where he had spent the night.

He wavered for a moment. What had Ciro declared? Had he said that he returned late, or that he went to bed early?

"That night," Marcelo responded, "my brother slept at my side."

"All right, he didn't sleep outside. But at what hour did he retire?"

"At sundown."

"You saw him. You're sure it was early?"

"Yes, *señor.*"

"Do you hear him when he comes home late? Does he wake you up?"

"Yes, *señor.*"

"Always?"

"Always."

"Your brother never gets up after going to bed and goes out again?"

"Never. Once in bed he sleeps like a log . . ."

"And when he stays out all night, what does he do?"

"Most often this is when he has some . . ."

Marcelo paused, not daring to say the word.

"Some what?"

All present smiled. They understood.

"Come now, speak up."

"Well . . . when he has some . . . some business with . . ."

"Some amorous adventure?"

"Yes . . ."

"Is this very often?"

"*Most* of the nights."

"In short, what did your brother do that afternoon, when he finished work on *Señor* del Salto's farm?"

"He came home, fell in bed at my side, and slept until the light of day."

Marcelo breathed freely when his testimony was over. Nothing was going to happen to him, they were going to let him go. After returning to the mountain, it took him four days to recover from his nervousness, and the fatigue of the trip.

Once recovered from the initial surprise, Ciro kept calm. He who has done nothing wrong has nothing to fear When they arrrested him he managed to control himself. He had no doubt that the murder was Gaspar's handiwork. But what part did Silvina play? None, he was sure. Perhaps the fright and anguish he noticed in her that night were caused by her knowledge of the crime, possibly after Gaspar had told her about it. On the other hand, where had the stains on his clothing come from? He vainly searched the corners of his memory.

At last he decided: bah! they were plantain stains. Yes, the moist plantain leaves a dark smudge on clothing. Without doubt they were plantain stains. It didn't seem strange, since he'd passed through a plantain grove that night.

As for the rest, as for telling about his unhappiness that night, that never! Poor little Silvina! Drag her into this? By no means; he would suffer persecution and jail before that. He decided not to even *mention* her; thus, testifying in a calm, unswerving manner, he insisted that he had gone to bed very early that infamous night, and had slept tranquilly until morning.

Andújar wasn't nervous either. It was natural that they should take him into custody, and he entered the jail feeling confident that he would be set free by noon. Had he been made suspect by a few details? Well, to suspect was not to prove; they would soon be convinced of his innocence.

Nevertheless, the crime caused him much thought. He couldn't understand why his cousin had met with such a tragic end. If Gaspar was—as he didn't doubt—the murderer, what happened between them? Why had Deblás, his pockets bulging with loot and a dagger in his belt, succumbed in a struggle with such a poltroon as Gaspar?

He tried, to no purpose, to fathom the intricate warp of the crime. In any event, he was rid of his celebrated cousin. The closing of the store would hurt him a great deal, but he would soon recover by setting his new business into motion and by adding to his property with land purchased from the neighbors; above all, Old Marta's coveted coffee orchard.

When she learned of the crime, Marta fussed about and damned the wicked.

Her impression of the crime was colored by her own distrustful nature. She, too, was exposed to a similar attempt. Her money, spread out in small heaps, was unknown to all; but she knew that at any moment her hideaways could be found and emptied.

When she became convinced that Gaspar had been the barbarous assailant, she felt no surprise. She knew that thief's talents well and believed him capable of anything.

Since someone else's loss often makes a person think of one's own safety, Marta spent many sleeplesss night worrying that she might be the victim of the next outrage.

In her mind, she counted and recounted her treasure; she thought of new secret spots to which she might transfer her money; she decided to take inventory, to make sure that not one single *céntimo* was missing from her treasure. During the tiresome tasks, she suffered a thousand frights, imagining herself surprised at every instant.

She looked for her gold amongst some stones in the forest and counted *onzas, media onzas* and *centenes.*[2] All intact. Further on,

---

[2]*onzas, media onzas* and *centenes,* old Spanish gold coins with the smallest in value, *centenes,* equal to 25 pesetas.

kneeling down in the thicket, she counted a package of *pesos.* Not one short. Then next to a giant *ceiba* tree, she dug up the earthen jar. She counted one, two, three times, perspiring huge drops, her heart heavy, almost breathless. Great God, there was money missing! She paused, mentally summing up the amounts left there at different times, and counted once more. Money was missing. The thirty-odd *pesos* from that good Sunday had swelled her deposits to two hundred and fifty, and now there were only two hundred!

The day clouded over for Marta. Feverishly she dug a hole in another spot and inserted the jar; out of breath and crying tears of rage, she huddled up in her hammock.

Then her imagination soared. Surely they had robbed her, they *were* robbing her, and they *would* rob her of every last *ochavo.* Spend a life of want and misery so that some rogue can rob her in a wink! Gaspar's name danced before her eyes.

She was positive: Gaspar had robbed and killed at the store; Gaspar would surely rob and kill her, too; everyone in the *barrio* knew the author of the crime, but the fiend was still free. She couldn't live like that, knowing that any night Gaspar might strangle her.

The old woman prepared her defense. She knew that she couldn't prove she had been robbed, nor was it wise to complain about it, because everyone would know that she buried her money. No, it was better to find some indirect means . . .

A satanic idea occurred to her. Since Gaspar had committed the villainous act at the store, since everyone knew that he was the owner of the *sombrero,* since all had kept silent, she would speak up, she would drive that scoundrel into jail, and then she could breathe easily.

With a shaky step, she started out for the headquarters of a platoon of forest police, a few miles distant. She asked for the chief and told him that she knew the owner of the famed *sombrero* and would like to testify before the judge. She was taken to town and soon afterwards Gaspar's name sounded in the case for the first time.

Marta's testomony resulted in an arrest warrant being made out against Gaspar, and two or three days later the police were searching the *barrio* for Silvina's husband.

The day was already in decline when the mounted police came up the hill towards Leandra's shack. Gaspar was seated at the doorstep, Silvina and Leandra were bustling about inside. Their sounds alerted Gaspar who peered down from the hilltop, along the narrow meandering path, and glimpsed the uniforms through the foliage.

Gaspar took off like an arrow fired by a bow. His silhouette vanished in the dense refuge of the mountainside, with its labyrinth of woods and plantations.

When the police arrived at the hut, there were no traces of the fugitive. Surprised and fearful, the women were incapable of a coherent reply. Where was Gaspar? They did not know.

The police, familiar with the *barrio*, combed every peak and dale. But Gaspar was not there, and no one knew his whereabouts.

The next day, Gaspar went down to the town and spent many hours by the docks. He was seen talking with the sailors and chatting a good while with the captain of a fishing smack that was soon to depart on an inter-colonial voyage. Nothing was known for sure, but everyone in the region suspected that Galante had shipped Gaspar off, freeing him from the hands of justice.

The judge's warrant was useless. The strongest loose end, the firmest handle to which the law could reach out, had been cut in the shadows by Galante, the rich land owner. Marta's testimony would have cast some light, but Galante's protection, setting Gaspar in flight, blotted out the true path to the solution of the crime. Truth, justice and the well-being of all suffered. Only the old miser woman rejoiced, at last free of the villain's presence.

The case did not progress. A tumult of contradictory evidence confused the issue, and the motive of the crime remained a mystery. Nothing came of the countless testimonies; it was almost as if there had never been a crime.

The two *campesinos*, Rosendo Rioja and Tomás Vilosa, accounted for their time, and described their presence near the store and their encounter with the store clerk. It was impossible to charge them with the crime.

Andújar proved his alibi. Many people saw him in town the night of the murder. Several of his friends were called to testify: a grocer said he had given him a room; the coachman of a public carriage returned him to his quarters late in the evening; the owner of an inn said he had dined there; finally, Andújar himself flaunted a signed receipt which confirmed that at the very moment the crime took place he was counting and depositing a sum of money for safekeeping in town.

The judge was puzzled by this coincidence: precisely on the afternoon before the assault, Andújar had removed his valuables. Was it chance? Foresight? Nagging suspicions paraded about before the judge's spectacles, but without further information, they remained airy fantasies.

The clerk proved he had spent the entire night in his mountain shack. His encounter with the *campesinos* fixed the morning hour when he started out for the store; the deputy *comisario* told in minute detail of the youth's alarm when he came to wake him; also, the locks had been broken, and the youth had a key, which discouraged suspicion against him.

Ciro was still in the focus of doubt. Marcelo asserted that his brother had remained in the hut all night; many *campesinos* testified that for some time Ciro wore no other *sombrero* than the one he had on when he was arrested; then there was the disparity between the size of the *sombrero* found in the store and the young man's head; there was not a single bit of testimony to involve him. Everything seemed to remove him from suspicion, except for the blood stains.

Ciro swore that they must have come from the resin of plantains; but when asked where, how and when he got them, he could offer no help.

In a firm honest tone, he testified that he couldn't explain the origin of the stains; next he said he was inclined to believe he got them when he came in contact with some plantain shoots that he had been carrying a few days before; thirdly, he said that he hadn't noticed the stains until the moment the judge discovered them.

Though his testimony was a bit vague, it was delivered in a calm, sure tone. The judge took notice and wondered: if he's guilty, why doesn't he lie? Why is he so indecisive about a point that implicates him so greatly?

The judge asked when he had last laundered the stained clothing. Since plantain marks are resistant to water, if they were old stains they must have existed before the last washing. Ciro offered the name of the *campesina* who did his wash; she came, but remembered nothing.

In the midst of such total darkness, only one road of proof remained: science.

In the back room of a drug store, a pharmacist and a doctor devoted themselves to the analysis.

Such difficulties! Such depths! An army of test tubes, glasses and pipettes marched by; a goodly quantity of alcohol was burned in tiny glass lamps that produced blue flames; a deluge of technical terms was squandered. The two professors cut Ciro's suit into tiny pieces. They talked of infusions, of the need to discover the hematin, of the negative action of ammonia, of the positive value of heat, of the water solubility of coloring materials, of hydrogen peroxide, tannin, iron protoxide, ethereal alcohol, green, blue and black precipitates, plumbic precipitates, of sulphured hydrogens that free the tannin from the plantain. It was a grand quadrille of Greco-Latin terminology, of cabalistic phrases, of unmalleable, necromantic technical terms.

At last they found the truth. It was blood, recently spilt human blood, that stained Ciro's suit!

The conclusion was a terrible blow to the young man. The result of the analysis drew the judge into a real labyrinth. What crime was being discussed here?

Could Ciro, in complicity with the dead man, have been able to smash down two doors, break open a trunk, quarrel with his accomplice, kill him with a pickax, and then lay him down upon the cot?

If that is how it happened, why hadn't Ciro stolen anything? Except for what was found in the dead man's pockets, nothing was missing from the store. If Ciro had committed the crime, how could the nature of the victim's wound be explained?

According to expert opinion, the blow had moved from left to right, entering at the front and penetrating to the rear. If a pickax is lifted high and discharged upon a target, if Ciro was shorter than the dead man, if the pool of blood proved that the wound had been inflicted near the bed, if the experts claimed that the blow was delivered while the victim reclined in the cot, how could Ciro have caused such a monstruous wound? Had the victim, armed with a dagger, stretched out on the bed expressly to receive the blow? Had he dozed off after the robbery, when he should have been keeping watch? If he was attacked, why didn't he defend himself with the dagger?

It was a puzzle, a true puzzle, which kept the judge awake for many nights.

Andújar and the clerk were set free. After Marta's testimony, the futile summoning of Gaspar, plus his previous prison record, opened a new path, which was abruptly blocked off by his escape. At last, all efforts turned out to be futile: the trial was provisionally suspended, and Ciro was set free.

Once back in his native mountains, the young man decided that it had all been worth it: Silvina was his, his alone . . .

Chapter Nine

A year had passed and the crops were ready for harvesting.

The coffee trees drooped under the weight of the ripe vermilion berries, which basked in the autumn sun.

On every farm men stripped the plants, gathering in the clusters; down every trail there flowed *obreros* and pack animals, carting the coffee to the settlements; in every hydraulic machine, the skins imprisoning the twin seeds were broken, the syrup in which they soak was washed away, the moisture was dried by the hot sun; the vellum wrapping was stripped away, revealing the luster which would be on view in the auction warehouses. All was life, activity and movement: mother earth imparted the vigor of her bosom to man's aspirations.

Work never stopped on Juan del Salto's farm. What a fine crop it had been! Many *obreros* from different regions swelled the brigades of pickers, so that the succulent berries would not fall and become lost among the rough stones of the mountain.

The *obreros* deposited the berries into baskets made from dried banana leaves, which hung from their necks. At times they girdled their waists with cords or vines, or fibers from the tropical *emajagua*. Most of them went barefoot; the more civilized wore shoes with thick soles. The women gathered their skirts almost to the knees; the men wore either sweat-blackened undershirts or went barechested. Some wrapped their heads with gaily colored handkerchiefs, others wore straw *sombreros*.

Interest was high. Entire families left their huts and took to the fields, to deal with the rows of shrubs that had to be stripped.

The restless mob swarmed over the mountains, laughing and singing, as though the crop belonged to all. From afar, it looked like a gigantic ant hill.

In the dips and crags of the land the scene was picturesque,

174

filled with the rustle of shrubs, the skirmish of trampled stones, as the *campesinos* struggled to keep their balance.

A few frail lasses at the summit were neglectful at times, allowing those below to see a goodly part of their legs and knees, which appeared and disappeared between the foliage like vague figurines.

A brigade of puny boys helped the adults, picking up the grains that fell from the shrubs or spilled from the baskets. At times, an *obrero* would pause at a single shrub that was abundant with berries; other times, he would bend the tiny trees, pulling them close to reach the berries on top; boughs became entangled, and the interlocking shrubs blocked the trails.

When some inept *obrero* failed to do a thorough job, the foreman obliged him to go back and pluck the ripe berries that he'd overlooked; when work speeded up, and sprigs and boughs were broken or mutilated, the reproachful tones of the vigilant overseer rang out. When an *obrero* skidded on the slope, some laughed and others came to his aid, while the fallen man tried to right himself and return to his post. It was hard, dangerous work, which many *campesinos* undertook, while singing short satiric or erotic verses in their unique jargon.

During the day the scorching sun sifted through the foliage and blended with the damp, warm soil, creating an atmosphere where one felt sensations of refreshing coolness, alternating with fiery gusts that toasted the skin.

At dusk, when the afternoon waned, the kindled splendors of the passing day died out, and while multi-colored clouds sailed across the sky, the night began, with its terrible mysteries and dreadful solitudes.

The *obreros* weighed the coffee gathered during the day. The stream of berries flowed from baskets to gray sacks, in which they would be hauled to the hydraulics. Two by two, the sacks were loaded upon the loins of the patient mules, and the convoy descended the slopes.

Once more, the eternal concerto of the fields raised its rustic psalmody, as the sun cast its last shadows.

For the time being, Juan del Salto was immersed in "practical" things; estimating the abundance of *fanegas* the crop would yield; calculating the probable profits. He was in a world of plus and minus signs.

The memory of last year's events had been cooled by the distractions of work. That bloody history worried him, but offered no surprise. He often thought about the perverse tableau played out on the stage of the countryside, and about the people's indifference towards good or bad; their silence, their complicity of silence.

Juan had seen how justice groped deep in the shadows, searching for the guilty ones, and how it fell back impotent before the wall of pale people who had no concept of evil, no precise notion of good. He knew all the details, all the suspects; the pestilent cloud had even reached the summit, where his farm rose skyward.

Then he stopped thinking of the others. He thought of himself, and grew cold and bitter: a chill of remorse, an embittered spirit, displeased with itself. Yes, he knew the suspects, but he, too, kept silent . . . the dreaded contagion was impregnating him, too!

In his solitude, he vacillated a hundred times. Why didn't he speak? Why didn't he shake off the yoke of the odious "system" and help clarify the truth, point out suspects, impart facts, indicate clues? He knew who Galante was, and Gaspar, and he knew of the bestial concubinage in Leandra's hut; he knew very well of Andújar's passion for wealth; he knew the name and background of the man found dead in the store; he had reasons to believe that Gaspar was a dangerous criminal . . . Yet, he kept silent. The law had asked questions, yet he kept silent. Why should he act like this? Alas, he was like the rest, one of many, a bad citizen, a sick man, just an atom in that undernourished, amoral giant stomach.

He felt ashamed of himself; he knew his duty, and he strained to shake off the cloud that debased him with its touch. He must be strong, he must follow his conscience! The common good commanded him to try . . . he must prepare himself for the sacrifice. He saw clearly what others ignored, he understood what others failed to comprehend. His duty was clear, unchallenged; he must help the cause of goodness, clear the nettle from the road which tomorrow's heirs must trod upon.

His dignity and pride commanded him to stir the inertia of that mass of people, to grasp the thread of their misery and pursue it burl by burl, unraveling the causes, until he reached the springs of so much misfortune. Despite the consequences, he must gather the facts and hurl them at the men of his time, and harpoon the body of the gigantic monster of evil. When he thought this way, he swelled with pride, as though he had already acted, without hesitation.

But then his glance would fall upon his desk, overflowing with symbols of materialism: he would spy a packet of Jacobo's letters in a pigeonhole; he would contemplate the sea of verdure outside, stretching from the summits to the cool river bank. And a vision bewitched him: the fulfillment of his hopes, crystallizing into reality and illuminating the image of his absent son. Why struggle?

To speak out meant to accuse, to pursue, to prove; to speak out meant to waste time stolen from his work, for the benefit of others; to speak out meant to create enemies, impose excessive expenses upon himself, perhaps jeopardize his own well-being, exposing himself to the snares of evil people, arming the hand that might deal the treacherous knife slash, kindling the torch that could yield disaster in his buildings, whetting the scythe that could lay waste his fields, kneading the calumny that could turn against him with mutiny. And what would come of such efforts? Would one man's impetuous act, during one moment in the history of the colony, be enough to cure this great wretchedness? He would be dragged down by the noxious current, crushed by harassment, scourged by the jeers of his brothers—his own brothers—still stubbornly blind. His efforts would be lost, without benefit to anyone. No, his son had first claim; he must stay calm and indifferent. To follow another course meant to create obstacles, to be quixotic, to undertake ridiculous adventures, jeopardizing his son's future. Egoism possessed him, squeezed him in its claws, sealed his lips . . .

There had been great changes in Leandra's hut. Gaspar's absence filled Silvina with glee, but worried Leandra. It meant one less to bring home sustenance! What would Silvina do all alone? No matter what type of husband he was, he was still a husband, he shielded them; with his presence there was always a man in the house.

Silvina disagreed. No, he was no husband, he was a disgrace! She felt happy without him, without the scald of his imperious glance. She roamed the trails freely, went down to the river, climbed up to Juan's farm, did as she pleased. The happiness of being alone, the joy of being free!

She had one fixed idea in her new life. Poor Ciro! She felt such pain when she thought of him. It was said that nothing had been found against him during the trial, but still he remained in jail. The stains, perhaps the stains! and the fact that a single word from her could explain the mystery and free her beloved filled her with sorrow.

She felt hopeful at times. Ciro would return soon, he would come looking for her and cover her with caresses.

One day, accompanied by Marcelo, she went down to the plain and visited Ciro in jail. She returned smiling, filled with hope. Ciro assured her that he would soon be free.

During the trip, Marcelo directed meaningful glances at Silvina. He could not forget what he overheard that Sunday in the shed; that Silvina was an accomplice to the crime; that Gaspar promised that she would do the stabbing.

Did it happen that way? He didn't want to know, nor find out. Would it bring him any profit to know someone else's affairs? As always, he shrouded himself in silence.

Galante rarely came to the hut. Leandra was suspicious and nervous, as though she were expecting some catastrophe. And it arrived: Galante came no more, he stopped being her man.

After her many supplications and theatrics, he replied that she could count on him no longer. It was all over: enough was enough. Abandoned, Leandra stood face to face with the visage of hunger.

Galante and Andújar were occupied those days with their new businesses. Their planned business was already a fact. Each of them would arrange his personal affairs, each would put up a share of hard cash, and take the necessary steps to change residence.

Because of this, Galante wanted to rid himself of all obligations and hindrances ... There were already too many people after him, nipping at his flanks; too many weeping women with their tales of woe. No, it was enough now; those entanglements had cost him money. So a cold, barefaced furlough was issued to Leandra, precisely on a day that Pequeñín—feverish from breaking in new teeth—was more deafening than ever with his tearless wail, as he lay face down on the floor of the hut.

Leandra was forlorn. Once more to struggle, to suffer. She had been abandoned many times, but never had her sorrow been so deep. She had behaved well with Galante; she had humored him in every way; she denied him nothing, not even the sacrifice of her daughter. But he had left her flat, without a *céntimo*, without even a caress for Pequeñín! What would become of them. They would die of hunger ...

Silvina comforted her; the misfortune had becalmed their longstanding conflict. Better to be alone than in bad company, she said. God provides for all. No use worrying; they would wash clothes, they would take to the fields, they would sew, and furthermore, Ciro would soon be free.

At last, one happy day, a great cheer was heard down the trail. It was Ciro, together with several friends, coming up towards the hut.

They had just released him. Since the trial had been temporarily suspended, they had put him out.

Silvina and he embraced strongly. Nothing was said of a new life, nothing had to be said. The young man remained there with them.

He was a real man, and though Leandra had once impolitely kicked him out, he bore no grudge. Brimming with joy, Silvina sighed, and rejoiced with a smile over his every word.

Leandra lowered her head in assent. Was there *someone* who would maintain them? Well, now they were not so unfortunate.

For many days the two youths lived in a great burst of jubilation. They strolled together, humming songs, hands clasped, arms around each other's waist, frolicking, laughing. It was an idyll, lifting its head from a swamp.

When Ciro saw the mat—Gaspar's old sleeping place—he felt

loathing. By no means would he sleep there: into the river with that rubbish! Since woodlice and centipedes often crawled between the timberwork of the huts, Ciro wanted a raised bed. He placed several boards upon some thick blocks of wood and improvised a simple bed.

The youths spoke once more about the event in the store; Ciro told her about his confusion and anxieties during the trial. Many times they had wanted to pull out his tongue to make him talk. But he didn't say a word. He was convinced that Gaspar was the killer, and that Silvina was frightened by the enormity of the deed that night. But, hah, he said nothing to the judge; for nothing in the world would he have implicated Silvina.

She listened, nodded, and voiced her gratitude for the young man's conduct. One night, in the privacy of their bed, Ciro brought up the mysterious problem of the bloodstains. Laced about his neck, stirred by an impulse to tell the truth, she revealed the secret. Ciro knew everything at last.

Thus the days passed. Upon leaving work, he closed himself up in the hut; she, close to his side, was affectionate, and admired his behavior in jail, a conduct which so resembled that of a *hidalgo*[1] ready to die for his fair lady; they were living happily at last, but in the midst of their happiness she felt a strange malaise, hidden symptoms of sickness which the pleasant calm of their new life could not contain.

Andújar's store remained closed for some time. The shopkeeper preferred to lose money from his paralyzed business, rather than leave his affairs in strange hands.

When he returned to the mountain, Andújar swept up the damages. The old, rotten food was dumped into a ravine, where the dogs of the region enjoyed a succulent feast. Old Marta hovered about the piles of garbage, too, while Andújar hovered about her.

The business of the orchard worried him. Very soon he would have to move to town; very soon he would liquidate the store

---

[1] *Hidalgo*, a man of the lower nobility.

because Galante said that they were nearly ready to start the new business.

It was important, then, that he take over the coffee orchard soon. But how could he convince the old woman?

Things had changed, however, in Marta's thinking. Falling victim to Gaspar's thievery had forced her to change her hideaway; an arduous, scary task. She knew that she would die someday. What would become of the farm then? She remembered how Andújar took over the old man's land; she realized that her grandson would never survive her; she realized that the orchard—ownerless—would fall into strange hands. So she conceived a greedy idea. Money was better than stones and clods of earth. When she died, the land would remain for whoever took possession; but the money could be fondled, stacked up, and hidden; in case of alarm, she could clasp it between her arms as she died. She must sell the orchard . . .

This change favored Andújar's plans. They reached an agreement after some haggling, as Marta stayed firm in her demands and Andújar gave ground.

Finally, they reached an accord: four hundred *pesos* cash, a signed deed, and strict compliance with one condition: the old woman reserved the right to live in the hut for the rest of her life. The hut would be hers, while Andújar cultivated the land and harvested the crops.

Andújar agreed. Why did he need the shack? Bah! A pile of palm leaves. Furthermore, the old woman would not live for long, and the shopkeeper wanted her to stay there, to avoid any danger of her removing the booty. He knew that sooner or later the fortune would end up in his hands: it was just a question of patience.

The pact was sealed, and at harvest time the orchard was already Andújar's. Marta stood sadly by as Andújar's *obreros* stripped her poor little coffee bushes in a few hours, making off with several *quintales* of berries, which she grieved over as if they were beloved offspring, children of her heart.

In the meantime, the little grandchild grew weaker. Soon, he could no longer rise from the bed.

Consumption had sapped him until he was like a living skeleton. It broke the neighbors' hearts to see him in such a state of lifelessness and misery, so some of them called in a miraculous healer of the *barrio*, who "sanctified" the child's belly.

The poor little devil was dying, yielding in the grip of slow, cruel hunger.

In December, some of the neighbors advised the deputy, a shopkeeper who was substituting for Andújar in the petty municipal post. The spectacle in the hut could not be viewed without feeling pity. For the charity of God, the doctor from town should be called in to prescribe something, to save Marta's poor little grandchild, if he arrived on time.

The deputy wrote a message, a *campesino* took it to town, and Doctor Pintado was charged with the superhuman task of giving life to someone at death's door.

Pintado made ready for the trip to the mountain. He was accompanied by Padre Esteban, who had also been called to fulfill his ministry at the bedside of a *campesina*. The two of them, upon learning of their mutual need to make the uphill trek, decided to set out together.

Both were glad to have company. The distance was great, the road rugged, and the swaying of the pack horses was tiring. It was pleasant to chat along the way, offering each other cigarettes, discussing the latest political news, contemplating the panoramas of the countryside.

When they reached the orchard, Padre Esteban had to continue up the mountain for some distance. They agreed to meet afterwards. Since it was already close to noon, some cold victuals bought in any small inn would do for lunch. Later, since it would be dark and the winding roads were dangerous, they would sup at Juan del Salto's farm and stay the night there.

They sent a note to Juan, notifying him that his two fine friends from the city would be coming to dine with him, hungry and tired from their journey.

Padre Esteban followed his guide, and the doctor was invited to enter Marta's hut.

The physician sat upon an upturned box, next to the pile of rags where the sick boy lay.

Marta was there, fidgeting nervously, as though she feared that the impressive scene would cost her money. At times she was contemplative, at times she made wry faces, demonstrating grief and alarm over her grandson's condition.

Outside, near the door, a crowd of *campesinos* waited, either attracted by curiosity, or to show the doctor their ailments.

Between his thumb and forefinger, Pintado took a corner of the tattered rag that covered the boy, lifted it, and uncovered the patient.

He beheld a skeletal body, a handful of bones wrapped in wrinkled, flaccid skin.

When he inquired about the boy's previous medical history, Marta could offer scarcely any information. She did not remember the child's age, the length of his lactation, or the illness that had killed his mother.

Pintado pressed no further. He knew from long experience that these people scarcely paid attention to such matters. Medical practice in the mountains was a combination of science and guesswork. He gazed intently at the boy, feeling astonishment over such a disaster. He took a fold of skin between his fingers, felt the pulse, put his hand over the heart, lifted up an arm, set the lips ajar. He turned around angrily. Why had he been called? Was he, perhaps, a reviver of the dead? The boy had been sick for years, and they had waited until he was near death before calling him. He directed himself to Marta and spoke of nutrition, of the boy's diet. He subsisted upon *salcocho,* that terrible, insipid plantain stew.

The sick boy, meanwhile, directed doleful glances at the people. His eyes were like two brilliant dots in the depth of a cave. He was a thin twig snapped from the massive tree of life, a being whose right to live had been trampled by misery and passion. Had he been able to resist, had his body triumphed over Marta's greed, that suffering infancy would have been the foundation for the future man. The child would have delivered into the hands of the adult the crushing heritage, the physical ailments, the sickly stomach . . . But no, the tiny grandchild was dying, the small twig, brutally torn from the eternal trunk of mankind, was shriveling up.

Pintado looked about gloomily. A sad conviction subdued him: he was powerless.

He offered some counsel. They should care for the little boy; he suffered from hunger, a hunger of many years.

Tearing a leaf from his prescription book, he wrote out a request for some drugs from the pharmacy. With a fretful air, he handed over the prescription, convinced that his efforts were futile.

He knew that all was useless; he knew that his mission was unfulfilled; he knew that all those present were incredulous or indifferent; he knew, lastly, that if some generous soul didn't offer to get the drugs in town the prescription would remain in the grandmother's pocket for a week, until someone presented himself to "do her the kindness." What did one day more or less mean to them? Alarm over the danger threatening a loved one, the urgency to avoid sickness, the anxiety until relief is found— they understood none of this, because in order to fear the prospect of death one must first know what it is to live.

Musing once more over the stoic attitude of those unshakable people, Pintado fell into a bad mood.

Later, outside, there began a parade of pale, feeble people before the doctor's eyes, appearing for this "chance" inspection; if the deputy hadn't called him to Marta's hut, this cluster of phantoms would not have appeared.

He had a prescription and some advice for everyone. They should eat, they should eat; they should cover their nakedness with clean clothing; they should beware of inclement weather; they should drink pure water and shun alcohol. Over and over Pintado repeated the message, like someone reciting from memory.

Among those in line were Leandra, carrying Pequeñín; Silvina, whom the physician examined thoroughly; Marcelo, whose heart he listened to with curiosity; there were many others, forty or fifty *campesinos,* who remembered that they were sick when they heard the news of the doctor's presence.

It was already night when the three friends found themselves united in Juan del Salto's dining room.

It was a jovial, happy meal. Padre Esteban told of his adventures along the roads of the *cuchilla.*[2]

He had tried to avoid looking down into the abyss, but his eyes became transfixed upon the precipitous cliff next to the trail. What fright! That was no way to travel! Juan argued that it was all a question of getting used to it, but his table companions emphatically decided in favor of the lowlands.

Chatting all the while, they ate heartily. Pintado drank glassfuls of crystalline water with relish, and praised the choice quality of that nectar. He lamented not having it at hand where he lived. Juan explained that the exquisite water came from very high, from steep virtually unexplored peaks, leaping from stone to stone, aerating itself, saturating itself with freshness, filtering and regaling itself with purity. They talked for a long time about the water.

Then they compared the advantages of life in the lowlands and in the mountains. The plain dwellers found everything up there serene and delicious; mountain life had its attractions. But Juan deflated their enthusiasm and recounted the practical inconveniences of life hundreds of feet above sea level.

After coffee, they sat out on the balcony.

The night was cool. They were already in December, the winter of the tropics, a winter without storms or snow.

The three companions puffed their cigars, chatting, contemplating the brilliant sky. The mountain landscape was lost in the shadows; it was impossible to distinguish the contours in the black diffusion of the night. Only the sky was luminous, with splendors that caressed the eye.

Doctor Pintado related the anxieties of his day's work. Once more he had witnessed, in all its nakedness, the great misery of the mountains. Such languid expressions! Such discolored tissue!

[2]*cuchilla,* mountain range.

Some, when they suffered from attacks of fever, turned an earthy color, and a yellow pallor flushed the life from their faces. And such hearts! Such palpitations, such creakings inside the organ where there should only echo the smooth attrition of life's flow! Pintado despaired that he was powerless to overcome the formidable barricade of superstition, indifference and disbelief that was the basis for such a disaster.

He mentioned a young man whose strength had been sapped by anemia. From the symptoms, Juan del Salto suspected that he meant Marcelo, and in fact it was, as the doctor recalled how Juan had recommended the youth to him at a previous time. Pintado said that there was a marked lack of blood in the youth's brain, and that any day he might faint dead away, or suffer a fit of delirium. Everything would depend upon the stimuli around him.

As for Marta's grandchild, all efforts to restore his life would be useless. They could find more energy, more vitality, in a fern leaf than in the young boy. It was criminal!

He spent a good while describing another case which concerned a girl, barely sixteen years old, who was suffering from symptoms of epilepsy, à treacherous ailment that skulked about at first, and then exploded with the rudeness of a hammer blow. Based on the meager facts at hand, he knew that the girl had been married since the age of thirteen. Her husband had abandoned her, and for the while she was living with a youth of the vicinity, who was said to be a convict. He knew that the girl's mother had several children, but managed to learn nothing relevant about her father.

Juan knew that he meant Silvina, and he told the doctor about the loathsome details of her home life.

Pintado offered his opinions on the subject. What had been done to her was bestial, he said. Premature sexual experience was harmful and debasing; the uterus was a sacred organ, blessed by Nature to serve as a merciful cloister for life. To bruise it, to press it into premature labor, was horrible ... it emaciated families, peopled the world with lunatics.

Padre Esteban intervened with his own knowledge of such atrocities: men throwing themselves blindly into lustful orgies, and the women, barely pubescent, succumbed. *They don't let them grow up!* Hearts void of religious feeling, brains empty of the concept of God! What had begun as a pleasant chat now became a lively debate.

It had never occurred to Doctor Pintado that the concept of God would invigorate the physical weakness of the mountainfolk. But Padre Esteban argued the point.

"That which is not taught," he said, "cannot be practiced. Neither individuals nor nations can guess which is the right road. It must be explained, repeated, engraved in their minds. Unfortunately, the concept of morals never reaches the *cordillera* . . ."

"Let us suppose that it did," argued Pintado. "Is it enough, perhaps, for the air to carry seeds in order to raise a forest?"

"With patience and time . . ."

"No; for the seed to take root, it must fall upon fit terrain; ready to receive it. If not, the current of air would be useless."

"But because the seeds fall, land that was once sterile can become fertile."

Juan listened, smiling. It struck him as unusual that Padre Esteban had taken so long to provoke the battle. And the collision could be huge, since Pintado was an avowed materialist, an unshakable pessimist, who accepted no other deity than Claude Bernard.

Though the wind blows for a hundred centuries," the doctor added, "where there are no atoms, there are no bodies."

"Where there are no beliefs, there is no society!"

"Let's come to an understanding," Juan interrupted. "Where there is no health there are no nations. Morality! How beautiful it is! But let's not become confused. Morality doesn't reach these mountains because it has no wings, because it moves along burdened by its own weight . . ."

"However it may be," the priest said, "the teachings of morality don't reach these people because they are never taught religion . . ."

"It would be more fitting," added Doctor Pintado, "if iron salts and manganese reached them."

"*Hombre,* what an outrageous thing to say! And what is your concept of the soul?"

"The soul needs reconstituents, too."

"Jesus!"

"Why so astonished?"

"Over your materialism."

"Yes, I'm a materialist."

"And by means of medicine you're going to save this generation?"

"No, this generation can't be saved; it's lost."

"How's that?"

"We may as well inscribe on their foreheads what Dante read upon the door to his celebrated inferno: *Lasciate Ogni* . . ."

"Bah!"

"Yes, lost forever. Our ancestors didn't think of the future."

"It's certainly lost as far as God is concerned. The immorality, the dissipation, the bad example, the materialistic atrocities of you—the neo-redeemers of the earth—this is what has brought us to such an extreme. But there is still salvation. With a strict regimen . . ."

"A medical regimen?"

"A spiritual regimen, because these are souls. Look, gentlemen: God and man live in absolute relationship. If man is offended, it is an attack upon God; if God is denied, man is destroyed, deformed, forced into evil. Does God exist? Well, the Creation says so, and reason demands that it be so; because if all of nature exists, gentlemen, *He* exists. One comes from the other. There has to be an absolute creator and a relative creature; infinite and finite . . ."

Pintado turned away disdainfully. Bah! It would be such a good "symphony" without Padre Esteban's interference! Relative! Absolute! A creature of blood: here you have an absolute replenishing a relative. But the priest continued energetically.

"Everything decomposes: the intelligence from ignorance; the body from disease; the will from vice. The close relationship between man and his Creator keeps the balance; in the intelligence with wisdom; in the body with health; in the will with virtue. . . . Relations between God and his handiwork are vital; to design against them means the death of man. Religion! Man is a composite of spirit and flesh. His purpose is the perfection of those two components. This is why man must care for the development, perfection and conservation of his body; from there comes the duty of observing the precepts of hygiene. Notice, gentlemen, how religion not only encompasses the soul, but also the factors of the physical problem to which you, friend Juan, devote so much thought."

"I'm not arguing the merits of each school of philosophy," he answered. "I limit myself to studying the problem, to fixing it clearly in my mind . . ."

"Let's not be deceived; religious culture attains those miracles—the health of the soul, the health of the flesh, and . . ."

"Those goals aren't achieved," interrupted Pintado, "by ringing bells during the morning prayer, or making *novenas* to San Crispín."

"But, *hombre*! What do you take me for! Do you think, perhaps, that I'm some fanatical, ignorant little priest? No, *señor,* like yourself I'm a man of science. The *novenas*! The bells! Don't you put on your glasses to see the patient better? Does the glass influence your clinical judgment? The prayers, the bells, the *novenas* are no more than glasses that help man to visualize the majesty of the dogma, since the myopia of ignorance and skepticism make such lenses necessary in order to see God."

"Come now, padre, let's speak plainly: mystical ceremonies lead nowhere. The church loves the hollow pomp of its routine. It seems to live by the formula: 'many branches, little fruit.' "

"On the contrary. Much fruit, because Jesus Christ damned the fig tree that bears only leaves."

"Nature lives in practice, not by principles."

"Agreed. But you should understand that science-religion is quite practical. Take the Commandments, for example. To violate them causes physical, intellectual and moral disorders, and therefore social disorders. Religion is to progress what the spark of life is to the body. Fill the belly of a cadaver with food and there will still be no digestion; take away the life from a thinking being and there will be no progress. Life comes from God, therefore God is progress . . ."

The priest exhausted the topic, explaining his plan of religion and morality, whose success was based upon proper schooling, good example, the missions' teaching of the catechism, the growth of the priesthood, and the practice of virtue.

Contradicting him, Pintado spoke of economics, of the need to encourage commerce and agriculture, to expand trade that would open the way to industrial growth, that would develop the region's water resources and enrich the productive soil. That, that was reality. The rest, humbug. Gold, money: that is the lever, he argued. Everything crystallizes into gold, material riches. He who doesn't obey this rule had better get on course. Was there a need for a civilized, free society? Well, the answer was money, money and more money.

Padre Esteban accepted economics as useful and necessary, but he granted it less weight than the holy purification of the soul. On this point, the doctor said that aside from the health crisis among these people, the best foundation for culture was public wealth, through which mighty intellectual and material conquests were achieved."

"No," said the priest. "I would raise a temple on every mountain."

"And I," said the doctor, "a bank on every hill . . ."

"And I," interrupted Juan, "would build a gymnasium in every valley. Once a race is redeemed physically, it can learn, imitate, plant, restore, trade . . . and also believe. Yes, padre, believe. It is easier for a people to emerge civilized and cultured from a gymnasium than from a hospital . . ."

Being a man of considerable learning, Padre Esteban discoursed upon the Greek and Roman civilizations: the gladiators, the discus, the javelins, the cyclopean architecture, the Colossus of Rhodes. But he always crowned man's greatness with the saintly nimbus of religion.

Juan insisted that first the people must be redeemed physically. They were like a "giant stomach," perishing from malnutrition.

"If that giant stomach would nourish itself," he said, "the race would improve, future generations would be healthy and robust. We must not ask a poor starving man for his tithe, for his alms; we must offer him free bread, not stinginess . . ."

The conversation spun onward and they moved to politics. The three friends were inspired by the progressive nature of the September revolution.[3] The jolt carrying the nation towards the promise of the future had inspired reform and more freedom for the colony. They were three self-confessed liberals. Freedom, political and economic freedom, no more guardianship. They spoke of rights and duties, of equality, of the need to equalize before the law all sons of the nation, all groups, all people.

While Padre Esteban and Doctor Pintado continued to discuss politics, Juan fell pensive.

A luminous ray from the lamp escaped through the open door, slipped over the balcony and gilded a segment of the mountain-side. It was a bit of fugitive light illuminating the blackness; containing in its luminous zone a slim, peaceful royal palm which stood serene in its slumber.

A few moths entered the parlor and flitted capriciously about the light. They paused at times, folding their wings, and testing with their long feelers the rough surfaces of objects which offered neither nectar nor fragrance.

"All this redeeming effort must be based upon the solution of the physical problem," said Juan, emerging from his abstraction.

"But even among sick people one can find brains bubbling with genius."

"Individuals, yes; but never in general. Perhaps I could draw upon an analogy. Fancy, if you will, a statue perched upon a pedestal. The statue is beautiful, endowed by the enchantments of art, and it remains as immobile as all stone does."

"All right, now what?"

"That is the race."

"*Hombre* . . . a race of stone?"

"I haven't finished. Now, in front of the statue let us put an artist who wishes to make it more beautiful and preserve it. His name is 'Restriction.' "

The priest and the doctor burst into laughter.

"What will the statue do?"

[3]Refers to the *Grito de Lares* in September 1868, a brief revolt against Spain, attempting to create an independent republic of Puerto Rico.

"*Hombre,* it won't do anything."

"Naturally. And though the artist shakes it and chastises it, and begs it to revolve about on its pedestal, the statue will remain motionless."

"This is nonsense."

"I don't understand where you're leading us."

"Patience. Now, let us suppose that we remove the artist named 'Restriction' and replace him with another named 'Expansion.' "

"All right, but . . ."

"This other artist would widen the base, would weave crowns of laurel for the statue's forehead, would bestow many good things on it, would give it wings . . . and what will the statue do?"

"What could it do? The same as before."

"Exactly the same."

"It would remain inert."

"Immobile."

"That is the point I wanted to make. What is needed, then, is to animate the statue. A heart that beats, a brain that thinks, nerves that transmit feeling. Only now could the statue appreciate the efforts of the artists; only now would it be able to choose between the two, whether to be enlarged, or expand by itself . . ."

"But where does this lead us? Into what tremendous maze are you taking us? How can black be the same as white? How can it be the same whether you stand still or prosper, expand or restrict? How can it all be the same!"

"Come now, padre, it's quite simple. There is no lack of indisputable evidence; look at reality . . ."

"Well, then, what is the answer?"

"This shouldn't be asked."

"If the statue moves for no one, what is the best thing to do?"

"I repeat: this shouldn't be asked."

"Why?"

"Tell me, doctor, what do you do when you attend to a sick person who has trouble breathing; an asthmatic, for example?"

"Well, anything that would facilitate breathing."

"Such as?"

"There are many measures to be taken."

"Would you close the windows and door?"

"'No, *hombre*. I would set them wide open to let in pure, clean currents of air. I would seat the patient upright to expand his chest and help support his respiratory movements . . .'"

"Do you see now, padre?"

"But *caramba*! That's just common sense."

"Exactly, and so is the regimen for the statue. If one gives air to a chest that can't inhale well at the time, oppressed races should be given freedom, even if they still don't know how to move about freely. One doesn't argue about regimen: one doesn't ask about morality, philosophy, social sciences or politics, to see which of these would be the best cure to spur a nation towards the glories of the future. It's enough to ask your own common sense."

The night flowed by as they laughed and joked, rebuilding the world. They soared through the voids of theory, and at last descended to reality. They were sleepy and tired.

Soon they were huddled in their blankets. It was cold: the night chill nipped at the skin, and they curled up in the warmth of their beds.

Before falling asleep, each one thought of something personal and practical.

Padre Esteban reminded himself that in his mass the next day he was scheduled to begin certain merciful *novenas*.

Doctor Pintado thought about the patients he hadn't seen that day, and about the fool of a deputy who had made him climb the mountain on a fruitless visit to a dying person.

And Juan mentally summed up the shipments of coffee collected that day: he calculated how much still had to be picked; he pondered the likelihood of good prices. Then he thought about Jacobo.

Chapter Ten

In May, Marta's coffee orchard displayed its gay finery.

Only Marta was suffering. In February, her little grandson had died; the small boy returned to dust and the spirit flew far off. A few charitable neighbors wrapped the remains in the shreds of a white sheet, placed them in a rough board coffin and carried it, uncovered, to town. They dug an anonymous grave in the parish cemetery, lowered the child to the bottom, and—once the hole was filled and the soil tamped firm with a shovel—the earth guarded the secret; the secret of an ignored life; a sad soul whose right to protection was equal to everyone's; the secret of an unfortunate victim immolated by crime, the terrible kind of crime that is committed unconsciously.

They buried him. No one knew, no one cried. When the gravedigger dumped him into the hole, he hadn't even the curiosity to look at his face.

Now that she was left alone, Marta suffered greatly as a dormant fondness for her grandson was reborn. There awakened within her a strange, unconscious affection of someone who loves, without bestowing goodness upon the beloved; who unknowingly torments the beloved; an affinity of the flesh, rather than the vibrant throbbing of the spirit.

At that time, the old woman was suffering from the inclemencies of asthma; the affliction had plagued her for many years, springing up and subsiding.

The grandson's death, her loneliness, the nocturnal terrors as she worried about her treasure, the daily scavenging on the hillside, and, above all, the crushing weight of the years, stirred up the old illness and Marta often had to take deep gasping breaths to suck air into her lungs. The last few days' work had been arduous. The earthen jar which Gaspar had defiled was moved from its resting place and buried beneath a coffee tree near the house. The piles of gold and *pesos* were taken to the hut, and buried in the earth below when Marta felt uneasy.

From her doorstep, with her gleaming little eyes, Marta kept a constant vigil over the tree trunk that concealed the jar.

The coffee trees, interlacing their branches as they rocked gently in the breeze, adorned the hut like an awning, filtering the sun's rays, carpeting the shadows with tiny leaves.

Up above there was verdure, radiant color, life, sunshine, swarms of butterflies harmonizing with the bubbly chatter of the birds. Below, the drab straw of her hut; the ancient wretched dwelling with its rotted foundation, sieve-like roof, and thin crumbling walls. And while the roses bloomed above, below there was sadness, gloom and ennui in the crypt where an old human being clung stubbornly to life.

One night, the asthma grew worse. Astride the hammock, her swollen feet dangling, her body pitched forward and arms spread wide, Marta spent the hours gasping for air. While the pain crushed her chest, a fixed idea disturbed her thoughts. Ah! She was being careless. She could barely move, and the jar holding her treasure was in jeopardy. Better to have it nearby, so that she wouldn't have to walk up and down the hill every day to make sure that no one was digging at the foot of the tree. She felt sick, very sick; she could barely reach the shed to start a fire and stew the plantains. Old people were helpless. She had to divide up the crumbs among the hogs and chickens, fix herself a meal, open and close the door, go to the river for water. So many tasks! And she was alone, alone with God!

Her strength was gone. If only someone could keep her company. No, for nothing in the world! Company, no! What good was *company*? The neighbors were snoopers, who called her a miser. Better to be alone. But for her own peace of mind, the jar should be closer, there below, next to her other savings.

She thought of death, but why should she die? She wasn't harming anyone, and so many rogues were enjoying good health! Perhaps her indisposition was nothing; with God's help she would "perk up." But if she was truly dying, would all her money end up in someone else's hands? No, a hundred times no! She hadn't scrimped so that some good-for-nothing should enjoy. No one must find it, so that if she closed her eyes her fortune would rot in the earth. She was no fool. She knew how to fix things so that no one would take their pleasure with what was hers, hers alone.

She felt a surge of hope. Bah! She had been ill so many times, and still she was alive. It was nothing. Perhaps the dampness, that lifelong cold of hers, she conjectured. Most important was to reach the jar, recount the pile, and keep it within reach . . .

She waited for daylight. Galvanized by her idea, supporting herself with a stick, she left the hut and began to walk slowly, with difficulty.

The coffee tree was close by—eighty or a hundred *varas* at the most—but it was on the slope of the hill, where the terrain was roughest; a difficult place, expressly chosen because of her distrustful nature.

Where the path was tolerable she managed to progress with an insecure shuffle; when she reached the slope she stopped, tremulous and hesitant.

She sat down to rest for a moment. Some hens and a hog had followed her. Accustomed to being served every morning before anyone, the fowl clucked and the pig grunted, protesting the unusual neglect that day.

Mortally weary, she tried to pull herself together. Her fatigue was intense; her eyelids widened as though they wished to open a pathway for the air; her stomach fluttered like an obstinate bellows; her chest barely stirred, unable to suck in the life around her.

But in her head an unyielding, imperious idea propped up her life. To reach the coffee tree, dig down next to the trunk, and perhaps regain her health by losing herself in the sight of the treasure.

New found energy made her rise. She gripped the stick, dragged her feet and moved a few paces. The pig, still grunting, crossed in front of her and nearly caused her to fall; the hens followed, picking at her dress, and eight tiny chicks scampered about her like persistent little beggars.

Close to the tree, the mountain leveled off into a small mesa. The branches sprouting from the dwarfish trunk hovered close to the ground.

Marta wanted to reach that point, rest a while and then unearth her treasure. Then, going downhill, the task would be easier . . .

But the grip of anxiety grew tighter. The flaccid skin on her face turned blue; perspiration drenched the old woman's body; her heart, throbbing turbulently, seemed eager to escape from its cell; her mouth opened instinctively for air; the vents of her keen nose expanded with every breath; her tremulous hands and feet were powerless to maintain equilibrium. Only in her mind was the rugged stanchion, the hindmost blaze of passion, angrily succumbing, unable to survive the body which for all its life had contained it.

When she reached the mesa, the old woman could go no further. She reeled, stretched her arms out forward, threw her head back, extravagantly opened her eyes and mouth, exhaled raucously and fell. She was dead. Lying on her stomach, her right arm extended towards the coffee tree, her fingers contracted, her head bent backward, her chin resting upon the earth and her eyes fixed horribly upon the tree.

Two or three days later, when the neighbors missed her, they found her there and drew back with horror. The putrefaction had begun and the corpse was frightening. The pig rooted about, boring its snout beneath the cadaver, stirring it, pushing it, as if it wanted to make her rise and satisfy its gluttony.

All over the region, tales were invented about the life and death of the miser, practically making her out to be a witch. No one dared come close to the orchard.

Only Andújar dared. Since he was living in the lowlands at the time, he issued strict orders to the foreman who looked after his farm that he be kept informed about Marta. He owned that land and wanted to dispose of the hut when the old woman died.

He came quickly, ready to begin the search. He was cunning. Alone, he demolished the hut. When he yanked out the rotted beams which comprised the small perimeter, he noticed the soft, fresh earth. He dug and the gold and silver surged forth. When he took his find to town, he made an accounting. The unearthed sum amounted to two thousand seven hundred *pesos*; discounting the four hundred that the farm had cost him, the transaction had netted two thousand three hundred pesos. All was profit.

But there was another cunning fellow on the mountain. Andújar's foreman, who had no fear of witches, observed his actions and made a search of his own. He was among those who found Marta's body. He found it strange that the old woman, deathly sick, should have such a whim to venture up the hill, since it led to none of her usual haunts. He noted, above all, that dead-eyed gaze which seemed to bid a final *adiós* to a loved one.

The foreman was rustic, but no fool. Nothing could be lost by trying. He set to work, and the jar—the celebrated earthen jar that Gaspar adored—showed its tempting mouth, and its bowels were replete with silver and copper coins.

A short time later, the foreman left his employ on Andújar's farm and opened another pious little store in Vegaplana; another pinhole of fraud, another source of swindle.

The days passed uneventfully in Leandra's hut. There was an occasional dispute between mother and daughter, but they dissipated quickly.

An air of relative happiness floated round about; in the immediate limits of the house, where neither fruits nor flowers grew, the angel of tranquility seemed to be resting there.

Pequeñín roved about naked, playing, exposing his pale lean body to the sun. He no longer cried defenselessly; in the kitchen he was already able to scrape the bottom of the cooking pot, and lick his hands clean of the last particle.

Leandra still pounded away at her habitual pile of clothing by the river bank. Hunched over the flat stone cast upon the shore by the everlasting current, she spent a good part of the day soaping the garments and muddling the water with residues of labor and slovenliness.

In the hut, Silvina did her share, devoting herself to the household chores. But at times she became irritated over the slightest trifle; occasionally she succumbed to inexplicable grief, and gazed numbly at the landscape.

Ciro worked a few days and was idle the others. To him, work was not a habit; he remembered it when his pockets were empty. He was pleased to meet the family's expenses, but when there was a way to elude work without causing any hardship, he ran off like a schoolboy.

When this happened, he would stay in the hut and settle back in the hammock, which groaned a monotonous singsong as it rocked back and forth. Other times, he sat at the doorway, leaned back on the floor and, while Silvina caressed his head with her tiny fingers, slept with the contentment of one who has enough to be happy and disavows the more adventurous world.

Ciro intervened when there was discord. Imposing silence upon Silvina and pacifying ña[1] Leandra, he would ridicule their squabble by laughing at their unfounded annoyance. He was a good man, but he was aimless.

In the productive weeks, Sunday was a great day. They would treat themselves to an abundant feast. They ate huge quantities of their favorite dishes, gorging their bodies as though they hadn't eaten all the previous week, consuming on Sunday the greater part of their resources, and then being obliged to live very scantily the next week. There were times that Ciro, earning six pesos, would spend four on meat. They would devour it as though they had never eaten before, stuffing themselves until it made them sick.

One summer day at sundown, they were chatting.

"Now then, what shall I bring you?" Ciro asked.

"At what time will you leave?"

"When it's still dark."

"And you'll be back in the afternoon?"

"Yes."

"Well then," said Leandra, "bring me half a *maná*[2]. . ."

"All right."

"Are you taking many animals?"

[1] *ña*: a familiar term for *doña,* a title given to a lady, roughly equal to "Mrs."

[2] *maná,* a root with reputed medicinal powers.

"I'm taking four of don Juan's she-mules, and to help me when I get there, Marcelo's going on the *macho*.[3]

"You're going for supplies?"

"Yes, a bunch of us. Two peons and five mules from Galante's, and two more men from Andújar's . . ."

"How that man spends! He throws it about like water!"

"Let him spend. That's why he has a business now."

"Has he opened a store?"

"No, woman. He's opened a warehouse by the sea shore, and it's filled with barrels and casks. Outside, above the door, he's painted a sign."

"What does it say?"

"Montesa went down there the other day and read it; on one side it says 'Andújar' and on the other 'Galante.' In the middle, there's a scribble like this, look . . ."

With his machete, Ciro drew a & in the earth.

"What does that mean?"

"Well it means 'and what' company."

They talked excitedly about the prosperity of their former neighbors.

Ciro awoke early in the morning, when it was still dark. He had to start out with the mules from Juan's farm. When he shook off his drowsiness, he lit a lamp and woke up Silvina who who gave him his clothes.

Ready to leave, he bid goodbye to Silvina, who sat up in bed and smiled at him affectionately. Caressing her, he gave her a kiss, as she playfully pinned him in her arms, refusing to let him go.

Trying to gently break her grip, Ciro appealed to one decisive recourse and tickled her. Overcome by laughter, Silvina opened her arms. They kissed once more and he departed.

The drove was on its way towards town before sunrise.

Eleven mules laden with bananas, led by six *campesinos*, festooned the undulating road which was more suitable for goats and mountain lions than for human beings.

The convoy carried a goodly load of fruits for sale, but its

[3]*macho*, a he-mule.

principal purpose was to return with a load of foodstuffs and miscellany needed on the farm. Leaving the fruit in the lowlands, they would return by sundown.

The drivers walked in silence through the darkness. Their bodies pricked by darts of damp cold, the men huddled against the packsaddles, letting the riderless mules walk ahead.

Ciro, who was in better spirits than the others, drove the retinue from time to time; Marcelo, last in line, shiveringly wrapped himself in a threadbare woolen overcoat which once belonged to Juan del Salto and, after passing through the hands of two or three owners, had been inherited by the youth.

Trembling with cold, Marcelo made a superhuman effort to keep pace with the others. Had he succumbed to the malaise which he felt, he would have stayed in his hut until the sun was high; but he had to work, to do something, to earn a living.

The road extended along the river's edge and swerved into the water at times. Elsewhere, rather than follow the capricious turns of the river bed, it zigzagged up the mountain, soaring to the peaks, rewarding the traveler's fatigue with a splendid view.

The men had leaped directly from bed to their packsaddles and undertook the journey without even a spoonful of nourishment. The lack of breakfast didn't bother the *campesinos*. They knew how to resist hunger, and they knew that the road was littered with small stores and taverns where—if they found nothing to eat— they would certainly find much to drink.

At the top of a steep hill, where the road rejoined the river, they paused in front of an inn. Someone suggested a drink: a draught to warm up the belly and invigorate the spirit. They leaped from their mounts.

Everyone, that is, except Marcelo, who rejected the idea. But yes, he would have a bit of coffee.

He could hear the sputtering of the hearth behind the inn, where the brew was being prepared, but the proprietor said that it was not ready yet.

The others quickly gulped down breakfast—half a glass of rum—without a blink.

Ready to continue, they refused to wait any longer. They

wanted to take advantage of the cool morning to cover a lot of ground. They would lose time if they waited for the coffee.

Marcelo, resigning himself to the painful void in his stomach, yielded to the majority and followed them.

Climbing and encircling the mountain, they made another hour's journey and at last, in a place where the road was mired in mud, they found another inn.

The travelers drank once more and Marcelo, vexed by his bad luck, learned that there was no coffee there either.

"But drink something, fool," said one man.

"Me? For what?"

"Because you look ready to faint, *hombre*."

"You shouldn't have come; you're sick," said Ciro.

"And what am I to do? I'm not going to die of hunger!"

"You need strength; eat some bread and cheese."

"No, no, right now I couldn't swallow anything. Just something warm."

"I can see now that you'll be a big help to me!"

"Drink, drink something," insisted another man.

"It's better that you don't," said Ciro. "It's no good for you."

"Nah! Drink does no harm."

"I say that it will . . ."

"Well, let him drink just a little. We're not all alike. Some can take more than others."

"But I never drink!"

"We drink our rum straight, true? So take it with water and it'll do you no harm. It's good for you . . ."

"No, I don't *ever* drink. But I'll take a little water."

Since the inn was a bit distant from the river, they took water from a nearby lagoon. They gave him a glassful of thick, brackish liquid. He drank, grimaced with disgust, and returned to his mount.

The journey continued, festooning the base of the mountains, climbing to the heights, wading the river, inching along the narrow cliffs where the animals performed miracles of balance.

Meditating silently with his head down, Marcelo let himself be led by his mule. He would have liked to be like the others, who did as they pleased, without anything ever happening to them. There they went, so joyful, so content, so strong and happy after gulping down their drinks. How lucky they were! They were truly bold men, who drew their machetes over the slightest affront, and spent the rest of their time laughing and jesting—while he stayed away from fights, huddled in a corner. Alas! He was sick, very sick. For three days he had been taking swigs from a "bottle"[4] given him to see if it worked a cure, but nothing yet.

The other *campesinos* walked along, laughing boisterously, enlivened by the alcohol breakfast.

Marcelo watched them enviously. As he moved along in agony—his tongue heavy, his body sluggish, with a mute pain in his stomach—they were happy. Men, real men! He was so unlucky, not being able to drink, so that he, too, could feel active and strong. They had wanted him to drink rum with water, but what if it was just as harmful as the pure liquor? No, he knew better from painful experience.

After three hours of travel they reached the plain, where the road was open and easy.

They took another rest period close to town; the convoy tarried at a store, where the *campesinos* drank again.

Marcelo looked more like an escapee from the sick bed than a man at work. No sooner did he complain about feeling ill than the mountaineers argued again that he should have a drink. Why, they wanted to know, was he so stubborn?

One of his companions gave him a glass of rum with water. "Drink . . . don't be a fool. You're as pale as a piece of paper."

"I can't understand why you're so afraid," added another.

Marcelo took the glass in his right hand and regarded it with suspicion.

Suddenly the painful memory assailed him: the drunken spree that afternoon in Andujar's store. He held the glass at arm's length. No, he wouldn't drink.

No one paid attention to his gesture. They let the glass remain in his hand.

[4]"bottle," apparently some home-brewed medicine made by a neighbor.

Then Ciro intervened.

Drink just a little, he said, perhaps it might strengthen him without any ill effect.

"It can't do you any harm. Why, it's almost all *water*!

"That's how women and children drink."

"Yes!

"*Ea!* Drink this little bit, and when we reach town you'll have a bite to eat. You'll see how much better you feel."

All right, Marcelo decided, he would drink; but no more than half the glass. He drank it down.

As they continued on their way, Marcelo felt better. He spoke with Ciro about the details of their work that day. They would unload quickly, let the animals rest a while, and then load up for the return. They would eat while the animals rested.

They had lunch in a little inn outside town, filling their stomachs with *salazón*[5] and *verduras.*[6] Marcelo, animated and smiling, feeling carefree, drank another glass of rum and water.

In good spirits, he helped Ciro. The cargo was positioned upon the mules to resist, as much as possible, the swayings of the march. Soon they were ready to return.

The sun was still blazing when the convoy set out on the return trip. They stopped many times to brace the cargo which became unsettled by the fitful terrain, or to adjust the *pita* fiber harnesses on mules, or to put the animals back in line when they strayed off.

The silhouette of a store by the roadside was a tempting surprise. To drink, yes to drink! They dismounted and joked over who would pay. Their *ochavos* were quickly being spent, but there were still a few "chips" left.

So they drank. Marcelo forgot the past. He felt fine, strong and content. He drank without any prompting.

The proprietor served him half a glass of *aguardiente*. Pleasurably contemplating the glass for an instant, he wet his lips in it, tasted the liquid with relish, and hesitated. It still seemed a bit strong, and he asked for some water to mix it with.

---

[5]*salazón,* dried, salted meat.
[6]*verduras,* root vegetables.

Later, when the march was resumed, he broke into song. His companions were chatting merrily and he, taking advantage of a widening in the road, passed them by.

As they entered the mountain zone, the road became rugged. When he approached the foot of a hill, Marcelo suddenly lashed his mount. The beast galloped forward, while stones rolled down the hill with a crash, falling like a small avalanche upon the other riders.

Ciro howled. No, stop that jesting; Marcelo knew all too well that Juan del Salto had told them to be very careful with his animals.

Marcelo was laughing. He had reached the top of the hill before anyone. As for *don* Juan, he was rich enough not to worry if one of his animals were crippled.

Prank by prank, Marcelo soon became the clown of the retinue.

Once, as they waded the river, Ciro gave forth a loud shout. The cargo was slipping from one of the mules under his care. The accident was irritating, because he had to walk into the middle of the river.

In a bad mood, Ciro pulled up his pant legs and stepped into the water. Several of the men helped, and they soon fixed the cargo, securing it with a cord that Ciro had cut in pieces with the knife he carried in his belt.

As they worked in the water, Marcelo whooped and laughed from the shore, ridiculing Ciro's annoyance. Ciro meanwhile scolded Marcelo, who preferred mockery to jumping into the water to help.

The convoy continued. With nightfall approaching, they reached the small inn facing the bemired road. Marcelo leaped from his mount and, before anyone could advise against it, he happily drank a generous dose of pure *aguardiente*. When it came time to pay, he sneaked outside and burst into crude laughter, obliging one of the other travelers to pay the bill.

Marcelo was now the buffoon of the group. He walked on ahead, telling childish jokes, upsetting the regular pace of the others, shouting, cruelly punishing his inoffensive animal.

"Stop it! Stop it!" roared Ciro. "That beast will throw you and give you a nasty kick!"

Amidst a chorus of laughs and crude jokes, Marcelo continued playing the idiot's role.

At a bend in the road, he dealt the hinny a severe blow. The frightened animal gave a bound, and Marcelo, who was not seated very firmly, tumbled to the earth.

He fell near the edge of the precipice and the alarmed *campesinos* thought for a moment that he had gone over the side, but they soon saw him weltering on the ground, hurling curses and threats.

Leaping down from his mount, Ciro ran to him.

"I told you! I warned you not to act that way!"

"Shut up!"

"Have you hurt yourself?"

"What does it matter to you?"

"Leave me be!"

"But don't be ill-mannered, *hombre*! Give me your hand. If not, get up by yourself."

Marcelo sprang to his feet.

"You're a crackbrained fool," Ciro said.

"I do as I want, understand?"

"But you shouldn't act that way!"

"Each to his *own* way."

"But you're drunk, and I don't want you getting hurt."

"Me, drunk?"

"Yes."

"The one who's *tight* is you! Look, I'm getting tired of putting up with you and your advice. Leave me in peace!"

"Well, act right. You're not supposed to carry on like this in front of people."

"Out of my way!"

"God save you! If you lift your hand . . ."

"What?"

"Stop showing off . . ."

"Showing off, nothing. I'll do it if you keep bothering me . . ."

"You'll do nothing, *hombre*. Get mounted and shut your mouth."

"Shut my mouth, eh?"

"Marcelo!"

Marcelo raised his whip and would have lashed his brother if Ciro, the stronger of the two, hadn't pinned his arms.

The men tried to separate them, but it was impossible. The two brothers, firmly grasping each other, fought and wrestled. Ciro gave a mighty push and managed to tumble Marcelo. They both fell, with Ciro on top.

Ciro snatched the whip from his brother, who howled and struggled to get up.

Enraged, Marcelo let out an angry yell, seized Ciro's knife from its sheath, and with a lightning movement plunged it into his brother's heart.

Ciro moaned and toppled over backwards. He was dead.

The *campesinos* fell back, horror-stricken. It was a stampede . . .

Instants later, they were gone. The mules, obeying their habitual routine, continued straight ahead in a single file; the hinny followed, trotting around a bend and vanishing.

On the road there remained only Ciro's corpse and his assassin. Marcelo's skin bristled, his eyes were inflamed. He glanced about, confused, then took a few steps away from Ciro's cadaver. He returned next to the body, unsure whether or not to flee. Then he fled, running uphill and into the woods.

The next day, another criminal case was begun. The documents found in the corpse's pockets identified him, and listed the names of those accompanying him, including Marcelo's.

This time the truth was easier to obtain. A multitude of witnesses passed before the judge, and though they were still hostile to the truth, the circumstances of the crime forced them to be explicit.

No one, however, mentioned Marcelo by name.

After the crime, he reached his hut, panting for breath.

It was already midnight. Frightened, stunned, nearly insane, he threw himself upon the floor and fell into a deep slumber.

Before noon the next day, the police surrounded the hut. They awakened him harshly and he broke into sobs. Ah, they were coming for him! He answered their call and, believing that the police would judge and punish him immediately, he joined his hands in supplication, cried bitterly, and with pitiful desperation confessed to his crime. He had . . . killed his brother!

Still sobbing, he was bound and taken away. When the people saw him pass, they felt no pity for his tears. They turned their faces, or regarded him angrily.

At last, the prison. The first night Marcelo spent alone in his cell, he believed that he would die. As he sat in the horrible, disease-ridden grotto, he knew that his woeful destiny was fulfilling itself!

Chapter Eleven

Two years later, Silvina was living in a hut situated in the heights of Juan del Salto's farm.

Things had changed a great deal. When Silvina learned of Ciro's tragic death she was rent by immense grief. Hers was such a hapless destiny! Life with Gaspar had seemed a century; happiness with Ciro a minute.

In the first painful hours of her grief, merciful neighbors came with affectionate words to assuage her sorrow, but it was useless. Silvina was deaf to consolation. Ah, poor she! Her tender, generous man, murdered by his own brother, leaving her abandoned to a life of misery. She couldn't resign herself to it. If God was just, why did He abuse her so cruelly? She wanted to die; cure the festered wound of her sorrows; put an end once and for all to her wretched life. What did life hold for her?

Young, almost a girl still, she felt weary and helpless before such misfortune.

Leandra, too, was saddened. It was true when Silvina said that theirs was a terrible fate! First Gaspar, who had run away; then Ciro's death. Hardly a few months had intervened between one and the other. Once more, they were alone and forsaken, without a man! And Leandra moaned and wept.

In the midst of her grief, Silvina had a sudden impulse. Although it broke her heart, she wanted a last look at Ciro. She decided to leave immediately. Accompanied by Leandra, she descended to the lowlands, making haste to get there on time.

It was the day after the crime, and the autopsy had already been performed. The two women arrived at the cemetery and saw Ciro stretched out on a crude table.

Silvina thought that she would go mad. The corpse's head was swollen; the cranium had been severed and, although the removed segment had been put back in place, the brain was still visible through the crack. The thorax had also been opened and the wall of the chest did not quite cover the hollowed out trunk of the body; exposed to view were hunks of lung, ribs cracked in half by the coroner's scissors, and the heart opened in two, skewered by Marcelo's dagger. The stomach had also been opened, revealing the labyrinth of intestines which had been yanked out of place and slashed by the surgical knife. Everything had been mangled and profaned by the autopsy.

The two women were deeply shocked. Leandra, pale and cold, her eyes arid, had never before seen such a horrible spectacle. Silvina, weeping uncontrollably, now had these heart-rending images to add to her sorrows. Poor Ciro! So generous, so good, yet destroyed in such a way; practically torn to pieces before being lowered into the earth for his eternal rest!

The women returned to their shack, and continued their sad life. Loneliness and poverty reopened the wounds of their grief constantly, but in the course of time the pain slackened.

Leandra continued her washing, but now with more ardor, because wringing the rags of others gave them their meager sustenance. Silvina was sad, and sickly. Her tears, once accompanied by outbursts of rage, were now silent and reflexive.

As the days passed, mother and daughter, faced by their harsh life, were irritable and their tempers collided over mere trifles. Finally, they came to live in complete discord.

One day, to Silvina's surprise, a man arrived to live in the hut, another *man,* some hungry soul to whose dominance Leandra chose to submit herself. Silvina began to wonder: wasn't she a woman, too? She felt repugnance when she thought about a new man; only Ciro dwelled in her soul.

But Ciro was dead, and their love was a packet of memories that would never be real, nor bring in bread or sustenance. She was young and still beautiful. Her mother, nearly an old woman, was "finding" . . . why shouldn't she "find," too?

Gradually, time clouded her memories, weakened her firm resolutions.

One morning, after a violent argument with her mother, Silvina decided. Inés Marcante had invited her to go with him. Without love, without even fondness, almost with loathing, she followed him, settling her nest up in the barren heights of Juan del Salto's farmland.

Juan was away at the time. Jacobo had graduated, and the doting father lacked the patience for his return: he boarded a ship, hurried to his son, and together they went touring Europe.

Montesa stayed in charge of daily tasks on the farm, which was administered by a friend of Juan's from the city. The old mariner was puffed with pride and self-esteem, eager to fulfill his duties to the utmost degree. He issued stern orders to his assistant foreman, tolerated no objections, and, as behooves a supreme authority, he even condescended to being amiable at times.

Andújar and Galante were wrapped up in their business ventures. They were fascinated by the world of speculation and plunged deep into its dark mysteries, where the only light that shines is gold. From time to time, Andújar visited his farm, but he now affected a certain disdain towards it. Now that he was a businessman, his "little farm" was just a trifle, a plaything.

Marcelo was never sentenced for his crime. Before his trial was over, he succumbed in jail. Lying upon the damp floor of his cell, breathing the venomous prison air, he offered little resistance, and died in a coma. His only joy was the knowledge that he would die soon, and find peace at last!

Silvina aspired to little in her new life. All she wanted was minimal care, a little consideration; she had lived a painful life, never knowing where was the dividing line between moral and physical pain, and after that life of tears and misery, she wanted only peace, tranquility.

But Marcante did not vibrate in tune with her wishes. Stupid and vain, he had never asked himself what a woman was. He'd had so many, so prodigal was he in his dissipation, that he came to believe women were honored if he deigned to protect them.

Thus, when the first misunderstandings came, the despot's hand rose up, and fell upon the victim's face.

Silvina was enraged. She remembered how Gaspar's tyranny had chained her, but this was not the same. With Inés Marcante she felt brave, strong, fit for rebellion. There was a noisy quarrel, and then calm. But from then on there were new misunderstandings and new reconciliations, chorused by hunger.

One day, Silvina could bear it no longer. The night before, with her husband away, Silvina went to bed; very early the next morning she awoke and found another woman asleep at her side. Ah, that shameless Marcante! She wouldn't stand for such a disgrace.

She screamed and cried with indignation, but Marcante laughed at her. He was enjoying the fact that two women wanted him. And the other woman accepted the challenge. They quarreled, and when they ran out of insults they resorted to their hands.

Marcante separated them and issued a firm decree. The two of them should live there together; whoever didn't want to could leave.

Desperate and furious, Silvina surrendered to tears. All right, she would leave before suffering such abuse.

Only one choice was left: Leandra. Her mother, who antagonized her, and made her suffer, but her mother after all.

That afternoon, barefoot, unkempt, wearing a torn, faded little dress and carrying a bundle of tattered clothing, she fled from Marcante's hut.

There was no one at Leandra's shack when she arrived: the man of the house was at work; Pequeñín was buying food in the store; Leandra was washing clothes by the river. It was dusk. The day languished in its final hues as it chased the sun. The pompous armada of clouds floated in the sky like a spectrum: towards the east it was dark, mournful and gray; to the west, where the sun still shone with brilliance, it was rosy and aflame, incrusted with golden fog and mother-of-pearl contours.

The landscape was a feast of colors. The sun glaced the earth with slanting rays, and as its brilliance tarried behind the mountains, the peaks and the air around them gleamed with atoms of light.

Galante's coffee plantation up in the heights was hooded by the dark verdure of the mountains. Below, Andújar's settlement was sad and lonely, without the sounds of bustling shoppers at the store. Further beyond were the squalid farm shacks, resting upon fragile foundations, thrown together with the kind of nomadic attitude that builds no home so as not to have to transport it when the imminent day of change arrives. It was an insecure, change-able village: over there, where a grove of woodland stood yester-day, one sees a hut; and where one finds it today, tomorrow one will see a pasture. Everything uncertain, fugitive, transient; good folk living in the eternal topsy-turvy of an existence without reason, like rootless plants, submissive souls letting themselves be dragged along by chance like straw snatched up by the wind.

Every detail of the panorama stood out on that melancholy afternoon. The coffee orchard in its forsaken sadness, the moun-tainous border to the south that concealed the village of Vega-plana, the bold cusps of the *cordillera,* swaddled in low clouds or piercing the mist with their jagged points; Juan's farm, nestling on the inclined plane of the slope.

And then the river . . . always the river! . . . flowing sonorously, caressing the pebbles in its depths which were reddened, too, by the sundown. Trees on the bank drooped over, shadowing the current; in times of anger, the flow licked at small timid greens that grew in the keys formed by piles of stones.

The river was like a living being, with its past hidden in the *sierras*; with a rebellious present spent flowing through the sinu-ous river basin; with an uncertain tomorrow in which, turbid from its dredgings, heaped with the earth's impurities, it must hurl itself into the sea.

It was a tireless voyager, a witness to all grief, but with neither voice nor words to reveal it to the future as it rushed into the ocean of time. It lived in coolness, among beds of crystal, its murmurs hauling away the sheaf of laments fallen in its currents, telling with its purl the bitter tale suffered by so many hearts . . .

Finding the hut deserted, Silvina threw her bundle upon the floor, grasped hold of the two small trees that had so often witnessed her ecstasies, and sighed dolefully, gazing at the panorama. She could hear the splashing from below, where Leandra flogged the clothes with a piece of wood and, from time to time, the crackling of the water, when she squeezed them dry in her hands.

Silvina let herself be swept away by memories, and each of them wounded her intensely.

First, she recalled her innocent amours with Ciro, Galante's infamous abuses, the horror of her marriage to Gaspar, the terrors suffered under his dominion. Her face bathed in tears, she sobbed bitterly.

Then she remembered Gaspar's threats, his shoves, his blows; the terrible event that lugubrious night in the store, her dread when she realized what had happened; the episode with Ciro on the mountain, seen hazily, relived not with the sweetness of a pleasant memory but like the silhouette of a frightful adventure; and, finally, her times of happiness with Ciro after Gaspar took flight, the profound jolt of her lover's death, her struggles with Leandra, her loathsome life with Marcante, her physical pains and illnesses, the sickly decay that weakened her and made her weary of life.

She cried for a long time, while the day shrouded itself in the gauze of dusk and swooned mournfully.

Suddenly she felt a harsh sensation, and before she could explain it, she lost consciousness. Up high on the mountain she saw a fringe of light, which seemed to be a sudden flash fire; she moaned, threw her head back and fell . . . a victim to an epileptic seizure.

She collapsed by the edge of the slope. as she writhed about, under the stimulus of her convulsions, she momentarily moved away from the edge of the cliff; but after an instant's calm her body shuddered spasmodically, her face contracted in a horrible grimace, and she writhed close to the edge of the abyss.

She quivered there above the danger, like debris subject to the whims of chance. She trembled above death, all alone, and then she hurtled over the edge.

The slope, cluttered with trees and thicket, opened a path for her body; green stalks doubled over, tangled shrubs parted, dry leaves crackled into fragments, heaps of straw moved aside, as she plowed through.

She fell with the weight of that which will never rise again. She tumbled head over heels, smashing and bouncing from stone to stone, slowed by a tree branch until gravity pulled her onward; dragging in her wake piles of stones that followed her, like an escort to the bottom in funereal homage.

Plunging headlong, she left a bloody trail, a crimson furrow. She was life returning to its origin, the borrowed breath giving itself back to earth.

Badly wounded, her bones shattered, disfigured, covered with blood, Silvina landed in a shapeless heap upon the smooth flat stone where Leandra was washing.

The mother bolted up, terrified. She looked for an instant, and that instant sufficed for the immensity of the tragedy to sink in. She shrieked. It was her daughter! Silvina had fallen from the cliff!

Standing there, lifting her hands to her head, she screamed for help, whined for mercy.

Silvina's body lay there destroyed upon the stone, like an alto-relievo carved in granite.

The tenuous afternoon light imparted to it the look of a sepulchral sculpture, a reclining bust to commemorate the most suffering victim of the cruelest of sorrows.

Her right arm was submerged in the water, and the brisk current kept it half afloat, moving it with an unsteady sway, frolicking with it, swaddling it in coolness, bidding it a final *adiós*.

Mutilated, inert, the daughter lay at the feet of the mother, the shred next to the tattered rag, the fetus next to the maternal cloister, where chance had shaped it with unfeeling bestiality.

Leandra, her eyes wide open and her breath anxious, stared at Silvina stupefied, and in that stance one saw the massive breasts that had satisfied Silvina's first hunger; her already gray hair, more from worry than from age; her voluminous stomach, swollen so often by motherhood, consecrated so many times by prolific Venus, twisted so often by the formidable pain that peoples the world.

There was the victim, the result, the sinner without sin, the guilty without guilt, the unconscious criminal whose fate had been determined the day of her birth, and who in turn had borne others like her.

The neighbors, those returning from work or passing along the trails, and a few *campesinas* who were also washing by the river bank, responded to Leandra's screams.

Between their commentaries and Leandra's heart-rending screams, the mission which charity and misfortune demands in such cases was fulfilled.

Night fell. A somber gust quenched the life of the day, benumbing the earth. The eyelids of the fields drooped, the woods in the distance darkened, the peaks on high were obscured, the vast sky blackened. In the mystery of the night, God wept.

When the last plaints of sorrow faded in the distance, the site was left solitary.

Only the river remained, murmuring, ever moving, ever restless, ever sounding, as though it dragged in its current the prolonged lament of an inconsolable grief, as though it carried dissolved in its waters the tears of a misfortune that no one wipes dry, that no one comforts . . . that no one knows about!

The End